Burial Grounds

Burial Grounds

Mark A. Daniel

Mark A. Daniel

Copyright © 2023 Mark A. Daniel

All rights reserved

The characters and events portrayed in this book are fictitious. Any similarities to real persons, living or dead, is coincidental and not intended by the author.

No part of this book may be reproduced, or stored in a retrieval system, or transmitted in any form or by any means, electronic, mechanical, photocopying, recording, or otherwise, without express written permission of the author.

CONTENTS

Prologue

Prologue

1971

Merle Walker stood outside his house with his old hunting rifle. The gun shook slightly in his eighty-four-year-old hands. The last quarter of the moon lit the landscape of rocky ground and gentle hills. The trees were sparse and twisted, water was a rare thing this close to Mexico.

It was very difficult for Merle to see, even with his glasses on. And it hurt to walk. But this had to be done. Hopefully he would be able to just frighten them away. He had only been forced to kill someone once, and that had been over forty years ago. It had been a boy, a young one. It was always boys who had to come and see, to snoop around where they shouldn't be. No one had found out about the boy, but there had always been rumors. That more than anything had helped to keep them away.

Merle made his way to his old white '57 Chevrolet which he had bought in 1963 from its original owner. He crawled into the old truck and started it up, then headed toward the cave. The road was bumpy, so he drove slowly to the small cliff which overlooked the entrance to the cave. He got quietly out of his truck and crouched behind a large rock.

There was a car parked about fifty feet from the cave's entrance. It hadn't been there long; Merle had come as soon as the dream had awakened him. He just hoped that his slow pace hadn't given the trespassers too much time. The barrier his father had built within the cave was thick, and it would take two men an hour to get through it. But Merle hadn't even checked the barrier in over three years. He didn't like to come out here, and he only came now when he had to. Merle aimed for the entrance to the cave and fired a shot. About thirty seconds later he fired another. Then he waited.

About ten minutes passed before the two boys came out of the cave. They ran out in a panic and jumped into the car. In an earlier day he could have picked them off if he'd needed to. But that was long ago, and now there was no need for it. Instead he fired another shot near the car as its tires spun in the rocks. The car slid back and forth until its wide tires got a grip, then it headed for the front gate and the highway. In the morning Merle would have to replace the lock on that gate again.

But as he stood to watch the car flee he knew something was wrong.

Even from this far away he could hear the cries. The ancient voices from his dreams were calling out to him, and he knew the boys had gotten too far. Perhaps he had slept too long after the dream. How far had they gotten? Had they gotten through the barrier? He prayed they had not, but he had to know now.

Merle got into his pickup and drove to the entrance of the cave. As he approached it he knew the barrier had been breached. He knew he had to go inside now, but he was terrified. His father had built the barrier over seventy years ago, after three of Merle's brothers had died in that cave. Merle had never gone into the cave in his youth because of the dreams. He knew what was in there, and he knew that the beckoning voices were a deception. The ranch had been his for sixty years, and he had been alone here since 1957, the year Katherine had come to the cave despite his warnings. Now he was old, and he knew it would not be easy to go inside. He hoped even more that he would have the strength to get back out.

Merle felt the cool breeze across his face, and he knew the breech was bad. Had those boys run out because of the gunshots, or because of what they had seen behind the barrier? Merle traded his rifle for the flashlight behind the seat. Then he headed for the open mouth of the cave.

It was cold inside despite the warmth of the summer night. His bones creaked and his joints complained as he crossed the boulders which had fallen from the ceiling. He walked across the floor of the cave to the small tunnel which led to the barrier. The voices became louder as he walked, and he tried his best not to listen to them. The floor of the tunnel was rough, and his sore ankles made it hard to walk, but he ignored all of these little pains, knowing they meant nothing in the greater picture.

Then he saw the barrier. The boys had done much more damage than he had imagined. There was a hole large enough for a man to crawl through, and cold air was rushing through the hole, carrying with it a foul stench. Merle walked to the barrier and began picking up the fallen rocks and closing off the hole.

Then he heard the train.

The earth shook softly, and he could hear the rumbling sound. He knew it was coming from the other end of the tunnel which was deep within the earth. That's where the beast lay. He remembered that sound from his youth. He remembered hearing his oldest brother crying out as that train overtook him. It wasn't really a train, but that's how it had sounded to a young Merle, and that's what it reminded him of now. He even tried to think of it as a train, because to think of what it really was would be too terrifying.

He threw the rocks into the opening quickly and frantically as the train approached. But his old arms were sore and weak, and he knew the rumbling sound was approaching too quickly.

He felt his heart racing, then there was a sharp pain in his chest.

He grabbed at his shirt, knowing that this was too much pain. His heart was giving out. He was not going to be able to fix the barrier in time. He would only have to pray that someone else would find it, someone with the strength to stop the terror before it escaped.

Then he heard the screaming voices and he looked into the darkness beyond the barrier. He let the terror take hold of him as the train approached.

Then the coldness turned to warmth, then tremendous heat.

He covered his face and closed his eyes as the ancient fire leapt from the depths and turned him into a fiery dancing man.

As he burned the voices continued to scream. His screams joined theirs as the fire burnt his flesh and bones.

And then there was the music of a thousand voices as the old man fell to the ground and twitched.

The fire consumed him completely.

Then the voices subsided.

And the last rock which the old man had put in place rolled back down the pile as if it had been pushed away.

One

1993

1

It was a very hot day, too hot for October.

The skies were a dusty blue and the only clouds which were visible were the high and frozen cirrus clouds which were thin and wispy, as if they had been lightly stroked onto the dusty canvass of the sky.

It was a great day for flying. But every day for the past two weeks had been a great day for being in the air, and a terrible one to be on the ground. In those two weeks the heat had set record highs in one south Texas town or another, and there was to be no change in the foreseeable future.

Buzz looked down to his right as he passed over Interstate 10 in his Cessna 172 aircraft. There were only a few trucks and even fewer cars on this desolate section of the west Texas interstate. The land below him had begun to take on more variety as he ventured away from the Northwest Plains and further into the Hill Country. It was a two-hour flight between Texon Oil headquarters in Odessa and the branch office in Del Rio. He was glad he didn't have to make the trip often.

Buzz walked in the Del Rio office where he oversaw all operations south of Interstate 10 and west of Interstate 35. This included Laredo, but not San Antonio which had its own office. The Del Rio office was just five miles from the border with Mexico, and for good reason. Texon had several joint ventures going with the government of Mexico as that country sought to better produce the areas in the state of Coahuila, especially near the Rio Grande.

But Buzz was not involved with that aspect of the business. He was responsible for directing exploration and well development for the areas in the eastern portion of the territory, as far west as a line that was formed by state highway 163 which ran from Comstock at the border to Interstate 10 at Ozona. Oil prices had been through a series of roller coaster rides in the past few months because of the situation in the middle east. Texon Oil had issued a policy which endorsed cautious optimism, with the emphasis on caution. The crash of oil prices in the early eighties had brought Texon to the edge of the precipice from which many oil companies in Texas had fallen. But Texon had survived by a series of debt and cost restructuring efforts, which had included a pay cut of fifty percent for Buzz. But that had been alright with Buzz, considering he knew many more people in the industry who had fared much worse. Now Texon was as close to healthy as it had ever been after the crash, and the windfall profits from $35 per barrel oil were helping to wipe out some of the more pressing short-term problems.

Today, as with most days, Buzz's flight path took him over millions of uninhabited areas. Most of it showed the scars of the drought which had hit south Texas in September. As he flew over the Pecos River he realized that it was lower than he had ever seen it. The limestone walls of the riverbed seemed deeper than he had thought them to be. In the distance he could see the Amistad Reservoir. Water from this reservoir served the countries on both sides of it. It had been formed when the Rio Grande was dammed up near Del Rio in 1969. The land surrounding the reservoir was flat. The only variety in the terrain seemed to be that which the rivers had cut through tens of thousands of years. The water was clear and very blue here, an irony considering its dusty and forbidding surroundings. After crossing over the eastern arm of the Amistad reservoir he would begin his descent into the airport at Del Rio.

As Buzz surveyed the terrain something caught his eye. He descended gradually to get a better look. There was an odd border where the trees stopped growing and the land became suddenly flatter. Buzz had been able to see a structure of some sort from a distance and he watched as an old wooden home became larger and more detailed. The land around the house was wild, but not with the thick growth which preceded the terrain before it. It looked as if the land surrounding the house might once have been cultivated, though it would have been decades earlier by the looks of a few post oak trees which had grown large in what might have been the midst of the fields.

He watched the house grow closer and saw that it was leaning heavily to the east. It sat near the top of a small rise and was built in a style more like the old homes he had seen in Virginia than those which were typical of this area. If the house was old enough it might have presumably been built in that style by some of the original settlers of this area almost a hundred years ago. The yard had become overgrown with mesquite and underbrush. The house itself had been assaulted in a few places by trees which had grown so close to the frame so as to push in portions of the outer wall. Part of the roof was caved in. Sunlight from above streamed through that hole in the roof. As he looked into it he saw broken pieces of wood which might once have been furniture lying about the room.

Then he heard the sound of the racing engine and realized that he had let himself come perilously close to the ground. He looked away from the house and pulled slowly back on the yoke as he tried to pull out of the fast descent into which he had put himself. He instinctively wanted to pull out faster, but knew he risked stalling or damaging the wings if he did so. So Buzz pulled slowly as the plane continued its descent, coming to within a hundred feet of the ground near a small hill to the east of the house. He leveled out there and then began to climb back to 2500 feet, hoping that his stunt would go undetected by San Angelo flight service. They would be less than amused by his lack of attention.

As Buzz leveled off he began to realize the stupidity of what he had just done. How could he have lapsed like that? Why had he lost track of his pitch and altitude while trying to look into the roof of an old, abandoned house? Certainly he had seen many sights of much more interest, and he had always been able to maintain his concentration. The incident bothered him until he made radio contact with the tower at the Del Rio airport and pushed it to the back of his mind while he prepared to land.

2

Buzz landed the plane and taxied to the company hanger. He secured the plane and checked it over before logging in with flight services. Then he walked to his car which was parked in front of the small terminal building. The airport was on the western side of Del Rio, as were the Texon offices. But it was too close to quitting time to go into the office. Tomorrow was going to be a busy day. The orders from Odessa were to begin more speculative efforts with the new and cheaper technologies which had most recently become available. He was to map out the five most promising of the capped sites in his territory for possible reopening and prepare recommendations on three new sites by the end of the week, which was only three days away.

Buzz drove past the office on the way to his home near the northern part of town. He had only been in Del Rio for six months. It had been part of a promotion which had seen his rise from a simple supervisory position in San Antonio to one of management in Del Rio. His house was actually owned by Texon and Buzz was only staying in it until his wife could join him again in May. They had been able to spend the summer together, but she had been unable to get work at either of Del Rio's high schools. Two teachers were scheduled to retire at the end of the current school year, and Margaret Shaw was on the top of the list of potential replacements. In the meantime she was determined to keep teaching, and so she taught at Southwest High School in San Antonio and lived in the house she and Buzz had occupied together for seven years. Buzz had suggested that she just take one year off, but she would not concede. She had insisted that the Texas public schools were in bad shape and that her one-year absence could not be afforded. When Buzz had suggested that just one person, namely herself, couldn't really make that much of a difference he got to listen to a speech on such things as the American Revolution, people dying for rights, and the importance of voting. An hour later, when the ranting had stopped, he was quite sorry he had made the comment and made a mental note not to use those words together in front of her again.

The evening was quite routine for Buzz. He looked through the refrigerator but found nothing desirable to eat so he ordered a pizza. There was something to drink, however, and he grabbed the six pack from the refrigerator and carried it to the living room where he set it on the coffee table. Buzz sat down in the easy chair which complained loudly as he lowered his two-hundred-and-forty-pound frame into it. He was not tall, just round. But he was not jolly. He had been asked only once to play Santa at a school play for the children by his wife when she had worked at the grade school. She had made sure not to ever ask him that again. The lines in his forty-three-year-old face showed his seriousness, which was uncharacteristic of the folks of Del Rio. He did not know his neighbors, nor did he care to. They watched him come and go and had stopped extending the invitations about five months ago. The most physical exercise he got was when he had to personally inspect a working site, which usually meant a mile or more of walking in a two-hour period. His evenings were spent in front of the television, usually with a six pack, looking through the various channels for any programs of interest. He never stayed on any one program for more than ten minutes unless it was on the Playboy channel.

Tonight the routine was much the same.

Except for one little thing.

His mind kept wandering back to the old house which had nearly brought him down from the skies earlier that day. For some reason he had come to think of it that way. He had been flying for too many years to just lose control. The house, or something near the house, had pulled him downward. At the time it hadn't occurred to him, but now as he sat mulling it over in his mind he remembered that he had felt drawn to the house, somehow entranced by it. He sat thinking this over while his eyes mindlessly followed the heaving breast on the work-out show. Buzz spent the evening staring at the television while his mind wandered between the programs before him and the events behind him. He came out of his state only when the delivery girl (a peach, as he would say) brought his pizza to the front door.

A couple of hours after nightfall Buzz pushed the 'off' button on the remote and waited for his eyes to adjust to the dim light which glowed through the curtains so he could navigate to his bedroom. He reached the bedroom and flipped on the small television at the foot of the bed so he wouldn't have to do it later, when he got out of the shower.

Thirty minutes later Buzz lay somewhat clean and completely naked on top of the covers. It was too hot to get under the covers, and he never slept with clothes on anyway. At night clothing just got in the way of whatever he wished to do, whether his wife was there or not.

He lay nude on top of the bed watching the television dreamily while the air conditioner hummed in the background. His eyelids were heavy, and they slowly began to creep down over his eyes. In less than twenty minutes his snores drowned out the cheap conversation on the late night rerun of yesterday's best sit-coms.

As the night wore on his mind began to work against him.

At first his dreams came to him as they usually did. They were nothing more than indistinct images, more feeling and dull emotions than color or substance. But as the night wore on they became more concrete.

The first time he saw anything clearly it was the house. This time he was inside of it, looking up into the skies. Buzz looked out through the hole in the ceiling and saw his own plane as it came down toward him. He tried to call out to the plane, to himself, but it was to no avail as the plane simply continued to descend. As the plane closed it began to lose its color. The yellows and blacks which normally covered the body and wings of the plane were washing out and turning into at first a dull and then a more brilliant white. As this happened the body of the plane too began to change. The wings began to collapse, then flex. The metal and wire melted and molded until they were almost fluid.

Then he stood staring into the skies, screaming in horror as the giant white hawk swooped down toward him. Buzz held his arms out before him to protect himself, but the giant bird converged on him, tearing through the hole in the roof as it wrapped its talons around him. He felt the sharp claws piercing into his sides as he grabbed onto the great bird's legs. Then he saw the lines of blood as they ran down his naked sides and began to cover his legs. Buzz held tightly to the legs of the great bird as it lifted him upward into the sky, afraid now that the bird would release him, and he would fall to the ground. It flew a short distance, then it did open its claws to let him fall. He tried to hold on, but his dreamy hands had no strength, so he fell. As he fell he rolled over and saw the ground coming rapidly toward him. He saw that he was not going to land on the rocky earth, but in a pit which had been dug deep into it. He fell and as he fell saw a man standing at the edge of the pit, beckoning him to come down out of the skies. Buzz screamed, but no sound came from his lips. As he passed the man who stood by the pit he saw clearly into his face. His eyes were wild with insanity, and his mouth was drawn into a maniacal smile.

Then, for just an instant, he saw that the face was his own.

Then the earth swallowed him up and he fell forever into the darkness.

And an hour later the dream began again.

3

The next morning Buzz awoke with only a dim remembrance of the dreams which had terrorized his subconscious mind the night before. He did notice, however, that all of the sheets were thrown from the bed, despite the fact that he had slept on top of them. He quickly decided that this had been due to the heat, and he thought no more of it. As he rose from the bed he felt a sharp pain on each side of his fat stomach. He wrote it off to cramps from sleeping too long in the same position. Then he showered and shaved and headed to work.

The drive through town was an easy one. Rush hour in Del Rio was like driving at almost any other hour in San Antonio. He drove to the tallest building downtown, the only building of its size not owned by a bank. Eight years ago many of the surrounding buildings had also been owned by various oil companies. The larger ones had left, the smaller ones had gone under. Texon stayed mainly for the prospect of joint ventures with Mexico. The Del Rio offices were also located centrally to many of the smaller operations which were too remote to be handled either by San Antonio or Odessa, but Val Verde County itself was not a great oil producing county. Last year only 504 barrels had been produced in the entire county. That was less than most Saudi wells produced in a day. The only nearby county which held any real production was Crockett County to the north. It had produced over four million barrels last year, a much more respectable level, though by no means in the same league with many counties in the Permian Basin territory like Gaines, Ector and Andrews counties which had produced over thirty-nine million barrels each. But the ventures currently under way in Buzz's territory had at least that much potential. The advent of true horizontal drilling had also added to the reserves and lowered the overall costs of drilling in the nineties.

Buzz walked to the elevator which he took to the second floor, much to the annoyance of the woman who wished to go to the fifth and did not understand why people going to the second could not simply use the stairs. He walked down the hallway, which was covered in a beige vinyl tile whose time had come and gone to a poorly stained door with a black plaque screwed to its center, its faded golden letters exclaiming the name of the oil company. He opened the door and walked in, a few minutes before nine o'clock. He walked past the receptionist without saying anything, as was the norm. She had given up greeting him in the mornings soon after he had come to Del Rio. Buzz walked down the poorly lit hallway to his office which was next to last on the left. It had a door, but one which did not lock. Buzz had requested a lock but Dave Ostrand, the only man who outranked him in this office, had explained that it was not the kind of image he wished the office to have. Buzz flipped on the fluorescent light. The humming noise settled into the back of his mind as he added to the noise by flipping the switch on his old IBM 286 computer. It hummed and spit and beeped at him for a few seconds then provided him with the menu he wished to see. It was a slow machine which was sorely outdated. Nowadays they made machines ten times as fast at half the price and size, but Texon was watching its money carefully. It hadn't begun spending those new profits yet, unsure how long oil prices would stay high. It was this philosophy which had kept them alive in the eighties. Furthermore, the Del Rio office was near the bottom of the list when it came to modernization. The Mexican officials who had toured the facilities in June, however, had marveled at the same machines which Buzz wished to toss from his window.

Buzz selected the spreadsheets software from the menu and waited while the various copyrights and introductions flashed on the screen. Then he retrieved a file which he had marked "capped". It was a file system better suited to a database format, but he had grown comfortable with the spreadsheet software and used it for virtually all of his applications except correspondence. After almost thirty seconds in the 'wait' mode the first location came onto the screen. Listed was information on the Davis well outside Uvalde. Information listed included the coordinates of the well, its beginning and peak production, and its production before capping. Also listed were accrued revenues and payments to the various holders of the mineral rights. It was a bad well which had barely covered the costs associated with its drilling. It had been deep, and production had been good at first, but within six weeks it had fallen to the status of a stripper well, producing less than ten barrels a day. This was the condition of the majority of the wells in the state, but most did not fall off so fast. The well had been capped at six barrels a day in 1983. The oil was thick and hard to transport and refine. This well was not a good candidate for reopening. He pushed the button on the right side of the keyboard which paged down to the next well in the file. It, too, was a low production well, one which had been a loss. Buzz paged through the information, quickly screening the wells which were not candidates for reopening and printing off the ones with possibilities. When he finished he had a stack of information on fifteen wells which were candidates for reopening. By lunch he had narrowed it down to five. He gave them to his assistant, along with a letter to be faxed to Odessa for review and approval. They would decide whether or not to begin the reopening procedures and would contact him when it was time for him to come into the picture once again, at some point after the appropriate contracts and releases had been signed by the holders of the mineral rights. The easy part was over. Now he would have to get to the tough work.

Recommending new sites was difficult and risky. The safe route was to areas near well developed and still producing wells. But the people in headquarters had made it clear that this is not what they wanted this time. They were interested in entirely new fields. What they wanted was to take three shots at opening a new and highly productive area using the new drilling methods. Picking three areas gave Buzz a better chance than if he had been restricted to one or two, but it also meant that he was under that much more pressure to make at least one good hit. It was his big assignment for the new job. It was his chance to become a hero, or just another mid-level employee in the company. There was also the risk, if all three ventures were complete loss, that he might be made an example of.

Buzz decided that the work would best be done after eating, as were most jobs. So he left the building by himself and headed across the street to grab a burger.

After a quick and greasy lunch he returned to his office and pulled a special atlas from his desk. It was a map of Texas with Texon's county by county production figures listed for his territory, as well as overall production by all venues. The book then provided a map of each county with the sites of all known wells marked. Red markers indicated the highest level of production, then there was orange, yellow, green, blue, and finally black for holes which had been completely dry. The county level maps were topographically detailed with elevation markers and indicators of rivers, roads, railroads, treed areas, and rock formations. He turned carefully through the pages, taking his first look at the areas which might make him a king or a clown. There was no way he would be able to make any decisions on the first look through. He would have to study these maps again and again until he found areas which seemed logical choices, keeping in mind his constraints such as lease complexity and site accessibility. Then he would make some phone calls to check the availability of the areas, then he would fly over the sites. It was a lot of work to do, and he only had until the end of Friday to do it all. Today was Wednesday. By the end of the day he would have to have some sites selected. Tomorrow morning he would have to get up with the sun and do his best to fly over as many of the sites as he could in a day. Then he would have Friday to formulate his recommendations and fax them to Odessa by two o'clock. It was a lot of work to do in a little time. But it was a test, and he understood it as such. Buzz was determined that he was going to pass at least this first portion of the test.

As he looked over the county maps the house came once again into his mind. He was looking over a map of Val Verde County, the one in which Del Rio was situated. There were very few well locations, only two of them were Texon, and they were marked in blue and green, low producers. As he inspected the map he followed the topography carefully, looking for where the old house might be. He became lost in the search, suddenly oblivious to his first task. He looked over the hills and valleys, tracing his flight path of the previous day back from the airport. The topography of the land northwest of the airport was fairly unvaried with few elevation markers. Then, just to the north of Comstock, there was a series of small hills. He remembered that these small hills covered much of the northern portions of the county, and a few of them strayed almost to the Mexican border. It was at the border of these small hills with the flat lands that the house had been. He looked closely at the area and found a large plot which looked suspicious. It was marked as the Aldredge Farm, though he had remembered no signs of any crops or livestock in the area. It was a fairly substantial farm covering three sections of land, over 1,900 acres. Buzz noticed that there were no markers on or around the farm, no signs of exploration by any company.

Then he decided that this was his premonition. A feeling of peace fell upon him as he realized in his own mind that the mystery of the house was a sign. Something or someone was pointing him in a new direction. He felt very strongly that his destiny was somehow linked with this place. It did not seem now that the house had been trying to swallow him up, but rather that it was trying to speak to him, to call him to a new and wonderful future. Buzz was not a particularly religious man, but he did possess a certain amount of superstition which allowed him to accept these ideas as facts. Though he had already made up his mind that he would somehow be able to justify the exploration here, he looked to the map for support. The earth in the area was limestone, which was perfect. There were layers of shale in some places which were thick and dense enough to act as traps for the oil. The hills in the area of the farm were evidence of the possible existence of anticlines, underground domes which would serve as traps for oil. The characteristics of the land and soil acted as great support. The only fact which worked against him was that while the majority of this county fit those characteristics, the county as a whole had been a very poor producer. The majority of Texon wells across the southwest produced more individually than the entire county of Val Verde had produced the previous year. There was currently no drilling going on, and there had been no active rigs there for the past six months. The most recent venture in the county, which had been by a competitor, had turned up nothing. It was as if the county was the one exception to which the textbooks on oil exploration alluded when discussing prime exploration areas.

But that had to be part of it. There was oil in the county, and lots of it. Buzz would be the one to open the locked door, and it would mean many things. Things like more money and more power. It was well known that a man who made the oil company rich became very rich himself. This was going to be his one big gamble with his career, and it was going to pay off.

It had to.

It was his destiny.

By six-thirty he had selected the two remaining sites and had plotted the best flight path which he would use the next day to take a look at them. He had made the phone calls necessary to check the mineral rights on each of the properties. Pieces of the rights on one of the sites he had originally selected were held by so many different individuals that he scrapped it. That particular lot had probably been passed over many times before for the same reason. The sites he had ended up with had no big problems with the mineral rights upon a preliminary inspection. It would take a couple of weeks, however, to check the rights on these properties thoroughly. Except for the Aldredge Farm. There was only one holder of the rights in that case, which was a rare thing anymore. Buzz had taken this as further proof of the bizarre nature of his find. Of the three sites he ended up with, two were easily accessible according to the maps. The toughest one to get to would be the Aldredge Farm. It was near no highway, and a half-mile path would have to be cut through trees and underbrush if they decided to proceed with drilling. For one other site this same problem had been sufficient to eliminate it as a possibility. For the Aldredge Farm site it was merely an inconvenience.

Buzz picked up his map and notepad and walked to the door of his office. He switched the light off and walked through the hallway which was now lit only by the low sun shining through the western windows. Everyone had gone home already, and he locked the front door as he left. Buzz carried his articles to his car as he went over the next day's plans in his mind. He had picked three fairly good sites. He would like to have picked a fourth in case one of the three turned out upon visual inspection to be no good. But five o'clock had found him with only the three possibilities he now had written down in his notepad. The people in Odessa had understood that he was working on a short fuse and had given him a little leeway. If upon closer inspection there were any problems with one of the sites he had selected they would let him select another at a later date. But that was most likely only good for one site. The crisis which pushed oil to its current high prices was one which might become better or worse at any moment. The quicker the new wells began producing the better. At thirty-five dollars per barrel, exploration and drilling costs were recovered on almost half as much production as had been the case just two months earlier.

He felt good about the places he had selected. He felt particularly good about the Aldredge Farm in any case. Even if the other two sites proved to be dry, the Aldredge Farm would surely cover their costs as well as many others which were being undertaken in the other regions.

Buzz got into his big white Lincoln and drove home. He ran the air conditioner on maximum as the heavy heat which had been assaulting south Texas all fall showed no signs of relenting. Once home he threw his things into a corner and grabbed a beer. He decided tonight he would cook, so he got two cans of greasy tamales out of the cupboard and threw them into a skillet. On medium they would be done in fifteen minutes.

Buzz got out of his work clothes and into his television clothes. When he was finished dressing, the tamales were finished cooking, so he threw them onto a plate and grabbed his last six pack of beer from the refrigerator. Then he sat down in front of the television and watched reruns of All in the Family while he slurped down the messy tamales and drank his beer.

But he wasn't really watching the shows as they flashed past him that evening. Instead his mind wandered back to the house which stood on the hillside thirty-seven miles to the northwest, calling to him.

Two

1

Helene ran the handkerchief across her brow to keep the sweat from running into her sparkling blue eyes. Then she raised her binoculars to get a better look at the paintings on the wall of the ravine. The images moved up and down as her boat rocked in the river. She looked away from the paintings and down to her pad. These were paintings she had seen before, on her trip the previous August. They were faded and to anyone else might appear simply as some streaks of clay or other similar geologic discoloration. To her well-trained eye, however, they appeared as they were, actual paintings made on the wall of the ravine over four thousand years ago. There were dozens of known sites in the area bounded by the Devil's and Pecos rivers, and that was probably only ten percent of the sites which were in the area. The bulk of the sites were still undiscovered. Most of them would stay that way. Many sites, discovered and otherwise, had been buried under water with the Amistad Reservoir project twenty-four years earlier. Thousands of years of irreplaceable historical information had been lost when the Rio Grande River had risen over the sites, burying and carrying away unknown archaeological treasures.

Even the morning sun was hot. Helene had come out early to get as much work done as she could before the blistering afternoon heat made that all but impossible. She had been waiting for the cooler fall months to come before she undertook this project so that the weather might be of little hindrance. But summer had hung on long and hard this year. Helene had waited until she felt she could wait no longer, then school had started, and the weight of her thesis had begun to make itself known. She had been studying archaeology for almost five years now, and by this time next year she hoped to be participating in the exciting work which was going on in other places of the world. Professor Stein had told her that it was possible she would get to participate in the work going on in Chad, which in her opinion was currently the most exciting archaeological work. It was a prestigious possibility, but another year of work stood between her and that possibility. This project was part of that work.

She reached behind her and pulled the cord on the Mercury motor which sputtered to life and began carrying her further up the Pecos River. She went slowly, looking carefully at the steep walls of the ravine for any caves or pits which might have been used by the ancient nomads of the region. These people had appeared on and off for thousands of years leaving behind them paintings and artifacts which told about a life which was like that of the Native Americans, with a few differences. There were sites where great herds of buffalo had been driven from the cliffs to provide more food and hides than could be used. Evidence of this was provided in massive amounts of organic remains at some of the sites. Paintings of these hunts, as well as of other important events of ceremony and of life appeared in the caves which the people had used as their homes. The people had found good food and shelter and had begun to change from their nomadic ways to those of a stationary people.

Then they disappeared. About four hundred years ago the records suddenly ceased. The most popular theories were that they had either become absorbed by tribes of the Lipan Apaches or Coahuiltecans which had passed through the area at that time, or that they had migrated southward, attracted by the Mexican settlements. Helene hoped to find out which of these was in fact true, or if there was another reason which no one had yet ventured to hypothesize. A possibility which she had considered was that these peoples had died of a disease brought by the explorers, much as the smallpox epidemics had killed thousands of Native Americans upon the arrival of the English settlers.

But it was only another idea, and there was as of yet no evidence to support it. But there was a similar lack of evidence for any other theory, so she decided that her theory was no less valid than those which had somehow become accepted.

She took the boat upstream another two miles but saw nothing like the great dwelling areas which she had toured the previous day which all lay downstream from her, including some old sites on the Rio Grande. But those sites had been well documented and contained nothing which she would find to be of any use in her work. She hadn't really expected to find anything by just boating up the river. Drawings and sites that easy to see would have already been documented. In fact she knew she had missed some of the lighter paintings which had already been documented. The problem with the accessible sites was that almost all of them had been rendered useless by the seekers of arrowheads and other artifacts. The haphazard digging which had taken place at virtually every site on the lower Pecos over the past hundred years had obliterated millennia of important records. The only hope she had of getting close to her goal was to find a previously unworked site. That was what most of the archaeological community in this area had been hoping for for some time. The odds of her being the one to stumble upon that new site were slim. The only other hope was that one of the private landowners who had so far refused to allow anyone to work a site on their land might change their mind. But that too was a hope which had lain dormant for decades. There were many sites, most of them unknown, which lay on private lands. Most of these were not accessible, or they had been turned into cheap tourist traps and destroyed by those wishing to turn a quick dollar. She had seen a sign on her way into Comstock three days ago which had exclaimed that she could dig for her own arrowheads for just three dollars. She had considered driving down that road and giving the proprietors of the site a rather sizable piece of her mind. Instead she had merely cursed them as she continued on her way to the river.

Helene took the boat back to the dock and put it onto the trailer. The noontime sun was out now, and the pounding heat was making every movement a task. She got into her Suburban and drove the boat back to the rental facilities. After turning it in and getting her deposit back she returned to her room to sit out the afternoon heat and wait until evening for her hike on some of the federal lands around the Amistad National Recreation Area. There were some old sites there, some she had seen, most she had not. Most were hard to get to, so vandalism had been at a minimal level. Professor Stein had provided her with a special map available only to those interested in archaeology which pinpointed some of the more remote and more interesting sites. One or two of them had little or no signs of vandalism. One of the sites had been slated for excavation in 1991, but its remoteness had caused some budget problems and the project had to then be put off until 1996.

When she got to her hotel room she noticed that the small red light on the phone by her bed was blinking. She picked the phone up and dialed the motel operator. She figured that the message was from Michael, her boyfriend she had left back in Austin. She waited for several rings, but no one was answering the phone at the desk. She assumed that this meant the operator was busy or on lunch break. Helene left her room and walked to the front office. She could see the old man in the room behind the counter watching a 1960's western which blared loudly. She heard the phone ringing as she entered the office and noticed that the man kept watching his show, unaware of the ringing phone. He was probably the operator as well as the office manager, and probably the owner.

"Excuse me," she said. The television was too loud, and she did not get the man's attention. She saw the bell resting on the counter and rang it several times. This seemed to break his concentration.

He had learned to block out my sounds, including the phone. But the bell usually meant business and he could hear it through almost anything. When he saw that it was Helene he knew that it was not new business. He got up slowly from the chair and walked to the counter where he faced the tall lean woman who reminded him of Christie

Brinkley, only he liked this one better, mostly because she was within touching distance.

"Yes, ma'am," he said in a thick Mexican accent. It was an accent which dominated these parts as two thirds of the inhabitants of Val Verde County could trace their roots to a town south of the border or could remember it from their childhood or their recent past.

"My message light is blinking," she explained.

The man looked at a row of boxes beneath the counter to the one with 107 marked in felt pen above it. He pulled the white piece of paper from the box and handed it to her, looking upon her with deceptively uninterested eyes. She opened the paper and read it quickly before thanking the man and walking from the lobby. He watched her carefully as she left, smiling slightly at the soft curves of her behind.

Helene returned to her room and picked up her phone. A week ago she had made the standard phone calls to the people who owned property on which there were viable and unresearched sites. It was always a fruitless task, but one which she felt she had to undertake. Many of the people were hostile, tired of being asked the question at least once a year. Some were not hostile but demanded a price which was too high. Each time she tried, and each time it came to naught. Except this time.

The piece of paper she now held in her hand read simply 'Walker - 555-2947.' She recognized the name as one of those she had called from Austin the previous week. It was rumored that the site at the Walker ranch was almost untouched and held magnificent treasures for the student of archaeology. But Mr. Walker was a stubborn man who wouldn't even discuss the possibility of having a group of people with picks and shovels tearing down trees and digging pits on his ranch land for any price. Helene had never heard more than a few words from the man's lips, and most of those words had simply been 'no'. As soon as the old man discovered the intention of the caller he immediately hung up the phone, every time. The possibilities ran through her mind as she dialed the number once again. The phone began ringing. It rang four times, then five, but there was no answer. Helene stayed on, hoping someone would pick up. As she was about to give up there was a clicking sound, then a long pause.

"Hello?" Helene said to the silence.

"Yes?" An old, cracked female voice came.

"Hello, may I speak to Mr. Walker?"

There was another pause, then, "Who is this?"

"This is Helene Morgan. Mr. Walker called and left me a message to call him."

Another pause. "Can you speak louder?" came the request.

"I said this Helene Morgan. Mr. Walker left me a message to call him."

"Oh, yes, Miss Morgan," some of the hesitancy left the old voice.

"This is Eula Justin, Merle Walker's sister. I'm afraid Mr. Walker has passed on. He left us all a few days ago." The voice cracked for a moment and Helene couldn't tell if this was from age or sorrow.

"I'm sorry," Helene said before she realized she had just said what she swore she would never say at the news of a death. It was so trite and meaningless. "I don't know who would have given me this message, I didn't mean to disturb you."

"Oh, no, no," the old woman said, "It was me who called. I got your number from the university. I wanted to call to tell you that you can come have a look at that old cave now if you would like."

Helene felt her face flush as the excitement of what she was hearing had its effect on her body. She suddenly felt ashamed of feeling the pleasure at the cost of Mr. Walker.

"I would really like that, Mrs. Justin," Helene said, not exactly sure how to proceed. "What would be a good day to come by?"

"Oh, any day really, except this Sunday. That's when they're having the funeral."

Helene didn't wish to appear eager, but this was too exciting, and she let it get the best of her. "Can I come by this afternoon?"

"That should be alright. Just come to the house first and I'll give you directions to the old cave. You might want to bring some old clothes and maybe some rope. There's some climbing involved. Will you be coming alone?"

"Yes"

"You really should bring someone. It's a little dangerous for a lady."

"I've done this sort of thing a lot in the past few years, I should be all right."

Mrs. Justin seemed a little hesitant but decided that it was Helene's decision whether or not to take the risk. She gave Helene directions to the house and Helene explained that she would be by in about two hours. That would give her time to make a few phone calls. The heat would be no better by then, but if the cave was as Mrs. Justin had described then she would be protected somewhat from the heat. She even decided that she would take a long-sleeved shirt with her in case the cave was deep.

When Helene hung up the phone she immediately called Michael and told him of her good luck. Then she called Professor Stein, who was at least as excited as she was and told her to log as much information as she could in case Mrs. Justin changed her mind later. He badly wanted to join her, but it was six hours from Austin to where she was, and he would have to wait until the weekend, which was still a few days off. But he trusted Helene, she was the best student he had encountered in the past five years, and this was her specialty. He wished her luck before she hung up. She told him she would call as soon as she got back to let him know what she had found.

Helene changed into clothes more suitable for hiking through rough terrain and climbing rocks and headed for the Walker ranch.

2

An hour later Helene stood before an old wooden door as it creaked slowly open. It was like a scene from an old black and white horror movie, complete with lack of color. When the door opened she met the gaze of a woman who looked nothing like her voice suggested she would. She was obviously quite old and moved with some effort, but her face was pleasant, and she showed the remnants of what must have at one time been great beauty.

"Please come in," she said in her old and worn voice. Her face and skin had withstood the ravages of time much better than her voice. Her rough voice had been the result of fifty years of smoking.

Helene walked into the big old home. The inside was beautifully furnished with well-kept antiques which must have been in the family for generations. There were wondrously finished tables and book-shelves, and a large and beautiful armoire. Helene followed the old woman into the living room where she then sat on the couch to which she was directed. At first she was hesitant to sit in such elegance, dressed as she was. The old woman sat across a small table from her in a large wingback chair which had recently been reupholstered. On the table between them sat a small silver tray. On the tray was a matching silver decanter and some smaller covered bowls which presumably held milk and sugar.

"Would you like some coffee?" Mrs. Justin asked as she raised the decanter.

"Yes, please," Helene answered. She really didn't want any, but the elegance of the moment forced her to comply. She watched while the old woman poured with grace that suggested years at the role of hostess.

"Milk or sugar?" the woman asked.

"No, thank you."

The woman set the decanter down and lifted her cup. "Me neither," she replied with a smile.

Helene picked up her own cup and took a sip. It was not coffee but actually a mocha of some kind. It was rich and sweet, and she was glad she had agreed.

"I can see that you're ready to get to work, so I'll make this brief." The statement sounded wistful, as if company was what the old woman really wanted. "I know you people at the university have been calling just about every year for as long as I can remember. It probably started before you were even born." She paused and took a sip of her mocha.

"Merle was simply against the idea of other people coming onto his land and changing it. He wanted it left the way he made it and no other. He wouldn't even allow a drilling team on back in '82 when they thought there might be oil here. Lord knows that's not really likely in these parts, but even if there had been a guaranteed strike he wouldn't have let them come on. That's just the way he was."

"I agreed with him for the most part, except on this cave thing. We lost three brothers, all of them in that cave." Helene's eyes grew wide as the woman told her story. "Merle thought it was evil. I just thought it was bad luck." The old woman reached forward and set her cup down. "Now don't get me wrong, I am a God-fearing woman. But I know the difference between superstition and science. I always thought it was a shame the way Merle stood between that cave and you people. It may be nothing. It may just be a few pictures on the walls like those on the river. But I resolved that if I did outlive the man that I would do what I am doing right now. I'm sorry I didn't call you earlier, but it slipped my mind until this morning. "

The woman couldn't have called much earlier than she had, since her brother had only been dead two days. Helene waited for more, but apparently there was no more.

"So you don't have any idea what's down there?" Helene asked.

"No. Can't say it ever interested me. But if you find anything that's useful I wish you'd let me know. Kind of set my conscience at ease after all these years."

Helene understood that it was simply Mrs. Justin's way of saying that she was hoping to win her last argument with the deceased.

"Well, I don't mean to rush you," the old woman said. "But I'm sure you're anxious to get down there. Let me tell you how to get to the place."

The old woman explained the route across the ranch to the cave. "Those directions are based on childhood memories. Since I've not been there myself they are general at best."

Helene set her half empty cup down. "Thank you for the coffee," she said as she stood.

The woman walked Helene back to the front door.

"Now, I want you to be very careful. And if you do slip and hurt yourself please don't sue me." She smiled as she said this.

"Okay"

"But really," the woman continued. "Please stop by on your way out so that I know you're all right. If I don't hear from you by nightfall I'll send someone out to check on you."

"I appreciate that," Helene replied.

The old woman said farewell and closed the door. Helene felt sorry for her. In their short conversation she had understood Mrs. Justin was a lonely woman, and that she had been so for many years. Even though she had not said as much, she was sure that the old woman's husband had been gone for some time.

3

Helene drove her Suburban down the gravel road which rose gradually with the terrain. She reached the top of a small hill and could see the outcropping of shale which Mrs. Justin had referred to. She drove past the ridge, then began descending a steep hill. As she descended she could see the entrance to the cave. It looked remote, but she would be able to get fairly close by using this old road. She understood a little of what Mr. Walker had been concerned about. If this was the best way to the site it would take heavy machinery to tear up trees and clear out the underbrush in order to make a path through which they could take their excavation equipment. But hopefully Mrs. Justin did not care so much about those things.

Helene got out of the Suburban and walked to the entrance of the cave. The ground sloped gradually downward until it disappeared into what looked like a giant slit in the earth. From an airplane this slit might look like a deep empty riverbed, only one wall of the bed was missing. She could see some boulders at the opening of the cave which had fallen from the cliff above her. Trees and shrubs had grown all the way to the edge of the low cliff. She could see roots dangling through the thin crust which formed the very edge of the roof of the cave.

Helene took out her flashlight but did not switch it on. She could see most of the inside of the cave though she was not sure why this was so. She walked forward and began to descend into it. As she entered the cave she realized that there were two small holes and one large one in the roof which served as natural skylights. It was not as bright as it was outside, but when her eyes adjusted she could see the entire cave fairly well. It was cool in the cave, not chilly but definitely an improvement over the sweltering heat she had just left.

Helene walked down the sloping wall until it leveled out at the bottom of the cave. She stood near the cave's center and was directly below one of the smaller holes. The hole was about thirty feet above her. The floor beneath her feet was mostly rubble which had fallen from the roof. Underneath the rubble was a thick dusty material which she knew to be layers of the remains of the ancient peoples. This was the first indication that this had been a shelter used by them. The second indication jumped suddenly out at her from the wall before her. Helene took in a startled breath, then froze in her tracks as she made out the outline of an enormous drawing on the wall twenty feet in front of her. She stepped over a small pile of rocks and then onto the soft and cool dirt which covered the space between her and the wall. There was a small mound underneath the largest hole in the ceiling which probably meant an often-used campfire site as the hole above it acted as a natural chimney. As she stood beneath the hole she felt a cool breeze which indeed seemed to come from behind her and then travel up and out the hole above. She walked the rest of the distance to the wall and then she turned on her light.

When she shined her light onto the wall of the cave she realized that what she had found was not a single giant drawing but hundreds of smaller paintings which spanned in style and content over a period of five thousand years. Some of the oldest paintings were indistinct and had been painted over several times, but they were of familiar objects such as the shaman and the buffalo. Most of the paintings were rough reproductions of those she had seen countless times in caves along the lower Pecos. But these were also different. These were new paintings which were in no journals or textbooks, and she could tell already that this cave contained the stuff that textbooks and theses were made of. Already she could make out almost thirty distinct drawings. There seemed to be no new pictures, and no singularly spectacular ones either, but there were lots of them, and many were well preserved. The air was cool but not damp, and erosion had been kept away over the years. There was no standing water anywhere and she ran her flashlight along the ground looking for a natural drain. Without one this cave would have been filled time and time again by the floods which had visited themselves upon this region across the centuries. This cave showed no signs of frequent flooding. She ran the light along the base of the cave. The floor was amazingly smooth. Where the wall of the cave met the floor it was fairly well demarcated as if artificially constructed. At the farthest corner of the cave the ceiling came slowly down and met the floor which also tilted downward. The closure was a gradual one and ended up in a small pile of rocks. If there was a natural drain this was the most likely place for one.

Helene turned her light back up to the walls and looked for more paintings, but there were only a few faded ones. The most prolific painting had taken place in the area she had first found. The wall there was easily accessible and smoother than in other places. It lent itself to the task of being painted more than any other section of the wall. Some of the paintings were fairly high on the wall, higher than a standing man could have reached on his own. She had seen this before, especially at Panther cave. It was assumed that scaffolding of some kind was used. Perhaps some boulders or even another person. Helene believed the latter was most likely the case. The highest painting was incomplete. She wondered if this was because the painter had moved on or died.

There were too many pictographs to record in the time she had so she began taking pictures. Each time the flash went off she had to wait for her eyes to readjust to the dim light inside the cave. She ran through an entire roll of film taking first whole shots, then closer shots of individual pictographs. The largest was of a giant shaman who seemed to have several spears in him. The best defined was in the polychrome style of 2000 B.C. and was of a deer, complete with antlers. There were several deer pictures overlaid and linked together across the eons in which they had been painted. She wondered if those who had painted the most recent deer had any idea of the thousands of years which separated their deer from those they painted over or next to. The ancient man had probably thought that it had only been a matter of months, perhaps years.

When she had finished taking pictures of the pictographs she loaded another roll of film and began taking pictures of the floor and the walls. The walls were limestone and the cave had been formed long ago by an acidic underground lake which had been around in the time of a much higher water table. When she had photographed her surroundings she turned her attention back to the small pile of rocks in the narrow space at the farthest end of the cave.

Helene decided that she would have a closer look at the small rock pile, so she walked toward what had to be the natural drain. The cave became gradually smaller as she walked toward the pile of rocks. Where the rocks were piled it was less than three feet between the ceiling and floor. She removed her pack and got to her hands and knees and crawled the final few feet. As she approached the rocks she realized that they were not limestone. They had not come from inside the cave. Someone had carried them here and piled them in a mound which was approximately two feet high. Some of the rocks had been tossed aside, and she could see that there was a hole beyond. She crawled to the mound and began tossing the rest of the stones aside. The hole became much larger than she had thought it would. She turned her flashlight toward the hole and looked inside.

What she had uncovered was a small tunnel, about two feet tall and twenty inches wide. The tunnel went back about six feet, then turned to the left. The rock was fairly smooth, more limestone. She set her flashlight down and worked at removing the remaining rocks from the entrance to the small tunnel. She figured that Mr. Walker must have put the rocks there, but only after he had gone down the hole once. Mrs. Justin had said something about her husband thinking of this place as an evil place. Had that been merely because of the pictographs behind her, or because his brothers had died here, or was there something down this tunnel which had led him to that conclusion?

Helene worked at the rocks and was glad she had brought her gloves as she moved the last of them to the right of the small hole. She picked up her flashlight and shined it down the hole once again. Should she try to go into it? What if she got stuck? The old woman had said she would send somebody if she didn't report back by dark, but that would be a lot of trouble. She looked the hole over carefully. There didn't seem to be any protruding edges or difficult angles which might trap her, and the formation seemed solid enough. Helene scooted back and got her camera from beside her pack. She aimed it at the hole and took a picture. Then she started back toward the hole. She didn't know how far this tunnel went back, and she didn't want to risk breaking her camera, so she left it by the pack. If there were things which needed to be photographed she would return with a disposable camera, or something of that nature.

Helene worked her way back to the hole and stuck her head into it. She carried the flashlight in her left hand as she crawled. Covering the first six feet was fairly easy. But then she came to a corner which she could tell was going to be a tight squeeze. Images of becoming stuck teased her again, but she figured that if in fact Mr. Walker had made this journey alone, so could she. She turned the corner and got flat on her belly with her arms tucked behind her. It was dark and her arms were behind her, as was her light. The darkness became absolute as her body sealed off the light behind her. The air became very cold and suddenly she felt as if she were being squeezed. It got harder to breathe, and she began to try and move too quickly as panic set in. The darkness compounded her fear and she pushed hard with her feet, smashing her face into the wall which curved sharply back to the right. Helene started to scream out, then stopped. She closed her eyes, even though it made no visual difference, and began to take a deep breath. She tried to move back but could not, so she pushed on, slowly this time. She moved her head along the right-hand side of the tunnel, and she felt the floor of it moving away from her. She realized how stupid it had been to go through without shining her light ahead of her somehow, though she also realized that this would have been impossible. She might be pushing herself into a great pit, or even a little pit with no easy exit. She might fall to her death, or even worse she might fall and become injured, then die slowly.

Helene closed her eyes and pushed these thoughts away. She could not back out. She pushed herself through further until her arms passed the smallest point and then she was able to bring them forward, along with the small but bright light.

Helene saw that the floor of the tunnel indeed dropped away from her, but only about a foot. The top was fairly level. She put her arms on the lower ledge and pulled herself the rest of the way through the small corner and into the larger portion of the tunnel. She crawled ahead to where the bottom dropped a few inches so that she could sit up and take a break.

Helene felt her face throbbing and reached up to feel where she had struck the wall of the tunnel. She felt the wetness of blood and found that it came from a small cut over her left eye. The cut was not bad, but the bleeding was fairly heavy. She didn't have any of her first aid gear, it was in the pack she had left at the small tunnel's entrance. She wiped her forehead with her sleeve and shined the light down the tunnel to see what was ahead.

The tunnel seemed to stay a more navigable size for as far as she could see, and it curved gradually to the left. She inspected the wall around her for any markings, but apparently the ancient people had not perfected the idea of a torch or could not keep one lit for long enough to do any work for the walls here bare. Helene got back onto her hands and knees and began making her way down the tunnel. After about twenty feet the cave straightened out and began to descend. The ceiling became rougher, and the air became colder. As she followed the tunnel into the earth the air also seemed to become heavier. Her breath became visible before her as the air grew very cold. She wanted to take another break but was compelled by her desire for knowledge to continue. That and something else pulled her on, something which she could not quantify, so she labeled it sheer excitement. But the excitement was tainted by a measure of fear which seemed to be growing. She did not understand why, but she was beginning to feel as if she wanted to turn back. But she could not. She continued down the tunnel despite her roughed-up hands and knees which were beginning to hurt from the rocky floor of the tunnel. She pushed the pain aside and followed the tunnel until she came to a small cavern.

The tunnel opened suddenly into a small chamber which she would be able to stand up inside of, if she could get to the floor of it without breaking any bones. The tunnel she was in emptied into the chamber from near its ceiling, and it looked like about a ten-foot drop to a floor covered with long dormant stalagmites pointing up at her as if to threaten impalement if she slipped on her way down. She began to turn around to make her way into the chamber when she realized that she hadn't brought the rope which Mrs. Justin had suggested. Once in the chamber she would be unable to reach the tunnel which as far as she knew was the only way out. She cursed aloud at her own stupidity. It wasn't like her to forget these kinds of things. But this was new and exciting, and that often increased one's forgetfulness.

But she almost felt a sigh of disappointment come from the room itself as she pulled herself completely back into the small tunnel. She turned to face the chamber once again and it looked like a giant maw, open and awaiting her arrival to mark its first meal in eons. Already she understood just from the emotions she was experiencing why Mr. Walker had declared the cave off limits. To a man of his stern religious beliefs these emotions were clearly not something sent from above. She understood this even before she saw the paintings.

Suddenly she noticed a series of small holes in the ceiling of the cavern which were black around the edges. She inspected them as closely as she could with the light she held in her hand. The black rings were indicative that they had been used as ventilation for a fire of some kind. She looked over the floor of the cave and found several smooth places where the stalagmites had not grown, but there was no evidence of any fire sites.

Then she thought she saw something out of the corner of her eye, and she turned the light quickly to her left. As she turned the light the shadows of the stalagmites danced across the opposite wall, startling her some. Then she saw the paintings. The paintings were faded and hard to see from where she was. She wanted badly to get down into the cave and look closely at them. Though she could not make them out she could tell that they were not the traditional paintings which had been discovered to date. Most of the shapes were not right for shaman or deer, though she could see a few of these traditional figures amidst the others. She could recognize them by their general shape, which was always the same. But the other figures were new ones, ones she had never seen, so she could not begin to guess what they might be without closer inspection. And she could not make a closer inspection until she returned with the right equipment.

As she ran her light across the figures she found a place where the small tunnel continued. It picked up again in a distant corner of the chamber, on the floor. There was a small hole there about twenty inches high. She shined her light on it, but it was too far away, and she could not see into it at all.

Then she heard a sound like a deep rumble of thunder and felt a gentle shaking of the earth beneath her. She lay still while her heartbeat picked up. Then her light began to dim.

A red powdery dust came from the hole across the chamber from her and began to fill the small room. She wanted to back away, to begin her retreat, but she also wanted to stay and see what was happening. The cool air around her became suddenly colder and a shiver from both the cold and the terror ran down her spine.

Then there was another rumble and with it came a high-pitched screaming sound. It sounded like the screams of a thousand angry voices coming from ahead of her. The dust blew violently about the cave as a strong current of air came from the hole across the chamber. She felt it as it came toward her, then rushed past her. The icy breeze tore past her body, and she felt a presence which she did not understand, one which she had never felt before.

Her lamp became dimmer as the red powder in the room rushed past her. It also rushed up the ventilation holes in the ceiling chamber. The breeze continued and with it came a terrible moan which shook the cavern walls.

Finally she had seen and heard enough.

Something large and hideous seemed to form in the mist before her as she turned and began to travel back to the entrance of the small cave. As she crawled her light suddenly went out completely. She dropped it and decided that she would be able to travel faster without it, which was what she desperately wanted to do at this point. She could feel the cold air as it rushed past her, and she felt a grip around her ankles which seemed to hold her back, though she knew she was making progress.

As she came to the last corner she felt as if the grip which held her ankles had made its way up her legs. Now it held her waist as well and she could no longer resist the urge to scream out. She screamed as she squeezed her way quickly through the small hole, paying no attention to the damage she was inflicting upon her arms as she pushed frantically with her legs. She made it quickly through the hole and turned to her right into the blackness. She followed the curve to the small tunnel as the grip worked its way to her chest and made it difficult for her to breathe.

Then she saw the lights coming for her. She scrambled forward, fighting the force which held on to more and more of her body. She felt her legs growing numb from the cold, or the grip, she knew not which. The small round lights danced before her and she grew fearful of them, but she had much more fear of what lay behind her, so she continued toward them.

She came to what she thought should be the end of the tunnel, but there was no daylight, only the light of the orbs which came for her. She could no longer feel the walls of the small cave around her, but she continued to crawl forward, away from whatever lay behind her. She crawled ahead, upward, not knowing if she would run into a wall or fall from a precipice. She crawled ahead until the orbs came to her. They came forward dancing in the darkness and finally they converged upon her.

"Are you all right?" asked a voice from ahead.

The grip no longer had hold of her. The orb which stood directly before her was no mysterious entity, but a small wattage bulb on the end of a steel casing. It was a flashlight. The man who had asked the question had good reason to ask. He stood looking into a pale face riddled with both confusion and terror as well as a little dried blood. At the sound of his voice the face softened.

"Where are we?" she asked.

"In the cave," the man answered.

Then Helene felt the soft dirt under her hands and realized that she was indeed back inside the main cave. She had crawled fifty feet clear of the tunnel.

But where was the daylight?

"Why is it so dark?" she asked.

"Because it's night," one of the other men answered.

She got slowly to her feet, trying to shake her disorientation.

"But it can't be," she said. "I wasn't in there that long."

"Mrs. Justin was a little worried," the first man said. "She tried to call you at your motel when you didn't check in at sunset. Then she called us up to come look for you."

"What time is it?" she asked.

"Almost nine o'clock."

"But it can't be," she said again. "I was only there for an hour at most."

They all stood in an uneasy silence for a moment. Then the quiet man finally spoke.

"Let's get out of here now," he simply said. "I don't like it here."

Helene walked ahead of the first man who shined his light on the path ahead of her as they followed the first two men up and out of the cave.

In her mind she asked herself again and again what had happened.

Each time she got no answer.

Three

1

The deep dark of the warm night was broken up by a dazzling display of lights. Where only the sounds of nature were usually heard now roared the sounds of pumps and motors and working men.

It was ten o'clock and the crew was working overtime on the hole which was to make Buzz Shaw a wealthy and powerful man. Although there was no need for him, Buzz was there as well. He stood in front of the great drilling rig which had taken them three days to haul in a piece at a time and set up. Now it stood a great tower, the shaft in its center twisting and sinking into the earth as the drill bit which now lay a hundred feet below the earth tore at the rock, spitting fragments of it back to the surface for analysis.

Though it had been the only of his recommendations to be seriously questioned, Buzz knew that below the surface lay his destiny. He had reveled in that feeling as he had seen the results of the seismographic testing which had revealed that there was indeed a drastic change in the density of the earth which lay beneath them. The test could not reveal for certain if it was oil, or water, or a salt dome. But Buzz knew and he pushed the project through. One of his other recommended sites had hit oil and was already producing. The third was still being drilled, though they had already passed three thousand feet, and nothing had turned up. One out of three wasn't bad. The oil coming from the first well would most likely cover the costs involved in the drilling of all three holes. But that left no room for profit.

But Buzz was convinced that soon the score would be two out of three, and that this well would cover much more than the cost of drilling.

He raised his hands to his eyes and rubbed them. He had not slept well for weeks. On nights when he did sleep Buzz was haunted by indistinct but persistent dreams. Last night he had been unable to sleep at all as he lay waiting for the morning. He knew that this would be the day that the drill was going to be lowered into the earth. He had personally supervised the digging of the mud pits and the erection of the rig. Now he stood watching, waiting for something to happen.

But drilling was a slow process, and it might be days before he saw results. Buzz walked nervously over to the shale shaker to inspect the cuttings as they surfaced. So far it was still just white rock, limestone. If there was a trapping layer, they had not hit it yet. He watched as the white cuttings surfaced and bounced around on the equipment which separated the large cuttings from the mud. The mud was to be recirculated back down the hole for lubrication and removal of debris.

Cal Price sat in front of the various gauges and levers which monitored such things as the pressure of the drilling fluids and the speed and downward weight on the drill bit. As more and more sections of pipe were laid into the hole the pressure on the bit increased. Allowing the motor to turn a bit too fast would shorten the life of that expensive piece of drilling equipment, or even break it or warp the direction of the hole. The hole had to be straight and true. If the bit began to wander in any direction then the hole could be ruined. Likewise the pressure gauge had to be monitored constantly. A sudden jump in pressure could mean trouble if the hole was not closed off quickly. Gushers were a thing of the past. These days oil was precious, and there was no use in losing hundreds of barrels into the air when modern technology provided ways to capture it. There was also the possibility of hitting an underground aquifer and losing drilling fluids into it. Then they would have to pour cement down the hole and make a casing to protect the aquifer against contamination. These were just a few of the things Cal had to keep track of.

The resounding clang signaled the end of the twenty-foot section of pipe which had slowly been entering the earth. Cal turned off the drill while the crew surrounded the pipe and added another section. The operation took no more than thirty seconds, and the drill was once again turning and the joint where the two pieces of pipe met disappeared below the deck as it too entered the earth.

Cal was good at this. He had been working rigs all of his life, and his tight muscles and broad frame attested to that fact. His father had worked in the fields, and Cal had been there too, helping out at an age when child labor laws might have been a problem had they been enforced. He had seen all kinds of wells and all kinds of men. He trusted the men who worked with him on the rig, most of them anyway. He could tell when he met a man whose life had been spent like his, and he knew when he met a man who was new at it, even before any work had started. But even after thirteen on and off years with Texon he did not trust the men who made the decisions about where and when to drill. One of them was here now. He was fat and soft, and he hung over then men with a hungry look, waiting for something Cal knew might never come to pass. In this part of the state Cal doubted if they would find any oil, at least any which proved to be of any consequence.

Cal supervised most of the work at the rig. Most of the time he did so without the assistance of a 'suit', which was one of the nicer terms they had for the people in corporate. This time, however, the fat soft man stood over him the whole time, as much as the man could stand over Cal's six-foot five frame.

There had been a time when Cal worked the deck, moving pipe like the men before him now did. He liked that work better, it was harder and seemed somehow more honest. But that work had been taken from him along with his right arm when his carelessness and the overzealousness of the drill operator had combined to wrap it firmly around an eight-inch-wide piece of drill pipe. The pipe had spun slowly around, crushing bone and rending skin as it went. By the time the crunching and screaming had stopped Cal stood looking at his arm, knowing somehow that it was not natural that it be wound so tightly around such a small pipe, cut and torn by the chain he had used to tighten it in place. But the pain was distant, most of it had stayed with the arm which was torn halfway from its socket at this shoulder. The site had been a remote one, and there had been a lot of bleeding. When he woke the next day he had found himself to be one limb shorter than he had been before the merciful sleep had overtaken him.

Now he felt as if he had slipped slightly away from the realm of hard honest work. Now he was almost a liaison between the men in the offices and those in the field. He didn't like to think of himself that way. More importantly he didn't like the men to think of him that way. But it was apparent that they all did. Many of them held a grudge against him. Not because he was missing an arm, but because he had contact with the men in the offices, and that somehow made him unclean.

The clang sounded again, and again the routine was performed as another twenty feet of pipe was prepared for its descent into the earth.

Buzz stood watching the cuttings. There was another man who was performing this task, but Buzz paid no attention to him as he watched the process himself. He knew that this man was well trained for what he was doing, but Buzz was sure that he had no idea what would happen when the mud turned black, and the shouts began.

But for now the sounds of clanging pipe and powerful motors turning ruled the night.

2

Cal looked again at his watch. It was getting late now, and the men would be getting tired soon. Even though they would not admit it he knew that their response time was slowing. Buzz had told him that they would drill until they hit, but Cal was not going to let that happen. As it was they were only at three hundred and twenty feet. It could be another three thousand before they hit, or they might not hit at all. He could push his crew a little longer, then he would call it off no matter what the fat soft man said. Cal knew the dangers of working past one's limits. It was a place he had been to personally.

Then his eyes widened as one of the pressure gauges dropped immediately to zero.

"Get clear!" he shouted, and the men scrambled from the platform.

3

Buzz watched the cuttings as the white rock began to disappear and a heavy black rock began surfacing in blocks and chunks. He reached into the shaking plate and picked up one of the larger rocks. He took it in his hands and tried to break off a piece. A small corner chipped off. It was shale. The mud and the night made it appear darker than it was, so he didn't know for sure if it meant oil or not, but if it became denser then there was at least the possibility that he had a good solid layer of shale which would trap in any oil, unlike the limestone which let the oil escape.

Then the mud suddenly stopped flowing over the plate.

A moment later he heard Cal shout his warning to his men.

Buzz knew enough to know that what was happening was not good.

4

Cal looked up to the top of the drilling pipe which was still secured. He had hit the stop button, so it was no longer spinning, but it was still moving slightly, nonetheless. The pipe stayed secured so the immediate danger of the pipe slipping or breaking was over. Cal also hit the button which stopped the mud pumps. All of his gauges died, and the machinery came to a halt. Cal looked to his men who were either looking at him or looking at the suspended pipe. The only sound now was the sound of the pipe as it clanged against the sides of the steel casing below them.

Then there was the sound of footsteps approaching him quickly from behind. Cal resisted the urge to turn quickly and meet the stare of the man who was coming. Instead he waited until the steps came up behind him and the eyes gazed over his shoulders.

"Why did you stop it?" Buzz asked, sounding almost desperate.

"What happened first?" Cal asked.

"What?"

"You heard me." Cal finally turned around to meet the gaze of the fat soft man. "You were watching the shale shaker like a hawk. What happened first?"

"You tell me, you're the operator here."

"The mud stopped flowing first."

"You didn't turn the pump off?" Buzz asked, knowing that the pump was not running now. Had the pump given out?

"Only after the mud stopped flowing."

"So quit playing games with me and tell me what's up."

Cal enjoyed confirming his preconceived ideas about the men from the office. Any oil man would have already figured out what he was saying. The men on the deck below who had been listening did now, and they each displayed their own signs of disgust.

"We're pumping mud down into the hole, and nothing's coming back up."

"So we've hit an aquifer or some porous rock then," Buzz commented, forgetting the brittle black rock he had held in his hands moments before.

"We'd be lucky if that was it," Cal said. He looked back to the pipe which had quit making its racket and now just swung lightly back and forth. "Ever seen a pipe swing back and forth like that?"

"No." Buzz was getting tired of playing the game. He knew that Cal was just trying to make him look stupid. He also knew that the man was succeeding. "Why?"

"Well, a pipe that's pushing down on a bit three hundred plus feet under the ground doesn't do that."

The picture still wasn't clear to Buzz. "So why isn't it pushing down on the bit?"

"Because the bit and God knows how much the pipe has broken off."

Buzz's face slowly paled, and Cal thought this made him look even softer. As much as hated what had just happened, he got tremendous pleasure watching the fat soft man go pale.

"So how do we get it out?"

"I don't think it's going to be that easy," Cal explained.

"What do you mean?"

"Well, the pipe didn't just break in the hole. If that had happened this pipe here would be jammed in next to it, and I think we'll be able to pull it out pretty easily from the way it's swinging. I'd be surprised if there's a hundred feet on the end of it."

"So where did it go?"

Cal looked at the pipe, then to his men. He sat silent for a moment, letting the fat soft man feel stupid just a little longer. Then he turned and faced him again.

"I think we've hit a cavern of some kind."

It all came together in Buzz's head now. Cal was right. They had broken through into a cavern and lost pressure as the mud escaped the system by flowing out the bottom of the hole. They had probably lost the bit and some pipe as well.

"Can we fish out the pipe?" Buzz asked.

"Maybe. Won't know until we try."

"Even if we can't fish it out, we can run a new bit down there and start and start drilling again at the bottom of the cavern. Surely you've hit pits like this before."

Cal had hit pits like this before, and he knew how much trouble they could be. He couldn't imagine that this hole was worth the time or the money they were about to put into it, but that was not his decision.

Buzz made a decision. "Let's pull out and try to get that pipe out of there."

"Not tonight," Cal said.

"What do you mean, 'not tonight'?" Buzz was becoming irritated by this man who obviously thought he had more control than reality dictated.

"I mean my men have been working this hole since early this morning, and if I push them any further there's going to be trouble in the form of injuries and more damaged equipment. They're tired. We'll start again in the morning."

Buzz's eyes widened and the color came back to his face too quickly. His cheeks turned red, and Cal could see the rage beginning to build. For just a moment it scared him. It seemed to be way out of proportion for the situation.

"We will work this hole until I say it's quitting time. Are you forgetting who the boss is here?"

"No, sir," Cal said, trying to maintain a somewhat respectful air despite the total disrespect. "But I'm responsible for the well-being of my crew, and they've had enough tonight."

I'm responsible for their well-being, Mr. Price, not you. If anyone here is injured it is ultimately my responsibility, not yours. This is my well, my neck on the line. You're just a pee-on button pusher who's far from qualified to make the kind of decisions you're trying to make, and if you can't do what you're told, I'll find someone who can."

Cal watched as the anger turned slowly to fury. It seemed odd to him that this man was possessed by this task. The situation was absurd. The fat soft man was not acting rationally. What he said was true. Cal could push his men until someone got hurt, or killed, and it would be Buzz's responsibility since he was the senior man at the hole. But Cal didn't want to put his men in that kind of danger. He cared for these men.

"These men here do have lives, you know," he started. He stood from his chair, towering over the much shorter Buzz who took a step back to compensate. "No matter what you think of them, they do have lives, and families. They aren't like pieces of equipment that you can simply replace when they break. I will not push my men any further. And I doubt very seriously that an office type like yourself who can't even tell when a pipe's busted is more qualified than I am to say when it's quitting time." He stared effectively into Buzz's eyes and watched them as they softened. Then he shouted in a voice loud enough for his men to hear, and loud enough to make the fat soft man before him jump, "It's quittin' time!"

The men began to secure the equipment and Cal turned away from Buzz to secure and lock his console. Buzz knew there was nothing he could say to make the men continue their work. He turned and walked away from Cal's back and headed toward his car which sat a hundred feet north of the mud pits, near the old broken house that had originally called him to this place. Tomorrow the work would begin again, early. And he would be here to watch it. Eventually he would see to it that Cal was taken off the job, maybe even off the payroll. But for now Cal was the most qualified man for the project, and there would be no way to replace him inside of two weeks, and Buzz couldn't wait that long. He knew Cal was good, but that didn't mean he had to like him.

And he didn't like him at all.

Buzz walked away from the rig, downcast and defeated. The excitement of the day left him and suddenly he was very tired. He completed the walk to his car where he got in and took one last look at the rig as the men tumbled off of it like ants escaping their nest for another home. Then the big lights which lit the rig went out one section at a time until the darkness reclaimed the area.

Millions of stars leapt out from their hiding places and Buzz looked to where moments before the rig had commanded the horizon. Now it was but a bulky and defeated shadow rising up from the dead ground.

Then he thought he saw something near the rig. At first he supposed that it was one of the men, but they were all in their trucks, heading back toward the road. He stayed in his car with the engine and lights off, staring towards the shadow of the rig, watching for the movement he had thought he had seen.

As he watched and waited in a trance-like state the darkness grew and sleep overtook him.

5

Buzz found himself in that terrible place again. It was a place which he knew well when surrounded by its awful elements, but when he was away he could only recall fragments of elusive images. Now he was in that place again, and the terror of it returned.

He looked around and again he saw the screaming and melting faces. He saw the images of a hundred dancing men, perhaps more, as they bobbed at the horizon of his vision. They did not seem far away, yet they were indistinct and blurred. Then the darkness fell away in blocks as a new light invaded his consciousness. He reached forward but could not see his own hand. He looked down and remembered that here he had no body. He tried to cry out, but he had no voice.

The brightness enveloped him, then fell away and left him in a shadow looking up through a hole toward the heavens. As he looked through the hole he saw the bird as it appeared on the horizon. He knew where this would lead and he tried in vain to change the dream, but the bird approached. Buzz struggled to break free of the images and he wondered if this was how Prometheus must have felt having his liver devoured by the eagle every day, then healing again for the next day and the next attack. Buzz's chains, however, were chains of the unconscious and he could not see them. They held him fast and would not allow him to escape this place. He had no eyes to close nor a head to turn away so he watched in terror as the great white bird grew larger, its fiery eyes trained upon the man who could not even see himself. Here Buzz could not cry out, nor could he run. All he could do was experience the terror as it swept over him and reduced him to nothing more than his bare emotions. Here he was not Buzz Shaw. Here he simply - Was.

The bird came to him and tore him from his place, carrying him up into the heavens. Though Buzz had nobody he could feel the hawk's talons as they tore through him and ripped his soul to shreds. He watched as once again the old house grew smaller beneath him. The bird carried him into the brightness which burned. The brightness grew to such an intensity that he could no longer see the bird, though he could feel the talons still tearing and ripping. Then he heard a scream and felt the talons pull from his soul. He felt the brightness rush past him and suddenly he saw the house beneath him approaching rapidly. For only an instant it was a speck, then it was the house, then he was upon it. The house rushed past him as he fell toward a pit which sat beside the house, the pit where now the earth had been penetrated by the hardware which he had brought to it. The pit was an open mouth, a gaping maw with eternal teeth and suddenly he was in it and the world was black.

And the screaming continued until it was all that there was.

And he saw the darkness before him, but he did not know where he was, nor did he remember where he had just been.

Then he realized, awake now in his car, that the screaming was his own.

He sat up in the car and tried to remember the dream which left his heart racing and his clothes soaked with sweat once again. The terror lingered, though now he could brush it aside with rationality and he did so. He looked around, disoriented for only a moment before he realized that he was still at the drill site. He looked at his watch and saw that it was just past midnight. He had fallen asleep. He didn't think he had been that tired, but apparently he had been. Buzz was glad he had fallen asleep here, instead of on the road. He looked to the terrain before him and reached for his headlight switch, the dream all but forgotten.

But then he saw something move in the darkness before him and a part of that dream came loose in his mind. Buzz did not turn on his headlights. He knew, somehow, that if he turned on the lights he would see nothing unusual. Whatever it was he had seen could be seen better in the dark.

Buzz got out of his car and retrieved his flashlight from the trunk. He would use it so that he could see the path before him, though he decided that he would not shine it down that path as it might obscure whatever it was he truly wished to see. He slammed the trunk shut and began to walk toward the outline of the rig before him. The darkness had a presence of its own and his light seemed to have trouble cutting through it. Buzz covered the distance between himself and the rig slowly, his eyes darting back and forth between the dark shadow of the rig and the path. As he approached the rig the beam from his flashlight grew dimmer. He held his hand out in front of the flashlight. It didn't seem to be losing any of its strength. The circle which it cast upon the ground, however, was growing smaller. Buzz had to walk more slowly as the rocks from the excavation work were strewn about the ground, making random obstacles to his journey.

As Buzz came to the rig, the beam of his flashlight no longer reached the ground. Again he placed his hand near the end of the flashlight, and again it seemed to be putting out about the same amount of light. He mounted the steps and walked onto the deck of the rig. The warmth of the evening fled and suddenly he could feel the thickness of the darkness which surrounded him. It was cold and it sent shivers throughout his body. He could feel the darkness prodding and probing him, it flowed around him like a mist, one he could feel but not see.

The fear which should have taken hold of him only tugged at the corners of his mind. In its place was something which quieted the fear and pushed it back into the recesses of his brain where it could barely be heard as it cried out its warnings. Buzz pointed the flashlight at the hole where the pipe had been earlier. Somewhere down that hole was the cavern, and somewhere in the cavern lay the rest of the pipe they had been drilling with. He leaned over and shined the light down the hole, but the beam did not go below ground level. He could see the ground, and the place where the hole was, but somehow light did not enter the hole.

Buzz got to his feet and walked to the end of the platform where he descended the short steps to the ground. Then he got onto his stomach and began to crawl. His mind continued its stifled cries of warning, but something greater urged him on and it was this voice he heeded. He crawled along on his stomach. His pants worked their way from his round waist as he crawled, but he ignored this and continued toward the hole. The air around him was cool and heavy and as he approached the hole he realized that he could see no stars through the opening in the deck. Buzz paused for a moment as his rational mind wrestled with his compulsion, but it was a short match, and he crawled the rest of the way.

When Buzz reached the hole he pointed the light into it, but still the beam would not pass the earth. He reached forward and pushed the flashlight into the hole, and the light disappeared completely. Buzz turned the flashlight back toward the surface, but no light emerged. He brought the flashlight back out of the hole and the beam came on suddenly as it passed the invisible barrier.

This was strange, and Buzz knew it was strange, but he also knew that it was wonderful. The things which should have been terrifying him were instead urging him on, calling him to the edge of the hole.

He crawled forward a little more until he could place his head over the hole and look down. He stared into the blackness of the pit and lowered his head past the barrier. As he did he felt an icy coldness bathe his eyes and a thousand needles pricked his brain. But he did not pull away. Instead he put his head in deeper. He felt the coldness run through his body and into his head where a piece of it nested in the front of his brain. He stared into the blackness below, waiting for something he did not understand.

Then he heard a terrible scream which was not his own. His heart raced as he realized that the scream had come from the cavern below. He tried to pull his head from the hole, but he could not as the thick darkness held him down.

"Oh my God!" he shouted out. Then he began to answer the scream he heard with one of his own.

Suddenly there was a soft rumbling of the earth and then a gust of icy air blew from the hole. It raced around his head and his nose and ears stung as if he were standing unprotected in a blizzard. The terror began to take hold as he pushed firmly against the ground. The hole was not trying to pull him in, but neither would it let him go.

Then there was a brilliant flash of light, and he felt a powerful shock which ran through his system. Everything came at him at once, all of his senses were assaulted. There was a loud clap and a thunder of voices, he could smell a bittersweet smell, like those black bugs which let out such an odor when he stepped on them. He felt the taste of honey, and of hot pepper, and of rotten meat on his tongue all at the same time and he almost gagged from the onslaught. It all happened in a matter of a couple of seconds and when it was over he lay on the ground breathless. His head was sore on the back where he had hit it on the steel structure above him when he had finally gotten loose. A moment later he realized that he wet himself. As he inspected himself with the flashlight he saw that he had also lost control of his bowels and that he had ejaculated.

He pulled his pants the rest of the way off and dragged them along as he crawled back out of the hole. When finally got out from under the deck he stood and pulled his pants back on. He stood feeling very uncomfortable and smelling of urine and worse. Then he shined the flashlight on the path in front of him and realized the darkness was no longer so oppressive. Buzz turned the light to the deck behind him and saw whatever had hindered the beam was no longer there.

Buzz turned around and headed back to the car, feeling quite uncomfortable as he went. As he climbed into the car he turned back to look at the old house which was about fifty feet away. Something in his mind clicked. The house had something to do with his dreams, but exactly what he didn't know. There was something inside of him now which had made that connection, something that had not been there just thirty minutes earlier.

Buzz wanted to go into the house, but his immediate desire to go home and clean up was stronger, at least tonight.

But even as he drove toward Del Rio the thing now inside of his head began to grow.

6

Jim Dewey's ranch was right next to Merle's. While Merle had stopped raising cattle long ago, Jim ran over a hundred head, which was no easy task on only twelve hundred acres. On many ranches the land's capacity was measured in cows per acre. Here it was measured in acres per cow. Most of what little greenery spotted the landscape was inedible grasses and plants, though there was a little edible material which grew in the places where the ground was just a little more hospitable. And usually Jim could plant five acres of oats or hay grazer, which he let them graze an acre at a time.

But this year his oats had dried up and blown away soon after they had begun to sprout. And the natural grasses, even the weeds, were brown and dead. With the heat had come only a little rain, and that had been too long ago.

Even the night brought no relief from the heat. It was no longer a hundred degrees, but it only cooled off to the middle eighties, which was not a comfortable sleeping temperature. Jim was not comfortable. Neither was his wife. The swamp cooler circulated air but did not cool it. They could not spare the water to make it work. The well was not dry, yet, but the water was slow to come and dirty when it did, sure signs that it was soon to disappear until the next hard rain, which was nowhere in sight.

Jim lay facing the window, looking at the fluttering curtains and thinking about his cattle, his land, his property taxes. He was glad he didn't owe anything on his equipment or his land because this year he would only make enough money to buy food and pay the electric bill. There would be no trip to Las Vegas, that would have to wait for a better year.

Then he saw the light outside. It was small, and it hovered about three feet off the ground. It was moving steadily across the landscape, as if someone was carrying a flashlight and walking through the night. Only it was moving too fast. Then it began to move faster, and suddenly it darted out of sight, around to the front of the house.

Then somebody knocked on the front door.

Jim rolled out of bed and instinctively grabbed his shotgun. Nobody he knew that had any good intentions would be at his door at this hour, and he was still unsure about that light. He put on his robe and walked to the door, his gun swinging by his side. There had been just the one knock and no other. He began to wonder if perhaps he had only been only partially awake, that some dream had made the light and the knocking. He opened the door to be sure.

As he opened it he lowered his gun. He recognized this old man. But then he remembered that Merle was supposed to be dead, killed by a heart attack, or that's what he'd been told anyway. He'd heard there had been more, something about fire.

"Good evening, Jim."

Jim could still see the light. It was inside of Merle, floating in his stomach and shining out of it. The light dimmed and disappeared, but Merle remained. He didn't answer the old man. Instead he looked at the leathery face which was covered in burn marks. His eyebrows were missing, and his clothes were soot-black.

"I need your help, Jim."

Jim looked but didn't answer. He felt as if he were dreaming, as if he should run but could not. Instead he faced this thing that stood at his door. He stared at it, dumbfounded, wondering what he was supposed to do now. Then a peaceful feeling tingled in his head and ran through his body. It calmed him and removed his fear. Then his thoughts began to come to him.

"Aren't you dead, Merle?"

"If I was, would I be talkin' to you now?"

"I don't know, Merle. You don't look so good."

"I'm an old man, I'm not supposed to look good."

Jim looked him up and down again. "But you look burned up. What happened?"

Merle looked down at himself as if he hadn't noticed. "My goodness, Jim, you're right. I do look a little singed." He looked back up at Jim and smiled, his lips burnt and oddly twisted.

Jim was confused. "What's this all about?"

"I'm in some trouble, and I need some help."

Something was tickling Jim's brain again. "What is it Merle?"

"Remember that old cave I told you about?"

Jim Remembered Merle's crazy stories about what he called the cursed cave. "Of course. What's going on?"

"Well, you were right. I am dead." The news didn't seem to trouble Jim now, now that something had gotten a firm grip on his brain. "Those dern kids finally got in there and messed things up, and then they did this to me."

"Jesus, Merle. Kids did that to you?"

Merle just nodded.

"Local kids?"

"I think so."

Jim looked up and down Merle again. Then he heard a soft voice behind him.

Neddie, Jim's wife of thirty years, had heard Jim get out of bed and then she heard him talking to someone. At first she had let him be, supposing it had to do with his work. But it had been some time, and Neddie was afraid there might be trouble. So she put on her own robe and walked to the front door. As she approached it she could see her husband standing, facing the night. He was looking up and down, talking as if someone was standing right in front of him. But there was no one there. Was he sleepwalking? If so, it would be the first time she had ever caught him doing this.

Merle looked over Jim's shoulder for a moment, then back to Jim. Jim wanted to look back too, but Merle's eyes were burning into him, and they demanded attention.

"I want you to help me. I need you to fix the cave, and guard it for me."

"Fix it? How?"

"I'll tell you later." Merle looked over Jim's shoulder again. "Right now I need another, more important favor."

"Jim?"

Jim heard the voice behind him. At first he thought he recognized it, but then the recognition faded. He tried to turn around and look, but Merle's eyes continued to burn him.

"I want revenge, Jim."

Jim looked into those burning eyes. "But how?"

The voice behind him again, "Jim?"

This time he was able to look away from Merle. He turned around to see who was calling him. It was a voice he thought he should know, but as he turned he did not recognize the face.

"Jim, who are you talking to?"

Jim watched as the fat kid walked across his living room toward him. How did this kid know his name? And what was he doing in his living room? Instinctively he raised his gun.

Neddie stopped. "Jim? What are you doing?"

"What are you doing in here?" he asked the boy.

"I heard you talking," Neddie replied. "I thought there might be trouble." She looked nervously at his gun. "Jim, don't point that thing at me."

Jim heard Merle's voice over his shoulder. "Revenge, Jim. I need revenge." Then he saw the long knife in the kid's hand. The kid looked at him with strangely familiar eyes.

Then Jim heard the word revenge again, and he pulled the trigger.

Neddie fell back with the impact of the shot. The nine double-aught pellets tore through her body and burst her heart and liver. She died instantly, her blood coloring the living room floor and part of the wall.

Jim heard laughter coming from behind him. He turned around and looked at Merle. His glowing light had returned.

"Only two more," Merle cackled.

"I thought there were only two?" Jim replied.

"There are two more."

Jim knew Merle was right. "I'll help you Merle. Tell me what to do."

Fifteen minutes later Jim was heading out his front door with his rifle and a box of shells. He locked his door as he left, not worrying about the dead kid in his living room. Something still bothered him about that kid, but he brushed it from his mind and headed toward the fence line, toward Merle Walker's property.

The light red mist encircled his feet as he walked.

Four

1

Helene sat in the coffee shop listening to the morbid conversation being carried on in the small booth behind her. Apparently an old man who everyone had known fairly well had hanged himself during the night. The man had never really gotten over the death of his wife according to one of the two women. It was most likely this which had driven him to the act. Helene didn't really want to listen, but the voices were too close, and she could not block them out merely with her thoughts, so she found herself being drawn into the role of eavesdropper.

Helene drank a second cup of coffee as she sat waiting for John Stein. Her professor was going to make the long drive to Comstock to see for himself what Helene had stumbled onto. He was bringing another graduate student whom Helene knew but didn't particularly like. He was a very competitive man who felt threatened by Helene's ambition as well as her excellence. In a way, however, she was glad the jerk would be coming. That way he would see firsthand the discovery which she, not he, had made. The animosity was a silent but well understood one, and one which he had initiated. There was no other student with whom Helene did not get along. She was the kind of person who gave everybody a fair chance. A person really had to work at getting on her bad side, and Todd had really worked at it. Professor Stein knew about the rivalry. He was probably bringing Todd for two reasons. First, Todd was his second-best student. Second, the professor probably wanted to humble Todd some by showing him what Helene, not Todd Dumfreys, had found.

Despite her extreme excitement about the whole affair, Helene had not returned to the cave since her initial encounter three days earlier. Her fear and her recurring dreams of what had happened on her last excursion had outweighed her enthusiasm. She might have been able to find a local to go back in with her sooner, but she decided it would be worth the wait to get her professor to go with her, if he would come. John had been reluctant at first, but when she had described the cavern and the drawings she found his hesitation had faded and his paper on restoring first century sites had become a little less important.

Last night her dreams had taken a different turn. At first it was merely the same nightmare. In this dream she had been reliving the terror of her scramble out of the cave which had taken place three days earlier, along with a little embellishment in the form of glowing eyes and reaching claws. But last night, sometime after midnight, the dream had been interrupted by something more powerful than a dream. It was more like an image or a vision. In this vision she had seen a man lying over a hole which led to a deep pit. From the pit there was flowing a variety of things which lit everything up to a hot, red brilliance. Something was coming from the pit, and it was a terrible thing which she could not comprehend. Then the man had disappeared and in his place stood a terrible creature, something which reminded her of her own idea of what a true demon might look like.

Then the image had disappeared suddenly and left her in blackness.

Less than a thousand feet away, at the gas station next to the cafe, a middle-aged man was describing that same vision. About a dozen other people in Comstock remembered that vision as well, and many more had forgotten it.

Helene sat in the diner for another half hour until she saw the familiar blue van pull in front of the cafe. On the side of the van were printed the words 'University of Texas Department of Archaeology.' Below the words a small orange bull's head, a longhorn, had been painted on by some of the students who had wanted to make sure that the van had been properly blessed by the school mascot. Helene watched as

Professor Stein got out of the passenger's side and closed his door. He turned to the cafe and waved at Helene. She saw Todd as he too got out of the van, but she did not look directly at him, and he did not wave.

Professor Stein walked slowly, and she could see the toll which the five-hour drive had taken on his aging joints. He was not an old man, he had just turned fifty-three, but he was old enough that such journeys were slightly harder on his joints than they had been thirty years earlier. Even Todd looked a little stiff.

The two men walked into the cafe, past the cash register to the table where Helene sat. Professor Stein sat across from Helene. Todd sat next to her. Todd knew this would bother her a little more, and that was part of why he did it.

"Well, Helene, it was as long a drive as I thought it would be."

"I'm glad you made it," she said. "I really wanted you to see this, it's really quite spectacular."

"Professor Stein says you found some new drawings," Todd blurted out. They were not drawings, they were pictographs. He knew this. The word 'drawings' somehow lessened the importance of what she had found, as might have the term 'chicken scratch.'

"Yea," she threw toward Todd, without looking at him. Then she reached down to the seat beside her and pulled a small envelope out of her purse. She reached across the table and handed the envelope to Professor Stein who accepted it with raised eyebrows. "I drove over to Del Rio where I found a one-day photo place."

Professor Stein opened the envelope and took out the pictures. They were not clear, and the lighting from the flash was incongruous as was the wall it was trying to light up. But he could see enough to know that this was an exciting site, and that the pictographs were good ones.

"I'm afraid my automatic camera wasn't so sure what it was I was trying to take pictures of," Helene explained.

"I brought a camera which will take excellent pictures," Todd explained, as if in rebuke.

To Professor Stein Helene said, "I spoke with Mrs. Justin again this morning to make sure we could still get out there. She's pretty much given us free reign to go out whenever and however often we like. She even told me that I didn't have to check with her anymore unless we were going to be bringing in heavy equipment."

"Did she seem reluctant about equipment?" the Professor asked.

"No," Helene replied, "she even said that she simply wanted to be notified so that she could have some men around to help direct the efforts so she could preserve the certain areas that she's partial to."

"That's great." He smiled slightly as he spoke and handed the pictures to Todd. "I hope her willingness to work with us stays at its current level."

"I've spoken with her about four times now, including once in person before I went down alone. She has continually stated how terrible she feels that our work had to be hindered for so long by her late brother's stubbornness."

"So he died and now it's okay, huh," Todd threw in sarcastically as he flicked quickly through the pictures and feigned disinterest. He knew that such blunt references to the subject of death disturbed Helene.

"Yea," she threw at him again, mostly ignoring his comments.

A waitress appeared and asked them if they were ready to order at which Professor Stein explained they had not yet looked over the menu. The young waitress flushed slightly and walked away, returning shortly with the paper menus.

They ordered and ate lunch, discussing and planning their afternoon carefully. The Professor had brought all the equipment they would need to get into the cavern and catalog what they found. They might do only some preliminary digging around to see what artifacts, if any, lay buried in the underground cavern.

Helene had told them what she had seen in the cavern, but she had not explained the things she had felt, and in the past three days she had come to discount these things. As the terror had grown more distant the reasons for it had become less real. Explanation had made their way into her conscious mind and now she truly believed that she had been imagining most of what had happened. But her subconscious had not been convinced and had reminded her of the terror nightly. Even now it knocked on the door of her consciousness, filling her with a feeling of uneasiness as they discussed the methods by which they would enter and explore the cave in a few hours.

2

Jim Dewey saw them coming. He had been sleeping in the shade of the brush when they drove up, and they had startled him at first. As he picked his rifle up from the ground and began to sight it in, he heard a reassuring voice. These people were to be let in. He was not needed yet. Still he sighted in on Todd's head and his finger tensed on the trigger. He wondered what it might be like to kill a man instead of a deer. But he would have to wait for another time. His drive to protect the cave was tremendous, and the only thing which kept him from pulling the trigger was his fear of the voices.

3

By two o'clock that afternoon the three of them stood at the entrance of the large cave. Professor Stein carried a rope around his shoulder and a small but powerful flashlight in his left hand. On his back and on both Helene's and Todd's set small backpacks which carried the tools they would need once inside the cavern. Helene and Todd carried their own flashlights.

The three of them stood at the entrance for a moment, sensing somewhat, though not understanding the magnitude of it, the ominous nature of what they were about to undertake. Helene stood looking into the dark cave, remembering again what her imagination had done to her the last time. Only now, with the cave before her, it seemed like it might have been real. Her nerves tightened up as she led the descent into the cave.

They walked into the pit with their lights trained ahead of them. Helene led them down the gradual slope to the place where the floor of the cave leveled out. Professor Stein bent down and grabbed a handful of dirt.

"This is fascinating," he said. Probably no one had disturbed this layer in thousands of years. He looked it over quickly but could tell nothing. A small piece of shiny black rock appeared as he sifted the fine dirt through his hand. Though it was small and represented just a fragment, he could tell that he was holding a piece of an arrowhead. Perhaps this arrowhead had killed deer or buffalo. It might have served its maker well, feeding him and his family until they finally moved on. The professor's mind ran through the places of the past in a second and a wonderful feeling came over him.

Helene stood and waited. If Professor Stein stopped at each location and reveled in it like this they wouldn't get to the cavern for hours. But that was why they had started five hours before sunset.

Still squatting he let the arrowhead drop back to the floor and looked up to the small hole in the ceiling thirty feet above him. Enough light came in to highlight the features of the rough ceiling of the ancient home. Then he stood and looked forward, waiting for Helene to lead on. A small but noticeable smile stayed on his face. He looked to Helene like a child who had awakened to a bountiful Christmas morning.

But Helene's face showed no such joy as a cool breeze which came from the hole at the end of the cave reminded her of what might be awaiting them. Her fear increased a notch, but she did her best to hide it from the men.

She led them onward to where the floor was level for several feet until it ended abruptly in the wall which shot back to the ceiling above them. Professor Stein's eyes darted about the area, following the beam of his light. He saw in his mind where the people had slept, where they had eaten and where the communal toilet must have been. He scanned the ceiling for smoke-stained holes which would have served as vents for the campfires, though it seemed that the large hole now behind him served this purpose. He threw the light quickly to the wall before him where the pictographs sprang to life for him. Todd was opening his pack and removing the camera equipment to take pictures which would show detail which Helene's did not. He pulled a small tripod from the sack and mounted the large format camera on it. Professor Stein walked to the wall for a close inspection of the pictographs while Todd finished setting up the camera.

"Fantastic," he said again. "Here," he said, pointing to a stick figure on the wall, "here is a shaman." He looked to the right and saw other familiar drawing. "Here are the deer pictographs, just like in Panther cave. They look almost as if they were made by the same hand. Surely they were made by someone who had at least seen the Panther pictographs when they were new. They're even from the same era." He walked along the wall, talking as much to himself as he was his students. Todd began snapping photos, moving his tripod along the wall after each series of shots. He covered the entirety of the painted wall, using up a whole roll of film in the process. When they returned to Austin he would be able to reconstruct this wall first in sketchings, then in a more detailed map. The final map would have to be completed in the cave, where the subtleties of the overlapping and overlaid pictographs could be captured.

Helene stood back from the wall, walking slowly along with her professor as he walked and commented. With him as her guide she now saw ten times as many pictographs as she had seen on her first trip. His keen eyes and observant mind, honed by years of this kind of work, revealed to her the faded images which her mind had dismissed as discoloring in the rocks. Again she felt as if she was unworthy of the work, unable to decipher with the perfection that her professor did before her eyes. But she knew that this too would come with time.

When the wall had been satisfactorily cataloged and Professor Stein had made the appropriate notes in his book, everything was stuffed into the packs except the flashlights. The professor looked to Helene, ready for her to lead on.

Helene took them to the corner of the cave where the floor sloped downward, and the ceiling did not meet the wall so abruptly. The ceiling and the floor worked their way slowly together, and they proceeded down the slope to the hole from which she had escaped just three days earlier.

The hole looked like an open hungry mouth, awaiting her return. Her fear rose quickly within her, and her resolve began to weaken. She stopped where the ceiling and the floor were five feet apart, slightly bent over. Then she trained her light on the hole before them and just looked into it.

"So there's the hole," Todd said mockingly.

"It's really tight in there," she explained. "I think you can make it through all right," she said to the lean Professor Stein. Then she turned to Todd, "But there's no way you'll make it past the first turn."

Todd was not fat, but he was definitely above the normal weight for his size. He caught the jab, and it was the first serious punch thrown that afternoon. He did not snap back because he knew she was probably telling the truth, and because he could think of nothing potent to say.

"You'll need the real camera," he pointed out. It was meant to put Helene back a little, but it didn't come off that way.

"Let's empty out our packs and repack two of them with just what we really need in there."

The three of them removed their packs and emptied them out. They then loaded two of the packs to the point to which they would barely zip shut. Helene and Professor Stein each picked up a pack and began to walk toward the hole. Todd followed to the point at which they had to get to their hands and knees. Helene looked back and received the pleasure she expected from the forlorn look which Todd quickly, but not quickly enough, removed from his face.

As she looked back to the hole she stopped and shined the light in. A cool and very gentle breeze blew past her and sent shivers through her body. She was ready to go. But she could not.

Todd caught the hesitation and had to comment. "Something wrong?" he asked from his sitting place ten feet behind them.

She looked back to Professor Stein, and he caught the soft but pleading look in her eyes. He could see that for some reason she was afraid. He knew her better than this and finally asked her the question which had been bugging him since his dream the night before. "Did something happen here that frightened you?"

She wanted to say yes. She wanted to tell him at least a little. But Todd was too close, and he would hear, and he would hold it over her forever. "No," she lied.

Professor Stein knew she was lying, and he also understood why. "Would you like me to lead?" he asked her.

The look of relief which flashed quickly across her face answered his question before the words came from her lips. Todd did not catch the exchange, and fortunately did not understand nor did he care why the switch was taking place.

Professor Stein got to his belly and began to crawl through the small hole, pushing his pack in front of him. Back at the cafe Helene had drawn a quick map of the cave, and as he crawled forward he went slowly, using the light to work his way through the darkness before him. When he came to the first corner he rolled to his side and made the turn to the left. He immediately saw the tight place which Helene had described. Just looking at it he wondered if he would be able to get through, or he just might get stuck. He had done this kind of thing before and any time there was a hole which offered less than a couple of inches leeway it provided the illusion that it would be impossible to get through. Experience had taught him to compensate against the illusion and as he did so he still wondered if he could get through.

But despite Helene's thin frame she did have fairly large hips, which John Stein did not. He realized that if she had made it through, he would be able to. But she was right, Todd's poor eating habits would certainly have stopped their excursion right here. Why she waited until they had arrived to tell him this was probably a result of the often not so silent rivalry.

John pushed his pack through, then picked the best angle to crawl through the hole. He put his arms before him, shining the light into the small hole. As he looked ahead he could see the wall which had given Helene her small yet noticeable bruise on her otherwise unblemished face. He crawled forward, using his knees and elbows to propel him. As he crawled he felt the stone pressing on him from all directions and was glad he had passed on the cherry pie at the diner. As he pulled his hips through the small opening he turned his body to the right to avoid smashing his own face. The corner was tight, but his head was coming into an area where the floor fell away and there would be room for crawling on hands and knees again.

He pulled himself into the larger portion of the cavern and waited while he listened to the struggling sounds of Helene as she made her way through the small passage. When he saw her pack appear he reached forward and pulled it into the area where he sat. He watched the beam of her flashlight as it danced on the wall behind him. Finally her arms, then her head appeared. He made room for her, and she slid into the larger area panting heavily more from fear of the tight place she had just been through than the effort she had put forth.

"Shall we take a rest here?" he asked Helene.

"No," she said between breaths, "It's pretty easy from here on out."

"I'd let you lead now, but I'm afraid there's not quite enough room to let you pass." He knew the excitement of a new find, and the sense of ownership which its discoverer had.

"That's okay," she replied. "Just tell me what to do when we get to the cavern."

He turned away from her and began to crawl forward again. There was more room here, but not enough to crawl along with the pack on his back, so he continued to push it ahead of him.

They made the gradual turn to the right until they came to the place where the cave straightened out and began to descend. Despite the terrible heat above, John was now glad he had worn a long-sleeved shirt as his breath became visible before him.

Finally he could see a place ahead of him where the floor of the cave disappeared. As he crawled closer he could see that the entire tunnel opened up. When he came to the end of the tunnel he could see the cavern into which the small tunnel spilled.

"This must have been cut by an underground stream which emptied into a small lake, or more like a small puddle."

"There's an exit hole at the bottom, on the other side."

"That's right." He remembered that she had pointed this out on her map, but he had forgotten it since she had not explored it.

John shined his light around the cavern, observing the rock formations and indistinct drawings. He saw the blackened holes in the roof which indicated that a fire or two had been lit in here. The vent holes went all the way to the surface, or at least they once had. The absence of any movement in the air suggested to him that they had been closed off some time in the past thousand years. Then he remembered feeling a cool breeze just before climbing into the hole, and this puzzled him.

"I'm going in," he said.

"Do you need me to hold the rope?" she asked him.

"I think we should both go down there. I don't think we need the rope to get down, but it would make getting out much easier."

Just then Helene heard a distant clinking sound, then another.

"Did you hear that?" she asked.

John stayed still and listened, and the sound returned. "It's coming from behind us," he explained, "I think Todd must be doing some work in the large cave to keep occupied until we come back."

She felt silly for having let the sound frighten her, especially since it was only Todd, but her blushing cheeks could not be seen in the dark cave.

John opened his pack and removed a few tools with which he fastened one end of the rope to the floor of the tunnel he was sitting in. He had also done some mountain climbing in his life and he used such equipment now to ensure a good anchor. He threw the rope down into the cave and it hit the bottom with a thud. Then he turned around and slid his lower body over the edge of the tunnel. He grabbed the rope and let himself down gently to the floor below. His foot hit a stalagmite, and he adjusted his descent so as not to straddle it. The trip to the floor was a short one. He turned and faced the tunnel where Helene handed down the two packs. Then he took the packs and backed away from the landing area while Helene repeated the procedure he had just executed.

She reached the bottom of the cavern and turned to face her professor.

"Would you like to lead now?" he asked her.

She wanted to say no, he was the experienced one, but she knew that he was giving her some responsibility which would be hers upon completion. He was again being the professor.

She walked across the cavern floor to the place in the center where there were no stalagmites on the floor. She shined her light on the ceiling and saw that it was not level, that had been an illusion provided from the perspective of the tunnel. Actually the ceiling was a rough dome shape with the peak being directly overhead. It was at the peak that the ventilation holes scarred the ceiling. The shape of the ceiling explained why the stalagmites had grown only near the wall of the cavern and not in the center. The moisture which had made its way from above came into the cavern, then traveled away from the peak of the dome before finding a place to drip to the floor. This also explained why the stalag-mites nearest the center of the cavern were also the largest, and a few of them had reached the point where they had met with their descending cousins to form limestone columns. From where she stood she could not see over the formations to the tunnel which continued at the base of the cavern, but she knew where it was. She inspected the walls which she could not see clearly from the tunnel but found no markings. She was waiting for the sharp eye of her professor to catch her in error, but he said nothing as she ran her beam across the walls to the place where the drawings were concentrated.

"These are the only drawings I see in here," she explained.

"It's not usual that pictographs will be made in a cavern of this sort anyway," he said to her, though she already knew this. "They are almost exclusively confined to the dwelling places, and I see no evidence that this was such a place."

She scanned the floor and realized that she had in fact been walking on a stone floor, not one covered with fine dirt. Even the place where the fires had been built was stone. Apparently there had been only dozens of fires built in the cavern, not hundreds or thousands.

Helene turned her beam back to the wall and made her way away from the center of the cave, back through a series of first large, then smaller stalagmites, to the place where the exit tunnel met the floor. When the tunnel came to her view the images from her previous encounter came into her head and she froze for just an instant, but it was enough.

"Do you want to tell me about your last trip here, now that Todd's out of hearing range?"

Helene looked down at the tunnel on the ground before her. As she stood she thought she could feel an icy breeze coming from that tunnel and wrapping her ankles. But the air was still, and her pants were quite thick.

"I just let my imagination get away from me," she explained, "that's all."

She turned to face him, and he smiled. He understood that for now she did not want to compromise her professional integrity, despite what she may or may not have experienced on her last trip down here. He bent down and unloaded the camera and tripod from his pack and began to set up in the center of the cavern. She turned away from him and looked again to the hole in the ground which must have once been how the water exited this cavern.

Which meant it continued.

But how far back did it go, and were there any more caverns? The cowboy who had stumbled upon Carlsbad Caverns in New Mexico had certainly had no idea that what he found would someday be a three-mile hike for tourists. Those caverns had been formed the same way. She may have seen only a small and insignificant portion of the whole system of caves and caverns.

And if this was the case, then how much more of it had the ancient people found, and what archaeological treasures might await them?

And what terrors?

The last thought jumped into her mind before she had a chance to prepare for it and again a shiver ran through her.

Then there was a flash of light which made her jump and she let out a stifled scream.

And again she blushed as her professor advanced the film to the next frame. He looked at her back as he did so, wondering what was in her mind that was making her so jumpy.

Helene walked away from the hole and toward the center of the cavern where she could be with her professor. Silently she was turning control of the situation over to him, and he understood. She was afraid he would be disappointed , but he understood some, and wished she would talk to him so he would understand more. He was certainly a scientist, but he had been touched by the supernatural more than once in his work and he had not closed his mind to many possibilities.

"You know," he said as he concentrated on the multi-layered wall before him, "once I was in northwestern India, near the Himalayas, working on an old site which had been in place for some time. It was thought that the site had been worked pretty well, but we hit a layer where it seemed a whole new culture had existed."

He paused and snapped a picture. He did not look at her as he spoke, to keep the pressure down. Instead he turned the camera a few degrees to his right and set up for another photo.

"One morning I went down to get a head start, I wanted to at least appear as eager as I was for professional reasons. When I got there, I found that one of the other men working the site had decided to do the same thing and had gotten there almost an hour before me."

Another flash, and another adjustment.

"I found him sitting in a corner, babbling something about a ghost. I figured he, being much senior to me and prone to practical jokes, was trying to pull one over on his young helper. I turned and began to walk into one section of the dig where there were some underground rooms capped with some heavy stone. As I walked from him I felt a feeble grip on my pants leg which I assumed was for effect."

He took the picture, then relocated the entire set up to get some pictures of the new pictographs and the small tunnel below them.

"I went into the room to see what this guy was trying to scare me with. When I turned a corner, about a hundred feet back into the cave, I saw a large and indistinct white cloud which I assumed was to be the object of my fear."

Finally he raised his head from the camera and looked into her eyes.

"I walked over to the thing to see what kind of sheet or projection it was. When I got to it my light went out, but I could still see it. Still thinking this was a hoax I walked to the object and placed my hand into it." He paused, knowing he was about to tell a story which he had kept to himself for fifteen years. "I put my hand into it, and I felt something, like an electric shock. It was cold, and upon contact my whole body went numb. I began to think that perhaps this was not a hoax, though I was still skeptical and turned to look for the projector."

"Then the white cloud suddenly enveloped me, and I felt something terrible holding me still, running through my brain, my nerves, everywhere."

Helene could see him growing a little tense as he related the story.

"I decided to run, to let the man have his satisfaction at having frightened me, but I couldn't move. I was frozen that way for perhaps five minutes. The entire time I felt like there was something inside me, something which wanted to push me out and take over, but which had lost its strength over the eons."

"Finally the glow weakened, and I fell to my hands and knees. I made my way like this to the entrance where I crawled out, the fear showing plainly on my face. A small part of me expected to find the old guy standing at the entrance, his hands on his knees as he tried not to fall over from laughter. But another part of me told me what to really expect. I saw him huddled in the same corner he had been in when I found him. In a feeble voice all he said was, 'see?'"

John stopped and searched her eyes to see if he had said too much, if he had frightened her perhaps, or if he had struck the right chord.

She had known this man for the past seven years and known him well for the past three. She knew that he was telling the truth, and she knew that it had taken him some effort to tell the story. He was a man of science, and while it was not forbidden to say such things, their expression could greatly diminish an important credibility. She doubted if either of the two men in the story had even related it to anyone else in the camp, nor had they spoken of it since, and she was right.

She stood in silence and watched as his eyes finally lowered, and he returned to the cataloging of the painted wall. When he finally turned away she found the strength to say something.

"Last time I came here, I felt like something wanted to keep me here,"

He did not reply, he simply took his pictures and let her speak.

"I left in a panic, and looking back on it now, I'm not so sure that anything did happen, other than just panic on my part. But I thought I heard some screams, and I thought I saw something come out of the hole and into this room, and I thought it had a hold of me as I tried to escape."

Saying these things finally helped her tremendously. She felt the burden of the events lighten as she shared them with this man. But as soon as she had said them she was sorry she had. Suddenly she felt again that it had been nothing more than her mind playing tricks on her and that she had damaged her own credibility by telling her professor these things. Maybe his story had been only to draw this from her. Maybe he was testing her. But the feeling only lasted a second. She knew him better than that.

"It may have been your imagination," he explained. "There are some very emotional things here for someone in our field. I must admit I have experienced some things which I believed to be supernatural, but now believe were nothing more than my excited mind playing games with me." He turned to her again. "But there are a few that I do not discount. I don't know which of these things you experienced, but I'm glad you shared it with me, and the knowledge of it will not leave this cavern."

She smiled at him, and he returned the smile, then turned his attention to photographing the remaining pictographs. Then he collapsed the equipment and turned to a closer physical inspection of the pictographs.

"This is fantastic," he said for the third, and not last, time. "There are the traditional old style shaman drawings overlaid with the polychrome rock art of about 2000 B.C., and some of that has been almost completely obliterated by the more recent red monochrome rock art. These later images even include one painting of a horse, which means it would have to date after the eighteenth century."

He stood close to the wall, shining the light closely on the images which had been painted onto the wall over a period of over five thousand years. He followed the images over the wall, making notes as to their apparent content and approximate location so that he could properly note them on the pictures he had just taken. Some of the pictographs were high on the wall, near the top. He had seen this phenomenon before and supposed that again a scaffolding of some kind had been used, possibly a human one. More probably some use had been made of the reaching stalagmites. With the help of Helene he balanced upon one of these to get a closer look.

He cataloged from the top to bottom. Most of the paintings were less than a foot tall, though one aggressive painting of the red monochrome period had covered up thousands of years of work. The pictographs thinned out as he approached the floor of the cave, and finally there was just one left, just over the entrance to the small tunnel at the floor. A portion of the picture had been destroyed when a piece of the tunnel's roof had fallen, pieces of that rubble lay at their feet. The broken image was hard to discern. John reached down and picked up larger pieces of the rubble which lay on the floor, looking for a piece of the picture. One large stone did have some red coloring on it, and after close inspection John was able to make out a set of talons.

"It's a hawk," he said.

The words ran through Helene like a knife. Her heart began to race, and her face flushed as her terrible dreams had returned to her mind, including a piece that she had apparently forgotten, the part about the hawk.

"I've never seen a picture of a hawk in any of the lower Pecos drawings," he said, beaming with excitement. "This suggests a whole new dimension, a more advanced and creative one of these peoples."

Helene turned quickly around and looked at the hole from which their rope dangled. She could hear something. John could hear it too. From somewhere behind them there was a soft scraping sound. Then the image of a great hawk clawing its way toward them jumped into Helene's mind and she had to resist the urge to head down the unknown tunnel on the ground before them.

Helene looked back to her professor who despite his years in such pits still registered at the least a startled look. The sound grew louder as they stood staring at the hole, wondering what was coming their way.

Then a beam of light began to dance within the hole before them, then the bloodied head and worn hands of Todd Dumfreys appeared at the top of the cavern. Helene breathed a steamy sigh of relief.

"I widened the tunnel a little at the right place," He explained, "and with a little work I was able to get through."

"Your face is bloody," John observed. The blood was thick and plentiful, coming from a cut over his left eye.

"I hit that second sharp corner just after the small opening."

Helene smiled slightly, remembering Todd's smile in the diner when she had explained the source of her bruises.

"That soft limestone was a little work, but I chipped enough of it away so I could squeeze through."

Helene knew that he had done so in a frenzy, unable to live with the thought of missing out on the exploration of such a discovery as this one. Her suspicion was confirmed when he turned and climbed down the rope, and she saw his ripped and dirty clothes. She thought to herself that he must have gotten stuck coming through and had to chisel his way out. This image pleased her tremendously.

"We've found some rather remarkable pictographs here," the professor explained to Todd. He quickly went over some of the more outstanding features of the pictures on the wall before them, including the hawk. He handed the rock with the talons on it to Todd who turned it around in his hand and worked at the age of it.

Finally Professor Stein turned his attention to the tunnel before them.

"Well," he said, "here's the part nobody had looked at for at least a thousand years."

Helene thought again about Mr. Walker and wondered if he had gone this far, and if the real terrors were yet to come. Professor Stein almost asked Helene if she wanted to lead but realized that her previous trip might have been a hindrance. Rather than make her do something she didn't want to do, or back out in front of Todd, he got to his hands and knees and pushed his pack into the hole. The floor was damp, and he assumed that water still occasionally ran this way as a drain from the larger cave behind them.

He turned on his bright light and began down the tunnel.

Helene got her pack and followed, and Todd waited until she disappeared before climbing last into the hole.

4

John crawled along until the roof of the tunnel began to work its way downward, forcing him to crawl on his belly. The ground was damp and very cold, and he wished he had thought to bring gloves. After about ten feet the tunnel turned sharply downward and he stopped for a moment, shining the light down the shaft to be sure he wasn't putting himself into a bad position. The tunnel continued downward at a sharp angle, but it also continued to be narrow, so he could grab onto the walls if he started to slide.

"What is it?" Helene called to him.

"It gets pretty steep here," he called back. "Wait until I call you before coming down."

He began to crawl down the steep tunnel. The sides had grown rough, and the bottom was made up of more and more small rocks and stones which dug into his ribs and made the crawl uncomfortable. But soon there were too many rocks, and he began to slide upon them. He tried to hold onto the wall of the cave, but he could not get a grip and he began sliding downward quickly, too quickly. If he came to a dead end now he would most certainly bruise himself, if he did not stop his acceleration, Helene and Todd might have to drag him out of the tunnel unconscious, if they could get to him at all.

The professor cried out as a large rock glanced off his head and pummeled his side as he slid past it. He was picking up speed. He tried pushing his legs against the sides of the tunnel, and this slowed him some, but he was still not in control.

Suddenly his head struck something hard, and his back pushed up against the top of the small tunnel. He came to an abrupt stop which jarred the flashlight from his hand. He saw stars but did not go unconscious. Something told him that he had to resist that urge, that danger waited for him if he did not.

Then he understood why.

He felt the floor of the tunnel fall away before him. He reached out beneath himself as far as he could, but could not feel the floor, just the ceiling and the large rock which his head rested against. Then he heard first his pack, then the flashlight, as they hit the bottom of the pit over which he hung.

Helene heard the cry when the rock glanced off her professor's head. She also heard the tumbling and sliding sounds and knew that something was wrong.

"Professor Stein?" she shouted down the hole. "Are you all right?"

She listened, but there was no reply. Then she heard a muffled voice speaking, but she could not make out the words.

Fifty feet down the tunnel, John Stein tried to answer the call which came to him, but his precarious position and the placement of his head on the ceiling, which was keeping him from falling into the pit, kept him from calling out very loudly as well.

"What should we do?" Todd asked.

Helene ignored him and took another rope out of her pack. She had picked it up on their way to the cave at the suggestion of Professor Stein, and she was glad she had. "I'm going to throw you a rope," she called down the tunnel. She tore the plastic package open and tossed the coiled rope down the pit. She hoped that fifty feet would be enough.

John heard the sound of the rope slapping the floor of the tunnel behind him, but it was at least ten feet away. He lay still. His neck was cramping badly, and it was becoming difficult to breathe. He tried to reach something solid with his hands, but the ledge of the pit was hitting him in the middle of the chest, and all of his weight was pressed down on it. He pressed his legs against the sides of the tunnel, afraid that if he let up he would fold in half and slide into the pit below.

Helene waited, but there was no sign that the rope had reached him. She decided that she would have to try again.

"What should we do?" Todd asked again. Helene was getting tired of hearing him, but she said nothing.

Helene coiled the rope back up and crawled down the cave toward Professor Stein. She would like to have left a rope tied around her ankle, but they had no more rope, and she really wasn't comfortable with the idea of Todd holding the other end.

Helene crawled forward to the point at which the tunnel began its steep descent. She stopped there since it might have been dangerous to proceed. Then she tossed the rope again. This time John felt the rope tickle his leg and crawl halfway up his frame. He reached back as far as he could with his left hand, being careful not to dislodge his head from the emergency brake. He felt the end of the rope with the tips of his fingers and got a tenuous hold of it, then it pulled away.

Helene coiled the rope up and looked down the steep tunnel. She could try to get a little closer, but she didn't know where she too might begin sliding. She shined her light along the walls of the tunnel, trying to decide if it provided enough anchor to proceed. She decided that it would have to, and she descended another ten feet and tossed the rope again.

This time John felt the rope as it bunched up next to his midsection. He quickly grabbed hold and took up the slack, tugging to let Helene know that he had hold.

"What's going on down there?" came a cry from above. Helene ignored Todd and began backing up the tight hole she had come down.

John knew that with this much slack she had to be at the descending portion of the tunnel, so he let her take all but the last foot of the rope, then he held tightly.

Helene considered what she would have to do. There wasn't enough room to turn around, so she couldn't anchor herself very well. "Can you hang on for about three minutes?" she called.

He felt the pain tearing through his neck and did not truly know the answer to that question, but he knew she had an idea, and he would have to let her go with it. He tugged once on the rope.

She understood his message.

"Don't pull on the rope at all until you feel me tug on it," she called down.

One tug came back.

She dropped the rope to the ground and set a rock on it so that it would stay put. Then she backed out as fast as she could. Near the entrance to the small tunnel her feet accidentally met with Todd's face. Apparently he had decided to come down and see for himself what was going on.

"Get out!" she shouted at him. He backed out quickly.

She backed completely out of the tunnel and into the cavern. Then she got up and turned around, placing her feet down the hole.

"What the hell is going on?" Todd shouted. Again she ignored him.

As she disappeared into the cave he reached out and kicked her head lightly for revenge and in frustration. She would have cried out under other circumstances, but the urgency of her task and her desire not to give Todd that satisfaction stifled her cry.

Helene went down the tunnel, feeling the walls with her feet. Finally she came to the place where the cave began to descend. She kept her legs high on the tunnel walls and reached between her legs, feeling for the rock which held her end of the rope down. She continued to scoot downward until the rock bounced from her hand and rolled down the tunnel. She scrambled for the rope and caught the end of it with her fingers.

The rock rolled down the tunnel, picking up speed as it rolled until it bounced once off the feet of Professor Stein, leapt the length of his body, and struck him firmly on the back of the head.

The impact was too much, and his neck gave out. His head scraped along the final portion of the cave ceiling, and he slid forward into the pit. He slid just over a foot when the rope tightened in his hands. For a moment he stopped. Then he began to slide slowly over the edge.

Helene held tightly to the rope and forced her legs against the sides of the tunnel. At first it seemed to work, then her feet began to slip. The weight on the other end became suddenly heavier and her descent continued. The floor beneath her was becoming a slick rubble against which she could not brace.

Then her left foot struck a small protrusion against which she could anchor herself, and her descent stopped.

John Stein held firmly on the rope, half of his body hanging over the edge of the pit. The rock at the edge of the pit was pressed firmly into his stomach and it was very difficult to breathe, and impossible to speak. He lay with his arms extended beneath him, back toward Helene. His weight pressed his worn hands against the rock just before the pit's edge.

He tried to remember how long after he had dropped the flashlight that he had heard its impact. He knew it had been too long, especially for a headlong descent. He mustered his strength and began to pull himself back over the edge of the pit.

Helene felt the pressure on her foot. It grew steadily and her ankle began to burn. She could not see her foot, but she knew that it was stretched into an unnatural position. She bit down hard, mashing her teeth together to block out the pain, but it did not work.

John reached forward and found the far wall of the pit. He pushed against it and pushed himself back up onto the ledge. He made his way slowly back until his body was completely on the rock. Then he slowly loosened the pressure on the rope, making sure that he would not begin sliding again down into the pit when he did. When he had released the pressure he tied the rope around his wrist and then pushed himself off his chest. He felt relief as the blood flowed back into the potions of his body that it had been forced out of.

He rested for a moment. Then he called up to Helene. "I'm all right," he called, "but don't go anywhere just yet."

Helene straightened herself back up. The pain in her ankle began to throb and she could only wonder how bad the damage was. She sat still, waiting for the next instruction. When it came it surprised her.

"Could you slide me down a flashlight?" he called her.

Helene called back up the tunnel to Todd, "Hey! Bring me a flashlight!"

She listened and soon could hear the laboring sounds of Todd crawling toward her. Soon she saw the beam of light, then the hand that held it. He had come down headfirst on his stomach, so she reached back over her head and waited for him to place the light into it. When he did so he used a little too much force, bouncing her knuckles off the floor of the tunnel.

She took the flashlight despite her knuckles which, like her ankle, throbbed thanks to Todd.

"How should I send it down?" She called.

That was a good question. Perhaps he should just climb back up and get it or get out. But his curiosity, which had gotten him where he was now and urged him to continue, won over.

"Put it in your pack and slide it down," he called back.

She emptied out her pack except for a few heavier items so the pack could slide. Then she placed the flashlight in it.

"Here it comes," she said. Then she placed it in the space between her legs and pushed it down."

"What's he doing down there?" Todd asked, knowing by now he would get no answer.

She heard the pack slide for a distance, then come to a thudding stop in the darkness below. She was sweating despite the coolness of the air.

John reached back with his free hand and grabbed the pack. He pulled it up next to him where he could get it open. Then he fumbled around inside until he found the light which he pulled from the bag and turned on.

His surroundings lit up suddenly and they were not what he imagined they would be. About a foot in front of him was a pit which was only about two feet across. The place where his head had impacted was not where the ceiling sloped downward but only a small stalagmite which hung over the pit. He slid over the pit and felt the rope tighten suddenly.

"It's all right," he called up. "I'm okay now, just give me a little more rope."

"There is no more to give!" she called down.

He looked his situation over carefully and decided to take the chance. "Then let it go."

There was a hesitation, then the tension in the rope slackened. He slid forward over the pit, knowing now that if he continued to slide he could brace himself on the ledge across from him this time.

Then he realized that this was not the end of the tunnel. He scooted forward as far as was safe until he could see under the stalagmite. The tunnel continued straight ahead. But he could not get to the other side with the stalagmite in the way.

Then he turned his light down the pit to see what he could see. He could make out his pack on the floor of the pit, about thirty feet below him. Next to it lay the broken flashlight. He started to turn the light away when something else caught his eye. Anyone else might have missed it, but the grinning skull was quite clear to the man who had spent years dating and recording such items. Then he saw another skull and decided that there had been a few others who had come this way and not made it past the hole, though how many could not be told since most of the bones had doubtless rotted away.

"Slide the pick down here," he called up.

"It's in the bag," Helene called. She had left it in for weight.

John backed away from the pit and pulled the chisel and goggles from the pack. Helene and Todd listened from above while the clinking sounds indicated his work. They continued for several minutes, then there was a crashing sound as the stalagmite fell thirty feet onto the pack at the bottom of the pit, crushing Todd's camera completely.

"Oh, well," John muttered under his breath.

"Are you all right?" came the call from Helene.

"I'm fine," he called back.

John crawled forward and reached the opposite side of the small pit. Then he pulled the rest of his body across it to level ground. He sat for a moment to catch his breath. He rolled his head around and grabbed his neck which still hurt tremendously. After a moment he called back up.

"The tunnel doesn't get any steeper than you see it, but the rubble makes it hard to keep from sliding. We might need a rope to get out of here, but my climbing gear has fallen to the bottom of a small pit, along with the rest of my gear."

Above him Todd cringed at the prospect of the crushed camera equipment.

"I'm going to try and bring the rope back up. Then Todd can stay up there holding to the end of it while you and I do a little more exploring."

He didn't wait for a response but began his climb back to the top. The area he sat in was bigger than the one he had crawled from, and he had room to turn around. With the help of the light he was able to make out good places to get a grip. He slipped back once or twice, but made it back to Helene, who was still rubbing her ankle, in about three minutes.

"Here," he said, handing her the rope, "hand this to Todd."

She followed his instructions.

"Todd, anchor yourself and hold on. We're going to need your help going down and coming up. I'll go back down now. When I'm there then I'll call up and Helene can start her descent."

Knowing well the rivalry which existed between his students, and Todd's outright spitefulness, he said to Todd, "there's a pit at the bottom of the slide. I'm counting on you to hold tight."

Todd understood that the professor meant this not only for himself but for Helene as well.

John went back down the tunnel, feet first this time, with the aid of the rope. Though the rubble was uncomfortable it caused no problems. He continued down the tunnel until he came to the pit, which was also where the rope ran out. He let go of the rope and let himself slide until his feet hit the other side of the hole. Then he rolled over and crawled back across the open hole.

"All right," he called up. "Come on down Helene, feet first just like you are, and come slowly."

Helene prepared herself for the descent. Her ankle still hurt, but it was not that bad, at least not bad enough to keep her from going on. She went down the tunnel the same way her professor had. When she reached the end of the rope Professor Stein talked her through crossing the pit and lent a hand as well.

Between them they had only the light he held in his hand. They looked quickly at each other, each noting how worn the other looked.

"You want to go on?" Professor Stein asked Helene.

"You bet," she said, trying to muster a smile. For the moment her fear of the unknown had left her, in light of the temporary triumph she felt at overcoming the last obstacle.

Professor Stein led the way, crawling now on hands and knees. The tunnel jogged to the left, then back to the right. They were no longer descending, but the air was frigid, and Helene supposed that a steak would keep for a very long time down here. As might other meat. Like maybe human meat.

The thought crept slowly into her head and shocked her again. She thought for a moment about becoming trapped and she looked back into the darkness behind her. But then she closed her eyes and took a deep breath, and the attack was gone.

"The tunnel splits here," John called back.

"So pick a direction, I guess."

He looked for any markings, or any signs of traffic, but there seemed to be none, so he went right. She followed him and the tunnel turned back slightly to the left.

John crawled into an area where the ceiling shot upward at a sharp angle. The wall to his left just disappeared. He crawled ahead just five feet and was able to stand, and it felt good. As he stood he turned the light back toward the tunnel where Helene made her way out of the small cavern as well. As he did he saw another tunnel, directly to the right of Helene. He walked to it and shone his light down it. He could see where it curved to the left and figured out that this was the second tunnel they had just seen.

Helene crawled forward to where John stood, and she too got to her feet. As she stood her ankle complained by sending a sharp signal up her leg. John saw this.

"Is your leg okay?" he asked.

"Sure," she said, "I just bent up the ankle a little when you were sliding into the pit."

"I need to thank you for that," he said. "You probably kept me from bashing my head in on some nasty rocks."

"Just remember that at recommendation time," she said, bringing a smile to his face.

He turned and looked ahead to where they had not yet progressed. Above him the ceiling continued its steep climb, then stopped abruptly against a loose pile of rocks which reached to it from the floor. At its peak it was about nine feet, but looked as if it might continue to a much greater height behind the loose boulders. The small area they stood in also widened out quickly and was about nine feet across at the wall. At the left portion of the wall John could make out the faint portion of a painting which disappeared behind the loose rocks.

"I think there's another chamber behind this wall."

"Why don't we just move the rocks and get into it." It was her dry humor at work, and John understood it as such.

"I think this is as far as we're going to get today, but I'll bet there's some wonderful paintings in the chamber beyond this wall, and who knows how many more chambers there might be." Images of Carlsbad caverns were now racing through his mind as well, only these caverns would be full of archaeological treasures.

"I no longer have my pad on which to make my notes, nor a camera to take pictures with."

"And we don't have any of the pictures you already took," she added.

He reached into his pocket and pulled out two rolls of film.

"I put the exposed rolls in my pocket. These include pictures of the cavern above us as well."

Her face brightened and for a moment she forgot her worries.

But it lasted only for a moment.

Helene heard it first. From the other side of the wall, through the cracks between the boulders, came a low and mournful wail. John saw the color drain from her face and was about to ask her why when he heard it too.

"Let's go now," she suggested.

John didn't answer, he merely began heading back toward the tunnel.

Then there was a hideous scream, soon joined by a hundred more. It was like the screams she had heard before, only now they were much closer. She could see the edges of the red cloud as it began to seep through the spaces in the boulders and her face froze in a terrified grimace.

Then there was a sound like thunder and a gust of wind which seemed to originate in the center of the room in which they stood. The force of the wind knocked them to the ground, and their flashlight went out leaving them in the darkness.

Yet they could see by the glow of the red cloud which seemed to be taking form in the room with them.

And Helene could stand it no more.

She let out a terrified scream of her own and turned for the tunnel. Already she could feel the tingling sensation at her ankles, which was not the pain from her earlier injury but the pulling sensation which she had felt on her last journey. Only this time she had so much further to go that she knew she would never make it.

But she had to try.

She rushed again trying to remember the trail before her. She crawled on hands and knees through the darkness while the grip which held her strengthened and moved its way slowly up her body. It seemed slower this time, perhaps because there were two of them. Perhaps this would give them both the time they would need to escape. She turned to her right, then back to her left, then left again to where the tunnel grew small and began to bring her up out of the earth. She could hear the crunching of rocks behind her which she knew to be Professor Stein and she wondered what he felt.

His legs felt numb, and they were getting hard to move. He too felt the grip which had held to Helene and now threatened to hold them both. What would become of them then he did not know, but he did not wish to find out.

They crawled ahead until Helene found the pit with her hands and fell to her face in the process. She hurried across the pit in a fury, her heart pounding in her head as she crawled. She grabbed the rope and pulled as she made her way up.

But there was no tension in the rope. Todd had dropped it when the screams had made their way to his ears. Helene slid back toward the pit on her stomach and her feet went into it. She cried out and John ran into her as he tried to cross the pit. He felt her sinking beneath him and tried to grab hold, but she was sliding too quickly. She forced her legs against the side of the pit which slowed but did not stop her fall. Then she continued to slide slowly downward while John fumbled in the darkness for the rope. One of her feet came loose and she slipped quickly, her head bouncing off the rocks behind her. She felt her hand tug upward and realized that she still had hold of the rope, and that Professor Stein had gotten hold of the other end.

He had crossed the pit and sat on the steep side, his feet against the far wall of the small pit. He held tightly to the rope as a heavy weight began to clamp down on his chest.

"Climb back up," he shouted.

Then she realized that there was a noise which followed them as well. He had shouted, yet she had barely heard him. The sound was heavy, like a train rumbling down the tracks in the night, it could be felt and heard, but not seen. Something very like a train was barreling toward them both, and she did not think they would escape.

She slipped further into the pit as John's grip loosened. The forces which held him were making it hard for him to breathe, hard for him to hold on, and she was slipping slowly away from him.

Then she saw the cloud again. This time it looked not like a floating amorphous thing, but like a creature of some kind, with intent. She saw it above her, enveloping her professor, passing through him and onward in its race to the surface.

She saw the light above her as it grew brighter, and she knew that the cloud and the train were not the same thing. The voices which had chased them from the small chamber now grew again, and with their screams joined in the scream of her professor.

She saw him suddenly lit up, the cave and everything around her was aglow with a brilliant flash of light. The coolness increased and she felt the pain of a thousand daggers piercing her chest. She looked up to her professor, hoping that he could hold on.

But then she saw the stark terror as it rose upon his face. It was a terror which she had never seen, and its magnitude reached down and touched her as well.

She felt the earth trembling and saw a few stones come loose from the ceiling of the tunnel, bouncing down toward her and crashing on the earth beneath her. She watched as her professor's face turned white. Not just pale, but actually white. Then it seemed paper thin as his mouth formed into a hideous scream which was overcome by the rumbling of the train.

Then there was a hot flash of air and John Stein's skin became almost transparent. Through it she could see veins and bone, and she wanted to look away, but could not. Then his face disappeared and was replaced by a wide mouthed skull.

Flesh melted from the terrified face and in the next moment he was vaporized as the train passed by.

She saw it only for an instant. It was a fiery red cloud with arms and legs. In it she could see the faces of the hundreds of voices.

But it did not see her as it continued upward.

And since John had been turned into vapor the rope fell to the bottom of the pit.

And so did Helene.

Five

1

Buzz awoke the next day and looked around the room. He noticed two things which seemed to be odd.

First, he awoke sitting on the edge of his bed fully clothed and smelling quite rank. Second, it was not morning.

He looked quickly around the room for his watch, but found it still wrapped around his wrist. It said four.

How could that be? He tried to think about where he had been before he had come home. The last image he could conjure was that of himself going to see if there was a problem at the rig. He remembered seeing the shadowy figure, and he remembered crawling under the deck of the rig, but then he only remembered waking up here. He tried to remember if he had gone drinking, and his head hurt like that might be the case, but he could not recall doing so. That didn't mean however that he had not. There were plenty of times he had gone out drinking and not remembered the night, or how he had gotten home.

His eyes and head hurt. Although it was four in the afternoon he did not actually feel rested. Instead he felt exhausted, like he hadn't gotten any sleep at all. His back hurt, and his legs tingled as if he had been just sitting like this all night.

He stood to go see if his car was parked out front when two things hit him, the pain in his stiff legs, and the bad smell. He realized suddenly that the terrible smell was coming from himself. At first he felt disgust, then nausea. He ran toward the bathroom but did not make it and threw up on the floor as he ran. When he finished he walked the rest of the way into the bathroom and looked at himself in the mirror.

His hair was a mess, his clothes were torn and dirty. Some of the vomit clung in lumps to his filthy shirt. He looked at the image of grossness in the mirror before him and suddenly thought of Halloween, which was only a few weeks away. Perhaps he would just stay this way until then and go as himself. It was an effective costume. It was sure scaring the hell out of him.

His face looked dark, almost bruised. Hey eyes were the worst. Deep dark circles surrounded them, and even the eyeballs themselves looked darker, as if they had somehow been bruised. His face was thick with a light stubble, and he reached up to touch his face when he realized that his hands too were sore.

He stood staring for a few minutes more, then stripped down and got into the shower. Pieces of what had been inside him flowed off his body and down the drain. He scrubbed and soaped for almost forty minutes before getting out. He left the clothes where they were. He didn't want to touch them now that he was clean. Instead he stepped over the smelly mess and walked to the mirror where he observed a clean man, but one which still haunted him. The dark circles around his eyes and his seemingly bruised eyeballs remained, as did, of course, the stubble. He felt better, but still sore, and extremely tired. He walked to the bed, which was still unmade, as it always was when he lived alone. He lay down on it to relax for a moment, and darkness crept into those bruised eyes of his.

When he awoke again it was six in the morning. That didn't seem right. Had he been asleep for the past thirteen hours? He stood and saw that he was still naked, though quite dry. The rank smells had soured in the room. He walked to the closet and pulled on a few old clothes. Then he left the bedroom and closed the door behind him to keep the stench closed up. He walked into the kitchen and opened the refrigerator but saw nothing he wanted.

Then he realized that he was not hungry. It had been a day and a half since he had last eaten, yet he was not hungry. But he was thirsty. He took a glass from the cupboard and filled it with water, which he quickly consumed. Then he drank another, and half of a third. Then he walked into the living room and sat in his chair for a moment to think.

His thoughts came to him slowly.

A whole day had passed, and he had not supervised the work at the drilling site. What might have happened while he was out yesterday? Had they found the pipe and the bit? Had they resumed drilling? What about the hole? Had they struck oil yet?

He felt his body turning itself up a few notches as these questions raced through his mind. He looked at his watch and saw that it was now six thirty. He decided that he would need to go now and see what was going on with his precious hole.

He went back into the room and got his car keys from his rancid pants. Then he made his way out of the house. As he walked across the porch he noticed the past few days' papers were beginning to pile up, so he picked them up to toss them in the house.

But then he realized that there were too many. He looked closely at them then saw something which both shocked and terrified him. It was not the headline, but the date. Today was Sunday. He had been in his house for two full days, and this was the third, not the second morning. Either he had slept for thirty-seven hours, or he had spent an additional twenty-four hours sitting on his bed, staring blindly into the bedroom wall. Somehow he knew it had been the latter.

2

Cal watched as the men finished capping off the hole which they had created three days earlier. They had spent most of the past two days first trying to fish the bit and pipe out of the cavern, then trying to start a new hole. The cavern they had hit was too deep, and the floor of it was tilted and made of some very hard stone. There was too much dead space to fill, and there was no telling how wide the hole was. If the anomaly which the seismographic readings they had taken before drilling was outlining the cavern then it stretched a half mile in every direction, and they were smack in the middle of it.

Buzz had disappeared. No one had been able to find him or reach him at home. The guys in Odessa had pulled the plug on the site. The one good well they had hit was still producing, and oil was still over $35 per barrel, so it looked like they were going to make money enough to cover the cost of the two dry wells, as long as they cut their losses here now. So they had given the orders and the equipment had been pulled. The pipe had been cut off below ground level and a steel plate welded across its top. Now all that remained of the site were patches of soft dirt where the mud pits had been.

Cal had been glad to see that cap go on the pipe. Since the day after they had hit the cavern he felt strange working in the area. The hole emitted some kind of smell, he couldn't place it, but it reminded him of walking into his grandfather's dusty old wine cellar. One day he thought he had heard sounds of muffled screams coming from the hole and had looked to the only other man who stood closer to the hole than he. That man was looking back at him. No words were exchanged, but they both understood what was being said.

They had worked quickly to finish off the capping work and now it was done. The last of the equipment was being loaded onto the big trucks which would carry them either to a yard for storage or a new site. As the final loading proceeded Cal saw Buzz's Lincoln as it came racing down the dirt path. He watched as the heavy man got out of his car and stomped toward him. He knew this was going to be even more unpleasant than dealing with Buzz normally was.

As Buzz approached he felt his fists balling up and his blood pressure rising. He walked quickly, but it seemed to take too long to close the distance between himself and the man he called the one-armed bandit before him. But the distance finally did close, and he stood there, less than a foot away, his dark eyes staring ahead into Cal's.

Cal knew that something was wrong. Something beyond Buzz's sheer anger. He looked into those dark menacing eyes and saw something which was more than just anger. It seemed also to be more than just Buzz.

"What the fuck is going on here?" Buzz shouted in Cal's face. "Just what do you think you're doing?"

"I'm capping the hole."

"I can see that, you stupid shit. On whose authority? Yours?"

"Randall Boggs."

Buzz hesitated for a moment. Boggs was not his boss; he was his boss's boss. "What happened?" he asked in a more civil, but still loud, tone.

"We couldn't fish out the bit or any of the pipe. The cavern we hit is too big, and it's sloped. Everything slid away from us, who knows how far it slid."

"So what!" he shouted. "That doesn't mean you can't start a new hole!"

"The floor of the cavern is tilted and hard. We tried to drill through the bottom, but the bit couldn't get a hold, and we just bent our drilling pipe. Almost couldn't get it out. Boggs said it was enough. Said to pull out. That was two days ago. He also wants to know where the hell you've been."

Buzz stood stewing. He was a kettle on high, just about to scream out as the pressure demanded.

But he just stood and stared at Cal with his dark eyes. Cal could feel them bearing down on him. They were not the eyes he was used to meeting, those eyes he could stare down.

Then the strangest thing happened. Buzz said something which sounded like it came from Shakespeare, or something similar.

"Fear, and the pit, and the snare are upon thee."

Cal felt the fear and he also felt something dark trying to burrow its way into his brain.

Then his reflexes took over. He wanted to turn away but could not. So he swung hard with his arm and brought his fist into the side of Buzz's face. Buzz went down, and the strange feeling subsided, but it didn't go completely away. It felt unclean, and it felt like it was in his head.

Buzz looked up at Cal from the ground, but Cal had turned away and was walking toward his own truck. The loading was all but complete, and he was going to trust the men to finish without him. He had to leave this place.

"You'll never have work again!" Buzz shouted at him. But Cal ignored him and walked away to his truck where he got in and drove away.

Buzz just lay on the ground watching him go.

Now what would he do?

He stood and walked over to where the pipe was now buried under the rocks and dirt. It was not only the hole they capped, but it was also his dream. Somewhere down there, beneath the rock, lay his salvation. He could feel it there now, calling out to him. He got to his knees and put his hands on the ground, trying to feel more. But it did not come, and he began to sob.

The trucks finally pulled away and left Buzz alone with his buried hole in the warm morning sun. He lay down on the ground and his mind began to work on its own. He got back to his knees and began digging for the pipe with his fingers. The ground was still soft here from the drilling and he was able to dig down about ten inches before hitting hard rock. He then peeled back a fingernail on the rock and cried out, pulling his hands from the hole he had dug.

Then he sat back and looked at the ground and then himself. For a moment his sanity returned, and he wondered what he was doing. He began to fear what had become of him, then there was a sharp pain in his head and his sanity fled him one last time.

He sat looking at the small hole he had dug. Then he looked around for a shovel or a pick, but the tools had all been taken.

Then he smiled as an idea came into his head.

3

Yvonne pushed the basket of clean towels down the cracked sidewalk. It was hot outside, but her job took her in and out of stuffy and hot rooms most of the morning. So far she had the remnants of three rooms in her basket of dirty linen and towels. There were less than half a dozen visitors in the small and old motel which was one of only three in the town of Comstock. Most of the time it was more than enough, but on a few weekends each year, like Labor Day and Memorial Day, there were never enough rooms, even though the rates were doubled for those weekends.

But it was not one of those weekends, and Monday would soon find the motel empty again, as it almost always did.

She pushed the cart to room six and she knocked on the door, but there was no answer. She knocked again louder to make sure no one was in the room. It was almost noon, and this was the last room she would have to clean. She took her key ring from the cart and put the key into the hole, making a lot of noise as she opened the door to provide a warning to anyone who might be running around naked. She stepped into the dark room and all at once remembered what the manager had said to her. He had said, "Yvonne, the lady in room six will be staying for a while and has paid us quite fairly. Her only request is that we not clean or otherwise enter the room. For this she pays us holiday rates." She remembered this not because she had a good memory, but because of what she saw.

All around the room were things she had never seen before, and many she had. There were candle racks like she had seen in church, and some other catholic figurines. But most of the items were foreign to her.

In the center of the room was a circle of burnt-out red candles which sat directly on the floor. Beyond the circle was another circle, this one of small straw figures, like dolls but cruder. These dolls wore carefully fitted clothes and all stood facing the center of the circle, held up by nails protruding from their butts. On the desk by the bed she could see more dolls being made. One of them was missing an arm.

She looked around the room with her mouth hanging open. Her knees shook softly as she felt what she could only describe as evil pervading the room. She abandoned her curiosity and turned to leave.

As she pulled the door shut she felt a sharp and bony hand upon her shoulder. She turned around quickly, dropping her keys in her fright. What she saw frightened her even more. What she saw was the inhabitant of room number six.

She looked into a terribly pale face which smiled a smile of yellow and crooked teeth, too many of them. The old woman's breath almost gagged the young girl, and she couldn't take her eyes from the pale pink eyes of the albino woman before her.

"Did you forget my request, Yvonne?" she asked.

Yvonne was now more frightened than she had been in the room, and she wished to flee, but that gaze held her in place. Yvonne tried to answer but when she opened her mouth all that escaped was a muffled 'ugh.' The woman before her had a tremendously wrinkled face which reminded her of a similarly wrinkled dog she had seen in a pet store in Del Rio. Her long and stringy hair was white, not blond, just stark white. And though it was hot outside the old woman wore thick black clothing which was worn and tattered, and it too smelled musty and old.

Then the old woman cackled. She did not laugh; it wasn't that deep. It was definitely a cackle, and Yvonne finally regained control of her legs which she used to flee. She left her cart in front of the old woman's room and ran to her Impala which coughed and sputtered before finally starting. She pulled out of the parking lot and left in a hurry, crossing herself and muttering her prayers as she went. The old woman watched in amusement as the car sped away, the woman inside calling on a God which would not hear her, but whom she would meet very shortly.

The old woman pushed the cart away from her door, leaving it in front of the nearest occupied room, and returned to her own room. She left the curtains closed as she had for the past four days, and she walked slowly to her desk where she resumed building the doll with one arm.

She paused only for a moment and closed her eyes. She closed her eyes and dreamt of a road which led to nowhere. Then she smiled and resumed her work.

4

Yvonne drove quickly to the southeast on highway 90 to Del Rio. She drove too fast, but she needed to feel the distance between her and the old woman as it grew. Still she could feel the woman's gaze upon her, even as she drove away.

Then she saw something which did disturb her. The road ahead curved sharply to the left. She had been on this road a hundred times in the past six months, and she did not remember this. She hit her brakes hard and turned with the new direction of the road.

Then reality returned to her, and she saw that the road did not curve here after all, and that she had simply swerved into the left lane.

And the large truck she had not until then seen smashed her door into her side, and her head into the dashboard.

And after her car had rolled over a few times her brains met the pavement.

5

Cal sat in his chair in front of the television watching the Cowboys deliver yet another loss to the Eagles.

But his mind was not on the game. It wandered back and forth between where he was and where he had been earlier in the day. He reached to the end table next to his chair and grabbed the bottle of Tylenol whereupon he downed his fifth pill in three hours. His head still throbbed near his forehead. It was a pounding pain, but one which pounded with a beat of its own. The source of the rhythm seemed to be outside of his body.

Finally, when the Cowboys pulled too far ahead to make it a game, he switched off the television and walked into his bedroom where he lay down to take a nap. The morning had been an eventful one, and tomorrow he would be starting up another job for Texon at a site which had been selected by the manager in the Del Rio office and which lay almost a hundred and fifty miles to the east.

As Cal lay on the bed his thoughts kept returning to the hole. He could not seem to push those thoughts from his mind, and they dogged him as he lay trying to relax.

Then he was pulled into sleep by something other than his exhaustion. The room around him faded to blackness, and he instinctively struggled against it, but it took him, nevertheless.

The blackness lasted for about ten minutes, then there was a light.

In the light he could see the hole again, only this time it was not capped. He walked to the hole to see why this was the case and noticed the smell of rotten eggs coming from it. As he approached the pipe he could hear someone speaking to him, but he could not make out what they were saying. He approached the open pipe and put his ear to it.

The voice was soft and distant, but he could hear in it a plea for help. It was a woman's voice, and for a moment he saw her soft hair and sparkling blue eyes. Somebody was down the hole. He listened carefully to see if he could make out any words, but he couldn't. He turned his face to the hole to shout down so that he could hear her. But before he could speak he saw a light coming toward him. The image was like looking into a tunnel at an approaching train, and the ground began to rumble.

As the light grew he tried to pull away, but he could not. The train approached quickly, and beneath the rumble he could hear the scream of a hundred voices.

Then the train hit him and threw him back. He felt the earth flying away from him as the blood red cloud emerged from the hole. It threw him away from the earth and into the heavens.

And it was very hot.

He awoke in a sweat, his heart pounding. The dream remained fresh. The pain in his head remained as he rose from his bed. Cal walked to the window and looked to the west, in the direction of the hole which they had capped that morning. He recalled the crazed look in Buzz's eyes, and he tried to understand what was happening. Whatever it was, it just didn't seem normal.

Cal decided to confront the thing which bothered him, which was simply the way he had always done things. He got into this truck and headed toward the site. A part of him wanted to stay behind, but another part urged him on.

He headed west on 90 toward the road which would take him northward to the site. On his way he had to drive on the shoulder as the county cops directed him past a tangle of metal and flesh which had been a big rig and a car of some kind. What kind of car could not be discerned by what remained of it, and he knew there had been a death here.

He continued down the road through Comstock and headed north to the Aldredge lease.

Twenty minutes later he was there. He turned off the main road and followed the dirt path which they had carved out for their trucks and equipment. It was still another mile to the site.

Everything surrounding this job had been bizarre. The site had been a poor choice and an expensive one to develop. Buzz had been an irritant and had seemed possessed by this site the entire time. Cal drove until he saw the roof of the old house appear over the horizon.

As he topped the small hill he stopped the truck and looked into the distance.

Near the hole was a backhoe. Black smoke poured from its stack as it labored, digging chunks of the earth out and pilling them in places around it. Directing the big piece of machinery was Buzz Shaw.

Something told Cal to go on, to see what Buzz was doing. Something told him that it was important work, and that he too could be a part of it.

But as Buzz looked in his direction Cal turned and drove away from the site.

In the backhoe Buzz watched as the pickup sped away. Then he released his grip on the pistol in the seat beside him.

6

Cal was confused by his feelings. It seemed as if a part of him had been touched by something terrible, the same something which had nested in Buzz's brain. As he drove away from the site and onto the main road he headed back to town. In his mind he tried to block out the pain he felt in his head, and the voices which he heard urging him to go back, to become a part of something important. But he would not listen. Not enough of whatever had gotten hold of Buzz had made its way into Cal's head. But there was enough to make life uncomfortable.

There was also enough to cause him to turn his steering wheel sharply to the left after he had traveled only a short distance from the Aldredge place. The dream of the pleas for help and the blue-eyed woman flashed in his infected mind. He stopped at an old iron gate which closed off a dirt ranch road. Cal felt that there was something here which might give him some answers, though he did not know if this urging came from his own mind or from the influence which had nested there. He opened the gate and drove down the dirt road, following it to a large house. He didn't think the answer was in the house. As he drove near to it he could feel the pull he had felt at the Aldredge site. Only now Buzz was not there to stop him. He drove past the house, in the direction of the pull. In his head the pain began to subside, and his mind seemed to be rewarding him for making the right decision. He drove on, following the road to a place where a small cattle path headed through the brush. He got out of his truck and started down the path. Then he stopped, returned to his truck, and retrieved the .357 from under his seat. Then he turned around and began walking toward the outcropping of shale which he saw in the distance.

Halfway through the thick brush he paused. He stopped and wondered to himself what he was doing here. He, the skeptic of all skeptics, running down a primitive path because of a feeling? He looked again toward the outcropping of shale and wondered why he was there. It all seemed ridiculous, but he could not completely discount it.

"Damn you, Buzz," he said aloud, "What have you done to me?"

He stared ahead, trying to believe that this was something that would pass. That tomorrow he would be working with his crew at a new site and none of this would be important.

But somehow he knew this was not to be the case. Something important was happening and was about to happen.

He continued down the path until he came to the cave. Then he began to understand.

7

Cal walked into the cave and felt the hot afternoon sun melt away. It was cool inside the cave, and it felt good. He walked down past the rocky decline to level ground. Then he looked at the dark walls of the cave, lit dimly by the sunlight which crept through a hole in the ceiling. He could see images on the wall, but it was too dim to make them out. He walked closer to the wall and could see that they were paintings like the ones he had seen on a boat tour a few years back. He wondered what the significance of all of this was. He saw a place where the cave faded away into the darkness and he wondered if the cave ended down there, or if it continued. He walked a short way into the darkness, feeling the ceiling as it closed down upon him. He followed it back until he had to get on his hands and knees, but still it went back.

Then his hands ran across something lumpy. He felt it out and decided that it was a pack of some kind.

"Hello?" he shouted. "Is anybody down there?"

There was no answer he could hear, but a chill ran through his body in reply. He wanted to go on, but not in the dark. He backed away from the darkness, taking the pack with him. Eventually he got into the light. He opened the pack and looked through it. He found a flashlight, and some rope. He tried the flashlight, but it didn't work. He considered turning and leaving, just driving away and leaving it all alone. But now he had to look further. He would have felt this way even without the voice in his head urging him on.

Cal left the cave and returned to his truck for his own flashlight. Then he walked back to the cave. The sun was low in the sky, but would not set for another two hours, so he felt he would be safe, though he did not know why daylight mattered.

Cal walked back to the cave and descended once again. He crawled down to the pack and examined it for anything he might find useful, but the rest of the items were things like rolls of film and a notepad. He took the rope and headed deeper into the cave, shining the light ahead of him. As he crawled toward the back of the cave he saw that it did continue in a small tunnel which he wondered if he would be able to get into, or, more importantly, out of. It was tight, but he had room to move. The air was still and stale with the smell of something rotten. As Cal continued down the hole he saw that it curved sharply to the right. He made it to this corner and turned his light to the right at which point he let out a yell.

There were a few times in his life that the big man had been scared enough to yell out, and this was one of them. In front of him was the face of a terrified man. His face was frozen in fear and his arms reached forward toward Cal. The smell was awful, and Cal wondered how long the man had been dead. His head was held up by a rock which protruded from the ceiling of the cave and pushed into the back of his neck. The face was pale, but dried blood covered it and the ground beneath it. There was a lot of blood, all of it dried, but it must have represented half of what this man had to bleed.

Cal looked the face over, and it reminded him of a face he had seen long ago in a similar pit in a hot steamy jungle. The image made him jumpy, and his hand twitched with adrenaline.

But he had to go on.

He reached forward and put the dead man's arms together, then grabbed onto the wrists. He crawled back to where he would have room to pull, then he pulled. He had expected that since the man had become lodged there that he would have to pull very hard, and that the body might have bloated making the task impossible. But the body popped out with a crackling sound and came toward him. It was lighter than it was supposed to be. It came toward him too quickly and its now soft head came into contact with his face. The head split open and a white and sticky substance flowed out of it. Cal pulled the light out from under himself and shined in on the dead body to see what was wrong.

He felt dizzy as what he smelled and what he saw assaulted him. The man's body stopped at the waist, just below the naval. It was as if the rest of him, whatever part of him had been out of sight, had been bitten off. The rotten flesh dangled in a ragged pattern where the separation had taken place. Cal was back against one wall of the tunnel and could not see beyond the body, or what was left of it.

Cal tied the man's hands together with the rope he had brought with him using his teeth to make the knot tight. Then he backed completely out of the hole, taking the other end of the rope in his hand along with the flashlight. He backed out of the hole and the process was a slow one, but finally he made it back to the now seemingly fresh air of the large cave. Cal backed to a point where he could sit up and began pulling the body out of the cave. As he pulled the rope the mutilated body appeared in the gloom before him. Cal pulled it toward him, then kicked it to the side. He crawled down next to it, noticing that the arms had become so rotten that they were tearing out of the sockets. It would have been much worse if it hadn't been so cool in the cave.

Cal untied the rope and resumed his exploration of the cave.

When he came to the point in the tunnel where the body had been lodged he found a pile of scorched bones. He looked them over carefully and deduced that the flesh had been burned off of them. It was as if someone had set fire to the back end of the man while he was stuck. Cal pushed the bones aside and squeezed himself through the tight hole, making the turn back to the right. It was very tight, and he would not have made it if the now dead Todd had not gone to the trouble of widening it with his pick. Cal squeezed through, holding the light ahead of him so he could see the tunnel. He heard a clinking sound as his gun fell from his pants. He reached back for it and brought it forward, pushing it ahead along with the rope. Finally the cave widened up some and he was able to get to his hand and knees with a little room to spare. He shined the light down the tunnel and could see that although it curved slightly to the right, it remained roughly the same size. He stuck the gun in his back pocket and began to crawl forward.

Cal followed the cave until it came to the small cavern. He saw that a rope had been secured to the tunnel floor and he used it to climb down. There were signs that people had been here, including a lens cap which lay crushed on the cavern floor. Cal picked up the cap and looked it over. The plastic was relatively new, and he decided that it had belonged to the man who had been fried on his way out.

Then he remembered that there had been no camera in the pack. Since he had not seen one so far, the camera was probably somewhere further along. Perhaps the man had been taking pictures when he had fled. But what had caused the man to flee? Cal looked around and tried to see where he could go from here, but he could not see any exit from where he stood. He walked around the cavern looking for an exit, and then he found the small tunnel near the floor. This tunnel was quite small, it looked even smaller than the one he had already squeezed through and he didn't think he could get into it.

But he knew he had to try.

Cal got down on his hand and knees and began to crawl again. His head began to sing to him, and he could feel that thing calling to him. He could feel the foreign thoughts in his mind agreeing with what he was doing, and it caused him to hesitate. But then he moved on.

Cal crawled to a place where the small tunnel began a somewhat sharp descent. He shined his light down it and considered if it was worth the risk. He had been with a man once in a similar situation. That man had gone on ahead of him, and Cal had watched as that man had lost control and slid into a steep portion of the cave, then into a large cavern, landing with a bone snapping crunch. The image jumped clearly into his mind and was his own, not an illusion from the false voices which teased him. He scooted to the edge of the decline and shined the light down the tunnel. He could see that it did begin to level out, but it also looked as if there might be a pit of some kind. The beam from his flashlight lit up the edge of that pit. And there was something else. There was something piled up at the edge of the pit.

As he squinted to make out the rubble he realized what it was. More scorched bones. From where he was it looked like there might be enough to make an entire body.

Cal wanted to go on. The voice urged him too as did his curiosity. But his sense of reality told him otherwise. He might become trapped at the bottom of the tunnel, or fall into the pit where the bones were, or maybe whatever had burned the two men might come after him as well.

In his mind Cal understood that this is what had happened. Something had come for them. He knew that it was the same something which he dreamt was in down the hole, and he wondered what the connection might be. Then he calculated the direction and distance he had traveled in this cave. Remembering that the cavern they had hit was a large one, a mile across, he deduced that the very edge of that cavern might be ahead, perhaps in just another few hundred feet. As it was he figured that he had already crossed the property line into the Aldredge ranch.

He stared at the bones and tried to think of a way to continue his journey. But no ideas came to him. He would have to leave, to go and get the right equipment for the descent, and it was a descent he would have to make. Tomorrow would not find him at the new site. Something was happening to him, which was taking control of a part of him, and leaving another part for him to work with. He knew enough to realize that he was jeopardizing his future, and he felt enough to know that what he was about to discover would make that irrelevant.

Cal began to back out of the hole when he heard the voice. It was weak at first and he thought that it was in his head. But then he heard it again, louder this time. He could make out only one word, and the word was a plea.

"Is somebody down there?" he asked. In any other place that would have been a stupid question considering that he had actually heard a voice. But he didn't know what to believe based on what he had seen so far.

"Help me," came a female voice. "I'm at the bottom of the pit."

The voice was female, and it was weak. He assumed the pit she was talking about was the one he could barely see the edge of.

"How deep is it?" he called down.

There was a hesitation, then a reply. "I think about twenty or thirty feet."

He could not throw her his rope. It would probably only make it as far as the edge of the pit.

"Can you wait for me to go get some equipment, and maybe somebody to help."

"I don't know," the voice answered.

"How long have you been down there?"

"I don't know, I can't see my watch."

He looked at his own. "It's five thirty, Sunday."

There was a pause. It was one of disbelief. Once again time had rushed by Helene as she had stayed in the pit. It seemed like only a few hours since the fiery train had passed, but it had been almost twenty-seven.

"I fell in here yesterday afternoon."

"How do you feel?"

"I'm tired and weak."

"Do you have any broken bones?"

"No," she replied. Her fall had been a relatively short one, and her landing a good one, "Just a bruised ankle."

He lay thinking for a moment. Then he asked, "What happened?"

"Please get me out and we'll talk about it."

He lay thinking of a way to get her out. He could not think of a way that didn't entail driving back to town for supplies and assistance.

"I don't have enough rope to get you out. And I don't think I can pull you out by myself."

After a moment of silence Helene said, "get the rope that's in the small cavern behind you."

Of course, he thought to himself. "I'll be right back," he shouted.

He backed out of the hole and into the small cavern where the rope dangled from the tunnel at the top of the opposite side. He walked over to it and looked it over. It was about ten feet from the bottom of the small tunnel to the floor of the cavern. Would they be able to get out without it? He jumped and reached for the tunnel. Grabbing hold with his hand on the first try. He hefted himself upwards with his one arm, leaning heavily to his right. When he had the height he threw his elbow onto the ledge, then pulled himself slowly into the tunnel. It was strenuous but possible. He looked at the piton driven into the stone and remembered the pick back near the cave entrance. He left his gun and crawled back to the surface where he retrieved the pick. When he reached the larger cave he noticed that no light was coming through the hole in its top. It seemed as if this had happened much too quickly, but he discounted the fact and headed back to the cavern.

When Cal reached the cavern and the rope he used the pick to dislodge the piton. Then he took it and the rope and climbed back down into the cavern. He made his way back to the point in the small tunnel where he had left his rope and shined the light back down the tunnel. This time he went in feet first.

"I thought you had left," came the voice from below.

"I had to go back to the surface and get something."

He tied the two ropes together and used the pick to pound the piton into the floor of the tunnel above his head. Then he threw the rope down the tunnel. It only went about halfway, which was what he had expected would happen, but had hoped against.

Cal grabbed onto the rope and let himself slowly down the slick tunnel. He held the flashlight between his legs, and he used his arm to hold the rope and descend. He could not see where he was going, so he went until his feet hit the pile of bones that used to be Professor

Stein. One bone slipped over the edge, and he heard it crash to the floor of the pit.

"Sorry," he called down.

"It's all right, you missed me."

"I'm going to throw a rope down to you. Do you think you can crawl up?" he asked her.

"I can try."

He threw the remaining rope between his legs, and it cascaded down the pit. He heard it slap the bottom.

"I only have one arm and I have to use it to hold onto the rope, so you'll have to do this in the dark," he called to her.

The announcement surprised her at first, but then she groped for the rope which she found near her feet. She tried to think if there was anything in the pack that had fallen into the pit before her, but she could think of nothing. She certainly didn't care to retrieve the camera, which was crushed anyway.

She began climbing the rope and was able to use the sides of the pit for a foothold as she made her way up. The pit narrowed at the top and she was able then to use both sides of it. She felt weak, her stomach burned with hunger, but she pushed this aside as she climbed to the top.

As she reached the top she saw the flashlight sitting clamped by knees of the man she could not see.

"I'd offer you a hand up, but I haven't got a free one," he explained. "But you're more than welcome to grab a foot."

She reached to his feet and grabbed on, pulling herself up and over the edge of the pit. The bones of her teacher and friend lay waiting for her, and she gasped in a breath at the sight of them.

"Take the flashlight," Cal said to her, and she grabbed the light resting on the floor near those bones.

Cal crawled back up the tunnel and Helene followed him, not pausing to speak. He reached the end of the rope and the pick he had left there. Helene was still beyond the sloping point of the tunnel, so he told her that she would have to remove the piton from the stone. He traveled past the piton and continued out of the tunnel as she began to pick at it. He emerged into the dark cavern and waited for her to appear. First the light danced on the tunnel wall, then the bulb appeared, and a moment later her face.

It was beautiful. Even beneath the grime and dirt and even the pain he could see the beauty and those eyes, and he wondered to himself what a girl like her was doing in a place like this.

"What went on here?" he asked her.

"Let's get out of here, and we can talk about it. I'm afraid if we don't hurry it might happen again."

Cal remembered the charred bones he had seen and decided that her suggestion was sound.

They walked together across the cavern and Cal lifted himself up into the ceiling level tunnel again, this time with a little more effort as his muscles were growing tired. In his head the voice began to complain and began to urge him to go back. But he did not wish to see his skin melting from his bones, so he ignored it and endured the pain in his head.

He leaned back into the cavern and Helene handed him the ropes, pick and piton. He reached down and used his arm to pull Helene up into the cavern while she climbed her best to keep his efforts to a minimum. She crawled into the tunnel in front of him and he backed up to give her room so that she would not fall. Then he turned and gathered the ropes.

"Can you get the rest of this stuff?" he called to her, "I'm at a bit of a disadvantage."

"Sure," she said, feeling uncomfortable about his reference to his disability, but feeling even more uncomfortable about what might be coming for her.

Cal led the way through the tunnel and Helene followed close behind. Once she thought she heard a rumbling sound, and it scared her badly, but it did not grow and it did not come for them, so she continued to crawl at a sane pace.

Finally they emerged from the hole together and sat at its entrance for a moment.

"You think we're safe here?" he asked.

She felt that this was true, but she did not like the chances, "I don't know." She paused, "I'm just glad that the numbskull got a hold of somebody before I died of dehydration down there."

"What?" Cal asked.

"Didn't somebody send you here?" she asked.

He thought again about the bizarre circumstances of his arrival at this place. "Not really."

"I thought one of the guys from our group had gone for help."

Then Cal knew who of whom she was speaking. "I'm afraid that your friend didn't make it out either."

"What?" Now it was her turn to be puzzled.

"I found the remains of another man at the tight curve back there."

"Oh, God," she uttered. She had been sure that Todd had escaped. Apparently he had not.

Cal felt it unnecessary to shine the light on the half-rotted corpse above them. He let her believe that Todd, too, had been entirely reduced to burned bones. But there was a stench that hinted at the truth.

She remembered what she had seen happening to her professor, and the scattered bones she had felt on her way out of the pit and pictured the same happening to Todd. Though she had hated the man, she still did not care for the image, and she wondered how close she had come to becoming similarly consumed.

Then Cal's light went out and they were again in darkness. And in the far reaches of the tunnel she could hear the sound of a distant train.

"We've gotta get out of here," she said in a panic.

Cal knew that she was right. He could hear the hideous laughter in his own head.

They crawled from the entrance of the tunnel and up to where they could stand and run. Then they did run, up and out of the cave. The sound of the train grew no louder, and the earth did not shake beneath their feet.

Cal stood in the darkness outside the cave and looked into the heavens, and to the millions of stars overhead.

"It shouldn't be this dark yet," he said.

"Time seems to pass differently down there than it does up here," Helene explained. "Although I'm exhausted and really need some water, my head feels like I was only down there for maybe four or five hours after the thing happened."

"Well, I'd really like to hear what the thing is, but I'd rather do it over a hot cup of coffee."

Helene agreed. "There should be a van around here somewhere," she commented.

"I didn't see one when I got here."

Helene looked around in the darkness, but there was no object which might be the van. She wondered where it had gone, and who would have taken it without coming in for them.

Together they walked through the brush to Cal's truck where he offered her a drink from his water jug. They climbed into the truck and Cal saw that it was two in the morning. He looked at his watch which said a quarter to six.

"Weird," he said, then he started the engine and headed to town.

8

Helene sat in the same diner where she had met with the two men who were now nothing more than charred bone and flesh. She waited for Cal who was calling to report the deaths in the cave to Sheriff Rodriguez. As Helene sat for a moment drinking her coffee, the events of the past several hours (or was it days?) finally hit her and she put her head down on the table.

Cal returned and sat across from her. "Are you all right?" he asked.

She didn't answer so he just drank his coffee and waited. When she finally raised her head there were tears on her face and her eyes were red.

"Were they your friends?" he asked.

"Yes, I mean one was," she said in a strained voice. "The other one was a jerk, but that still doesn't mean I wanted this for him."

"So what was it?" Cal asked. He had wanted to ask again in the truck on the way into town, but she had simply sat in silence in a mild state of shock. He had let her relax then, let her come to grips with where she had been and what happened. Now he wanted to know some things. He knew that she might not be ready to talk about it, but he had to know.

She took a drink and looked into her cup, as if it might hold some answers. But there were none, and she was ready to talk.

"The first time I went down there I was scared to death by things I thought I felt and saw. Now that I've been through this, I know that those things were not just my imagination." She looked up at the rugged oil man. "I don't know exactly what happened, but I can tell you what I saw."

She hesitated.

"Look," he said, "I saw some pretty bizarre things down there tonight." He thought again about the top half of Todd which was still lying in the cave. "And I've experienced some things which I don't understand. But something important is happening, and I feel like something needs to be done, but I don't know what it is. I've been driven by a force I don't understand to do and say things which have little meaning to me. Didn't you wonder how I found you tonight?"

Her mind began to grind again as she realized what he was saying. Todd had never made it out. She had assumed that Todd had gotten this man. When she had heard of Todd's demise she had thought about that instead of where this man had come from.

"How did you find me?" she asked.

"I found you by accident."

"How did you know about the cave?" she asked.

"I didn't. I don't know how I found it, or why, but I did. And I can still feel it pulling at me. I don't like it, and I'm hoping you can give me some answers."

This was getting even stranger. The same thing that had killed Professor Stein and Todd had apparently saved her, though most likely by mistake.

"How did you find it?" Cal asked.

"Well," Helene responded, "I wasn't called to it or anything, not consciously anyway. I've known about that cave for years. The department has known about it for much longer."

"Department?" he asked.

"Oh, I'm sorry, the archaeology department at U.T."

"I see."

"Anyway, we finally got permission to take a look at it while I was down here, and that's what got me into it."

"So what happened?" he asked.

"Well," she began, trying to figure how she was going to tell the story, "after my first trip down there I called my professor. I wanted to go back in, but not by myself. It turned out there was a treasure of pictographs and remains which would be quite valuable to our work."

"Pictographs?" Cal asked.

"Those paintings on the walls in the cave and the small cavern."

"Oh, yea." He remembered them now. He wondered how they fit into all of this, if they did at all. "So you all went down this time?"

"Yea, we went down on Saturday. We explored the cavern and took pictures and on our way out is when this thing happened."

"You went further into the cave?" he asked. "Further than the pit I found you in?" Cal had wanted to do this himself. Whatever had been calling to him was back there, but he had opted out, this time. "What did you find?" he asked.

"The cave goes back about another fifty feet where it dead ends in a pile of rubble."

"Does the cave go beyond the rubble?"

"I'm sure it does," Helene replied, "the cave had just begun to open up. Near the pile of rubble the top was probably ten feet from the top to bottom."

"Of course," he said. It had to be the outer edge of the same cavern they had hit from above. The voice that was calling to him from the cave was the same one that he had heard as he'd left the drilling site. But why him? Why did he hear this voice and no one else?

Then it hit him that someone else did hear that voice. He began to piece together the fragments of the past several days and it started to make more sense. It explained a lot of the things that Buzz Shaw had said and done. But what was he doing now? Was the voice louder in Buzz's head, or was Buzz just weaker? Cal would like to have believed that he simply had a stronger will, but he didn't feel that this was right. Buzz had heard the voice when there was no hole. He had watched and waited while the hole was drilled through the earth. Had he known what he would really find, or had his mind convinced him he was drilling for oil? Or had something or someone else convinced him of this? Cal decided that he had somehow caught just a small portion of the madness which had consumed Buzz Shaw.

And then he remembered the shock he had felt coming from Buzz's dark eyes before he had left the site.

"That bastard," he muttered.

"Of course what?" Helene asked. "And who are you calling a bastard?"

"Oh, finish your story and I'll tell you. I think you may have some more to tell me that might help me give you a complete picture."

"Well," she continued, "when we got to the wall there was a terrible sound, one that I recognized from my first trip. Our lights went out and I panicked, I headed out as fast as I could."

Cal remembered her urgent tone when his flashlight had gone out.

"When I got to the pit I fell in. Todd was supposed to be holding onto the other end of the rope, but he had taken off already. I slid into the pit, but my professor grabbed onto the other end of the rope and kept me from falling in. He was sitting there, holding onto the rope when it hit him. I saw it above me." She began to shake as the image returned. A part of Cal wanted to say that it was all right if she wanted to stop, but another part, a larger part, needed to know the rest. "It was like a big red cloud, and it rumbled past like a train. As it did I saw his face begin to melt off. Then he dropped me, and I fell the rest of the way down. I was almost to the bottom, so I didn't really hurt myself, but I couldn't get out." She closed her eyes and tried not to see the image of her professor's melting face which had jumped back into her head.

"Did you feel anything?" he asked.

"You mean besides sheer terror? Sure. I felt like I was being stabbed with giant icicles. It was cold, and bright. But it didn't come down the pit, it continued toward the surface. I guess it was going after Todd."

"Or it was going for the surface when it hit him."

She looked back up to him. "I guess that could be." She took a sip of her coffee. "So who's the bastard?"

He thought she might have forgotten that comment. "There's a man who's been looking over my shoulder the past few days while me and my crew were makin' hole outside of town, not too far from where you were trapped."

"Making hole?" Helene asked.

"Yea, you know, drilling for oil."

"Oh." There were times that she felt ignorant despite her extensive education. "So what's he got to do with this?"

"I don't know," Cal said. "I think maybe he was trying to get to where you were going, but from another angle."

"I don't understand."

"We've been drilling about a mile from the entrance to that cave. At about three hundred feet we hit a really big cavern and lost Our bit and some pipe. We couldn't fish it out and we couldn't restart it. This guy was over our shoulders the whole time, pushing us like his life depended on it."

"So how do you think he fits in?"

"I don't know."

"Why is he a bastard?"

Cal thought about why that expletive had left his mouth. As he remembered the reasoning seemed unsound, but he shared it, nonetheless. "Well, I was thinking that maybe whatever was making him act so strange had rubbed off on me somehow. It's not very likely, but the thought ran through my mind."

"I see." It did sound strange to Helene, but it didn't sound impossible, not after what she had experienced.

She finished her second cup of coffee and looked at her watch, which read six p.m. But although it felt like six p.m., the trauma of the past six hours (or was it thirty hours?) had drained her strength.

"I need to get back to my motel room and get my stuff together, call a few people, figure out what I'm going to do."

"Okay," Cal said, and he signaled the lone server for the check.

"What are you going to do?" she asked him.

"I'm going to wait until sunup, then I'm going to go back and see what's going on at the site we capped off yesterday. I saw Buzz there earlier today. He was digging in the same spot where we'd capped the hole."

"What do you expect to find?" she asked him.

"I don't know, but I don't think Buzz is going to quit now. If he has the same thing I do, only stronger, I think he'll find a way to open that hole back up. Whatever else he'll do I don't know, but I need to find out. And I need to stop him."

"Why?" Helene asked.

Cal thought for a minute. "I don't really know. But I think it may have to do with your red cloud."

Helene saw the train again in her mind and a piece of her horrible dreams came back to her "Let's go," she said.

Cal paid the tab and took Helene back to her motel. It was three thirty in the morning, but the sky cast an eerie red glow, nonetheless. It looked almost like the final minutes before sunrise, but sunrise was over three hours away, and the sight frightened Helene even more.

Helene thanked Cal for all he had done for her, and he gave her his number in case she needed anything else while she was in Comstock. Then Helene went back to her motel room and went inside. It had been cleaned and the bed was made. Her things were all stacked neatly near the dresser despite the mess she had left them in. She sat on the end of the bed, trying to understand what had been happening to her, and not coming to terms with it all. The light flickered for a moment, and for a moment she expected to hear the train. She wondered then if that would haunt her for the rest of her life.

As she picked up the phone to call her boyfriend she had the terrible feeling that it was not over yet.

9

Helene dialed carefully and then waited for the call to go through. It took a long time for the connection to be made, and then there was a lot of static. Finally the phone began to ring. After five rings there were some loud clicking sounds and a pause.

"Mmm?" came the sleepy voice at the other end.

"Michael?"

"Helene?"

"It's me, Michael."

"I can't hear you very well," he said, "where are you?"

"I'm still in the same motel in Comstock."

"I thought you would call me yesterday, what happened?"

"Professor Stein and Todd Dumfreys came down yesterday morning. They're both dead now Michael."

"What?" His voice livened up as he came fully awake. "What's going on? Are you all right?"

"I'm fine," she lied. Then she told him what she had been through since the previous morning.

"What are you going to do now?" he asked her. "Are you going to come back?"

"I think so," she said. "I think I need to get away from here for a while. I'm not handling all of this very well, and I don't know if I can stay sane or not." Her voice was beginning to shake as the terrible images haunted her again.

"Do you need me to come get you?" he asked.

"No, I can drive all right."

The static grew worse and there were some loud clicking sounds.

"Michael? Are you still there?"

"I'm still here."

"What do you think I should do?"

"Well, whether or not these things happened as your mind tells you they did, I think your work there has been affected too much. I think you need to get away from it and go back later."

"It did happen like I said Michael, and don't you patronize me."

"I'm sorry, it's just really strange."

"Of course it's strange. You think I'm making this up?" She was beginning to shout now.

"No, Helene, I didn't mean that at all. You're getting out of hand, cool off a little."

"Boy you're being a lot of help..." she was cut short by another loud clicking sound followed by a screech which made her pull her ear from the receiver. "Michael?" This time there was no answer, just silence.

She hung up the phone and waited for a dial tone, which was a long time in coming. Then she tried to call him again. It took a minute for the call to go through, then all she got was a fast busy signal. She hung up and dialed the operator, but she got only dead silence.

She slammed the phone into the receiver in frustration and the old phone let out a weak ring in complaint. Then she laid back on her bed and covered her eyes with her hands and wondered why it was her world that had to fall apart.

As she lay back she finally began to relax, and the terrors of the past day loosened their grip upon her conscious mind. They lulled her into a light sleep, where they then began to wreak havoc upon her unconscious mind.

10

Jim Dewey snickered as he ran away from the junction box which lay outside the telephone switching station. In his left hand he carried the small butane torch. Behind him the junction box was still smoldering.

He ran to his pickup and headed to the east end of town. Merle had given him new instructions, and he would need some time to pick just the right place to set up.

11

Cal got home and decided that he was not ready to sleep, since it was late in the evening by his internal clock. Still he set his watch to real time. Then he took a shower and shaved and thought about what he would do for the next several hours.

He decided that he would in fact check on the Aldredge site at sunrise. This would mean missing the job near Ozona, but it was a price he would have to pay. Somehow he knew that he would not have been able to go to that job anyway. The pain in his head seemed to increase with the distance he put between himself and the cave. He'd tried to call in and leave a message at Texon, but the phones didn't seem to be working.

Cal spent the next few hours thinking about what he was going to do, and wondering what it was he would find. He watched the cable news to see if anything new had happened in the Middle East that would affect the price of oil, but it was still the same old game of "stare down in the sand."

He felt himself growing tired as he sat in the chair and morning approached. He watched the images on the screen as they grew blurry, and as daylight began to color the sky his heavy eyelids closed.

And he saw the tunnel, only this time it was large enough that he could stand in it, or else he was small enough. He walked down the corridor which now seemed familiar in a way it shouldn't have. He walked around the corners and down the declines toward the pit where he had found Helene. As he passed through the small cavern he noticed paintings which he had not noticed before. They looked bright, almost fresh. He passed them by and continued down the tunnel, past the pit.

Now he walked into an area where he had not been before. Still that eerie air of familiarity stayed with him as passed the walls. He turned the last corner and walked to the place where Helene had said the stone wall had been, only there was no wall. Instead he stood before a gigantic underground cavern, bigger than any he had ever seen. Shadows danced on the walls of the cavern and a bonfire burned in its center, which was half a mile away, yet he could see it clearly. He could also see the naked men dancing about the fire, their shadows dancing like horrible monsters on the walls.

Then he was in the fire, looking out at them. He did not burn but instead gazed in all directions, as if he had become the fire. Then he began to float upward as if he had now become the smoke. As he drifted toward the ceiling he could see an opening which he had not seen before because it was night. He drifted toward the hole and as he reached it he saw a face peering down from that hole.

The face was old and haggard. The hair was white, and the skin and eyes were pale. The face glared at him, then it began to laugh a hideous laugh, and Cal knew there was something terribly familiar about that face.

Then he realized, despite the pale features and wrinkles which disguised him, the face belonged to Buzz Shaw.

The face spoke to him as he floated. "I know you are infected," it said. "But I know you want to work against me. You will either join or die."

Buzz's face began to melt, then it burst into red flames which spread out into the night.

Cal then fell from his place, back toward the fire. Then he found himself outside the cavern, behind a wall of rubble where no wall had been before. He felt the earth beneath him begin to rumble, and there was a terrible ringing sound which came to him louder and louder.

He tried to run, remembering what Helene had told him, but he could not. His feet and legs moved violently, but he went nowhere. The ringing continued, rhythmically growing louder until he felt something touching his leg, then...

...then he sat up and kicked his dog off his bed. The ringing continued and he reached for the phone.

"Hello," he said.

"I'm sorry, did I take you away from something important?" the voice asked. It sounded as if Cal had run to the phone, the way he was breathing heavily.

"No, I'm okay. Who is this?"

"It's Helene."

He hadn't expected to hear from her so soon. He looked at his watch. It was a little after seven in the morning.

"What's going on?" he asked.

"I thought maybe I'd missed you. Are you still going to the drill site?" she asked.

"Yep."

"Can I come?"

"You bet." He looked out his window where the sun was just beginning to rise. It felt as if it should be buried on the other side of the earth. "I'll pick you up in an hour."

"Great."

Cal said good-bye. Then he apologized to his dog and jumped into the shower.

Six

1

The old woman sat rocking back and forth with her eyes closed. She hummed old songs which she had learned from her mother, songs which had been passed down through the generations. The words were not English, but a mixture of old Spanish and some long dead language.

It was almost morning and the sky glowed red through the curtains. It was hot and there was no air conditioning in the small room, but she was used to weather like this. She came from a small town several hundreds of miles south of Mexico. She had come to answer the calls of her ancient ancestors, ancestors who had been pushed southward by their visions of the white hawk. There they became mixed with the tribes of South America and eventually with the Portuguese and Spanish settlers.

But this woman's blood was as close to that of her ancient ancestors as walked the earth. Through time it, too, had been corrupted. But the ceremonies and the stories had been passed down intact. The time had come to drive the white hawk away. The land had to be healed and reclaimed. She was to help the vengeful spirits in their war.

One small candle lit the center of the room. She sat amidst the dolls she had made before the journey. The doll of the changing fat mam, the pale woman, the one-armed man. There were other dolls, some which had already been maimed, others which awaited their time. One doll lay outside the circle, its bottom half burned away. She could not do this work without the help of the spirits, and they could not break free without her help.

She held the one-armed man in her hand and tried to see his face. He was a problem. She had helped the spirits work on his mind, but he was resisting, and he had met the woman. Together the two of them could cause trouble, but they were only human, and this could be used against them. She relaxed and sang her songs until she saw the face of the one-armed man. He was in the old, abandoned house where the spirits had tried to break through once before. For now she could only try to frighten the man. But as the fat man continued his work, as the spirits were released from their underground prison, she would be able to do much more.

Then she would be able to touch the entire town.

2

Buzz sat in the giant backhoe, looking into the pit he had dug. After the first five feet he had hit the hole which had been drilled into the earth and it now lay gaping at the center of the pit. He could see that something seemed to be seeping slowly out of it, something red and misty, but this did not discourage him. He knew that there would be forces which would try to stop him in his great quest for his own salvation. But they would not turn him from his work.

The pit he had dug was suitable for a very deep pool, but not much more. He was going to have to go much deeper.

He turned off the engine and got off the digging machine, dismayed that he hadn't seen this earlier. He had been so anxious to simply dig that he had not thought things out carefully.

Buzz looked over the edge of the pit and longed to jump into it. He felt the earth, or rather something under the earth, calling to him, and he wanted to join with it again. Something inside of him now belonged down there. But he could not get through the hole. The hole was too narrow even for a child.

Buzz looked back down into the pit and the call was so great that he decided to take the chance. He sat down on the slope which provided the gentlest angle and slid down the wall of the pit into the heart of it. His foot caught on a stone near the bottom, and he fell forward onto his face. He got a mouthful of dirt and spit it out. But he did not get up. Instead he lay there, feeling the warmth which emanated from the earth or what was beneath it. He dug his hands into the ground and held to it like a kitten might hold to its mother while nursing. He closed his eyes and tried to see. Home was down there, somewhere. He lay like this for an hour as the stars slowly left the sky and the sun made its appearance in the east. Then he rose to his feet. The longer he delayed, the later the reunion would be.

He climbed up out of the pit and walked to his car. If he was going to continue his work he was going to have to get equipment which would work better. The hole was getting too deep for the backhoe. He didn't really have the money to rent a steam shovel, but that was what he needed.

Then he realized that he didn't have the money because the company could afford it, and he could provide the account number and sign off on it. Texon would find out eventually, but by then he would be finished with it.

Buzz started up his car and headed back to Del Rio to see if he could find that steam shovel.

3

Cal saw Buzz's Lincoln pass them going the opposite way as they got within five miles of the drill site. Buzz, however, had been too preoccupied to see Cal.

"I knew he was still there," Cal commented.

"Who was where?"

"That was Buzz's car that just passed us headed into town. I'll bet he was at the site all night."

"What is he doing?" she asked.

"I don't have any idea," Cal replied. "The last time I saw him he was digging at the drill site with a backhoe. I can't imagine what he was up to."

They drove the rest of the way to the Aldredge Ranch, then pulled onto the dirt road. As they turned the last corner Cal's eyes grew wide.

"Jesus," he said, then, "Excuse me." He always excused himself when he swore in front of a lady.

Helene looked at the mound of dirt near the big backhoe and saw the edge of the hole Buzz was digging. "What do you think he's up to?"

"Well, I think he's not just looking for oil, that's for sure. But if he's going to try and dig a three-hundred-foot pit with a backhoe he really has gone crazy."

Cal drove up to the pit and got out of his truck. He walked to its edge and looked in. Behind him Helene got out too, but she had become preoccupied with the old house. It was a familiar house, like one she had seen in an old movie at midnight, or in a magazine. Then she knew where she had seen it. Once again her dreams had been giving her glimpses of reality, and she was becoming convinced of the greater connection between all these things.

Cal looked into the pit and felt a slight urge to go down into it, though there was no reason he needed to. He turned and looked behind him to see what Helene was up to. She was walking toward the house, apparently intrigued by some aspect of it. He wondered if perhaps she too had been touched by something which sought to control her.

"Hey!" he called to her. "What are you doing?"

She turned to face him. "This house looks familiar. I mean," she debated telling him, then decided that she said too many strange things to worry about it, "I mean, I've dreamed about this house. I want to look inside."

Cal looked at the house again and pieces of his own dream returned to him. She was right. The house fit into this all somehow.

"Wait up!" he called as he began to jog toward her.

Cal caught up with Helene about fifty feet from the front of the house and she began to walk toward it once again, this time with Cal beside her.

"This is all getting really strange," she said, looking ahead to the house.

"It got strange some time ago. Now I think we just feel like we have to sort it out."

"What do you think it all means?" she asked.

"I really don't know," he said. "I'm just a simple oil man who's gotten caught up in some strange shit, excuse me."

They stepped up onto the small porch together and Helene reached for the doorknob. She expected it to be locked, but it was not. The knob was hard to turn from rust and disuse, but it did turn, and the door did come open.

For Cal this was a wonderful and terrifying experience. He had grown up in Comstock and had known about the house since his childhood. It had been the haunted house of Comstock, even though it was actually outside of the city limits. He had dared and been dared to enter the house on more than one occasion. He didn't personally know anyone who had entered the house, but he'd heard stories of those who had gone in and never come back out. But of course those were the kind of stories they told you as a child. Now he was simply very glad that it was daylight as they walked into the musty old house.

The door creaked loudly as it opened, just as the doors on all haunted houses were supposed to. A dank, musty smell assaulted them as they entered.

"This place is pretty spooky," Helene commented.

"Yep," Cal replied. "It's got quite a history."

Helene had assumed that Cal had not known about the place until a few days ago. "You know this place?"

"Sure. I grew up around here. This was our haunted house."

"Have you been inside before?" she asked, knowing her younger brother had entered just about every 'haunted house' in their many neighborhoods in his youth. They had moved frequently, and it was his way of getting the initial approval he needed to become a part of the new community.

"No." Cal answered. "I don't think anybody's been in here for a very long time."

She found that hard to believe, but the dust was everywhere. It even lay a half inch thick on the floor and had no footprints but their own as evidence of visitors. The pain in Cal's head was very distant now.

Helene knew something was very wrong. Then it struck her. The furniture was strewn about and in disarray, it had been damaged by age and moisture, but it was there.

"Hey," she said, "there are some pretty nice antiques in here."

"Yep."

"Doesn't that seem a little odd?" she asked.

"I don't know," he replied. "If this house had been near San Antonio or Houston it would probably have been ransacked and burned down by now. But this place is kind of a monument here. It's not really sacred or anything, but it is on private property, so it's left alone."

She walked around a small table and into the living room. "Somebody owns this place?" she asked.

"Sure," he replied.

"Who?" she asked.

"It's always been called the Aldredge pace, so I guess the Aldredge's own it."

"You mean you were drilling on it, but you never met the people?"

"Sure, that's usually how it goes out here."

"Oh." She decided to keep quiet for a moment before any more stupid questions could escape her.

She walked around the living room, looking closely at the pieces of furniture which had been damaged, but long ago. Pieces of what had once been an end table of some kind were in the fireplace, as if for kindling. She would have thought this the work of a vagrant, but it didn't look as if any attempt had been made to light the fire.

Cal didn't enter the living room as far as she had. Instead he stayed at the edge of the room and made his way to the staircase which led upward. Sunlight crept through the windows and rays of light shot through the newly distant dust, adding a somewhat sacred dimension to the room before him. He watched Helene as she made a quick investigation. But then he looked back up the stairs. There was something up there which he needed to see.

Helene turned and saw that Cal had begun walking up the stairs. She had wanted to look through the room at the other end of the living room first, but she also wanted to be with Cal while he was exploring. Part of that came from her years in the field of archaeology. If some wonderful discovery was made, she wanted to be present when it happened. This was not from any desire to be first. There was a special wonder at being in a location of discovery, a magic much greater than being in a place which had recently been discovered. For some reason she felt that what they had seen had not been seen by human eyes for a very long time, at least long when compared with the age of the house. Perhaps not so long when compared with the events which seemed to surround it.

Then she realized that she had made a connection between her experience in the cave and this house. Why she felt that way she didn't know, but knowing she had come to that conclusion did not lessen her belief that it was so. There was a quality to the house, something she could distinctly feel, which was very much like a feeling she had experienced in the cave.

She walked back across the living room, stumbling on a broken chair leg, and walked up the stairs. She met with Cal at the top, though he did not turn to talk to her. Instead his eyes seemed to be focused ahead, on something which she could not see. He walked on, she followed. Cal walked down the hallway to a doorway. Then he reached out to turn the knob, but it would not turn. He tried harder, and the knob broke off in his hand.

"Shit," he exclaimed, not bothering to apologize this time.

He took a step back and lifted his foot from the ground. Then he kicked hard against the door. There was a crash and a splintering of wood, then the door flew open.

The room was cooler than the rest of the house, and Helene could feel a breeze coming through the doorway. The room also provided a lot of light. Cal stepped into the room and looked up. Above him the ceiling was torn away in a circular pattern. He looked through the hole and into the morning sky, which was bright and blue. He turned his gaze back to the room and saw something which made him stop.

Helene stood just outside the doorway, and she saw the expression on Cal's face. His mouth opened as if he were about to scream, but he did not. He began to raise his arm, then his expression relaxed, and so did his arm.

He looked closely at the sheet draped over the bedpost at the end of the room. For a moment he had seen a figure there. For a moment he had seen an old woman with white hair and a pale face. He had seen her smiling at him with a hideous smile and raising her finger to point at him.

But it had only been the wind as it had gently lifted the edge of the sheet.

Still his heart raced as he walked over to the bed and took hold of the sheet. He pulled at it, but it tore away in his hand. He looked up and saw that it was tied to the post as if it had at one time been a noose of some kind. One which had been poorly constructed and which time and the weather had pounded against. The bedpost itself had been beaten not only by time but by human tools as well. Though the marks were old and brown, a knife had taken small pieces of the bedpost away.

"This is where they say he killed his wife," Cal said, still looking ahead.

"What?" Helene asked.

Cal turned to face her. "A long time ago a preacher lived here. The story that was always told in school was that he killed his wife while she laid in bed, then hid her body away somewhere in the house." He looked back to the bed. Though there were no bloodstains, he could imagine where they had been. The mattress was no more than a mess of moldy fabric, all of the feathers had fled decades before.

He looked around the room and imagined he could see the madness which had once resided there. Then he walked to the window and looked out toward the pit that Buzz had dug. Somewhere in his mind Cal knew that it was right, that the pit had to be dug. He could imagine himself in that pit digging, digging with a shovel and pick. He knew that this was absurd since it would be almost impossible to reach the cavern with these tools, but these tools represented something purer than a backhoe or a steam shovel. He could see that the pit could be dug no deeper with a backhoe and wondered what Buzz had planned now. An earth mover would take too much area to get to the depth he needed. The only way to really do this now was manually, with a shovel and a bucket. But even with those tools it would be months of non-stop work before he could get all of the way down. From the looks of the work Buzz had done already, going nonstop is exactly what he had been doing.

Helene could see into the room and out of the window Cal was looking through. She walked slowly to him, looking out the window at the pit. She could see the pit well from here, but the feelings it gave her were unlike those which ran through Cal's mind and body. Hers were feelings of danger, maybe even evil. They were the feelings she had experienced in the cave, and they were dark and eerie.

Suddenly Cal turned around and faced her. His eyes were wild, and his breath was fast. He started to mumble something which sounded as if it were from Shakespeare, then he stopped, and his eyes returned to their normal state. Helene began to wonder if being alone in an old house with a man she hardly knew was such a great idea.

Cal looked at Helene and his first thought was 'what is she doing outside the window?' Then he realized that she was in the room with him, and he had turned to face her. But he did not remember doing this. All he remembered was one moment looking out the window, the next looking at Helene. And she looked frightened.

"What happened? he asked.

"What do you mean?"

"I mean, why do you look so worried?"

"It's nothing," she said, worrying that Cal was perhaps a little crazy. "Maybe we should go now."

"Helene, stop this and tell me what just happened. Did I say or do something strange which frightened you?"

She looked at his eyes, which now looked sane and normal, perhaps even a little inviting. "You turned from the window and started mumbling something about hell and the pit. Then you looked at me as if you wanted..." she hesitated.

"Wanted what?" he asked.

"Well, you looked crazy, that's all. You don't remember?"

"I don't remember anything more than looking out that window and into the pit. Then I was looking at you."

"Are you nuts?" she asked, deciding that directness might be best at this point.

"I have some bad memories of Vietnam. I have bad dreams, and sometimes late at night I drive on the wrong side of the road just for the hell of it, but I don't think I'm crazy." She looked only a little comforted. "I've never had anyone tell me that I did or said something which I didn't remember, except for a few nights when I stayed at the pub too long. I don't have flashback syndrome or anything like that. Besides, they say you remember those things."

"So what was it?" she asked.

"I don't know," He turned and looked out the window again. "But I think it's something Buzz has much worse, and I think he gave some of it to me."

"What do you mean?"

He turned back to her. "One day I had to tell him that the drilling was over. He went wild. About then I felt something odd, something dark coming from him. This sounds weird, but you've been through weirder, so I'll keep going. Something came, well, like out of his eyes and into mine. I felt it getting in my head and turned away. But whatever got in is still there. Remember me telling you how I found you in the cave? This thing in my head is what guided me. It also gives me a headache when I get too far away from this area. I don't know what else it does, but I'll bet my mumbling spell came from it too."

Helene wondered if this made him dangerous. She decided she would wait and see. And keep an eye on him.

Cal and Helene rummaged about the room but found nothing which might help them understand what was going on. Then they returned downstairs and looked around. There were various kitchen utensils in the drawers, and some old, cracked china. Had the situation been different Helene would have wanted to take some things, a lot of things, with her. But that was not what the two of them were here for, and there was something which begged her to leave everything alone, as it had been for so long, so she did.

After inspecting the house they went back outside and walked around it. Helene turned the back corner first and saw the cellar doors. They were closed, but there was no lock in the latch. She walked over to them with Cal close behind. She grabbed one of the handles and pulled, and it broke off in her hand. The wood was gray and cracked, split by decades of extreme heat and cold.

Cal punched a hole where the handle had been and pulled the door open. The rotten smell of eighty years of mold and rust did not assault them, which seemed odd. Despite the morning sun Cal could not see much in the cellar so he retrieved his flashlight from the truck.

"Why did they make the floor so close to the ceiling?" Helene asked. There was only about three feet from the floor of the cellar to the bottom of the house.

Cal got down on his knees and shined the light inside. It revealed a series of shelves and crates, many of which seemed to be cut in half by the floor.

"This is not the floor," he explained. "The floor is probably made of concrete, and it's probably another three feet beneath this dirt. Over the years the winds and rains have brought in the mud and dirt, filling the cellar halfway up. I imagine in another hundred years it'll be completely filled."

He shone the light around. It had been a long dry summer, and the floor looked solid.

"I think we can go in," he said.

Helene was curious. "Let's go."

Cal led the way into the cellar. He crawled along the pathway made by the top of the shelving which protruded from the ground. The shelves had ancient jars of preserves, most of which had been broken and the contents eaten by animals. Cal could see a source of light coming from the back of the cellar, the front of the house. He crawled in that direction and found the window. It was broken and had provided a way for the animals to get in and the smells to get out. He crawled toward the window, passing more preserves and some old rusty tools half buried in the dirt.

Helene looked her surroundings over with the eyes of an archaeologist. It was like finding a portion of a buried city, only this was pretty fresh compared with the cities she had in mind. She crawled behind Cal and followed him to the window. He crawled to the shelving which was built up just under the window and looked out of it. As he was gazing out, Helene's eye caught something which Cal's eye had not. It was her years of studies and work which revealed the barely visible white object protruding slightly from the dirt to her right. She crawled to that object and began to dig around it with her hand. Cal heard the noise and turned to see what she was doing.

"What have you got there?" he asked her, shining the light on the place where she was digging.

"I think it's a bone," she replied, clearing away more of the dirt.

"What kind of animal?" he asked.

She was silent as she uncovered more, wanting to be certain. Finally when she was, she answered him. "Human."

He left the window and got beside her, holding the light closer. "How can you be sure?"

"It's what I do," she explained. "This is part of the first finger of the left hand of a human skeleton. And there's no telling how much more of it may be under the dirt."

Cal was silent and watched as she gently and expertly cleared more dirt away. Finally she stopped.

"It appears to go straight down, though I doubt it's connected to the entire skeleton. It was raised and buried in pieces by the water and wind and dirt." She looked down now at the skeleton of a hand which was jumbled but complete, except for the small finger. She could judge from its size that it belonged to an adult, though she could not determine the sex, and she told Cal this.

"How long has it been dead?" he asked.

"I really can't tell. How long has the house been empty?" she asked.

"About eighty years."

"The only way to be sure would be to dig down until we had recovered the entire skeleton. The lowest point at which we recovered bone would be a good way to judge how long ago this person died, assuming that the accumulation of this dirt has been fairly constant, and that's really a pretty big assumption. Loads might have been dropped at once during a flood."

"Probably not this high on the hill," Cal explained. "But I'm not interested in digging down to see how old it is. It could be anybody. This house has been empty and unexplored for so long it could be ten or fifty years old."

"Or eighty," Helene threw in.

The image of the preacher's wife screaming on the bed while blood colored the walls and headboard jumped suddenly into Cal's head. It was a violently bright image, as if not an imagining but a remembering. For an instant he was no longer in the cellar. For that second he was somewhere else, and a strange room surrounded him, like the screams of the dying woman. The image startled him, and he dropped the flashlight.

"What is it?"

"I think I know who it is," he said.

"The preacher's wife?" Helene asked, remembering the story Cal had told her upstairs.

"You saw it too?" he asked.

"Saw what?"

"Well," he hesitated. His instinct was not to say. But considering they were quickly becoming a team, he decided to continue. "Well, I just had this picture in my head of that woman. She was bloody and screaming, and she was on the bed upstairs.

"What do you mean by 'picture'?"

"Well," he looked out the window. Then he looked back to Helene. "For just a second it was like I was there. I was in the room looking down on the woman."

Helene just looked him over, watching carefully for any signs of the craziness which she feared, but it did not surface.

"This may or may not be her," Helene said, "but I'd like to get out of here now and take a look at the work out friend has been doing."

"Sure," Cal agreed. In his mind Cal now knew that it was the preacher's wife who lay in pieces below them.

Cal and Helene left the cellar and walked around the house to the area where Buzz had been working. Mounds of dirt stood on either side of the hole. It was getting hot already as the sun rose above the hill. Helene looked down into the pit.

"You really think he's trying to dig down to the cavern?" she asked him.

"I'm sure of it."

"Why?" she asked.

"Because for some reason I want to do the same thing. But for some other reason I know that it would be bad."

"Bad? Bad like what?"

"I'm not sure," Cal replied, looking deep into the pit again. Again he heard the soft voices calling to him, begging him for his assistance. Promises of wonder and power lay somewhere at the bottom of the pit. "I'm not sure, but I think we'll let something very bad out."

"Didn't you already open up a hole to the pit?" she asked. "Why didn't it get out then?"

Something clicked in Cal's mind, and he began to put some things together.

"It was Buzz," he said then.

"What?"

Cal turned to her suddenly, frightening her again with a wild look.

"It was Buzz, Buzz didn't leave the night we hit the cavern, at least I didn't see him leave. We all got into our vehicles and took off, but his car was still sitting there when I pulled away. I don't think he left then. I think he stayed and went to the hole. I thought I felt something too that night, but that was one reason I insisted on shutting down. I sensed the danger and called it quits." He looked beyond her as he put the puzzle together. "Then he stayed and went to the hole, and something did get out. It got out and into Buzz. But there's more down there, much more, and it's waiting to come to life."

His wild eyes turned back to Helene, and she saw that they had changed. It wasn't just their expression or how he held them open, they had actually changed. His irises had lost their color and were as pink as a rabbit's. His face had lost all its color, and he hissed out his next few words.

"It is bigger than you could ever imagine, and there's nothing you can do to stop it!"

Spit flew from his mouth as he hissed the words, and he suddenly took hold of Helene and threw her into the pit. She screamed as she fell. Then she landed hard on her back, hurting her arm against the side of the pit and losing the wind from her lungs. She felt the terrible burning sensation as she struggled to take a breath but could not. She gasped for air, but it would not come. Her head felt as if it would explode, and her vision blurred. Then she was standing, bent over. She relaxed and eventually her breath came back to her in deep gasps for air.

"Don't panic," came a soothing voice. "Relax and you'll be fine, you just had the wind knocked out of you."

She remembered what had just happened and turned to see who was in the pit with her. It was Cal and she drew back her hand to rake her fingernails across his face.

But his eyes had returned to normal, and a look of surprise, not aggression crossed his face and she brought her hand forward into a soft slap. Then an almost sheepish look came to his face.

"I threw you down here, didn't I?" he asked her.

"Yes," she answered, still gasping for air. She looked at him sternly, and he shied from her gaze.

"I'm sorry," he said. "That's no way to treat a lady."

She waited a moment to catch her breath while he stood in silence. Then she asked him if he didn't remember pushing her.

"All I remember was talking about Buzz and figuring out what had happened the night we hit the cavern. Next thing I knew I was looking down into the pit at you on your back. I had the sneaking suspicion it was my fault."

"It was," she confirmed, still wary of him, watching his eyes closely.

"I think it's this place," he explained, "and this pit. I think we should leave, or at least I should."

Helene agreed and Cal helped her climb from the pit. They came out on the side opposite the house. The slope was gentler and easier to navigate. When they reached the top Cal apologized again, and Helene was about to accept when something at the base of a nearby tree caught her attention. She walked toward the tree and Cal simply watched her. When she reached the tree she found more bones. She stood over them and looked at the jumble. There had to be at least six or seven bodies represented by the mass of crushed skulls and scattered arms and legs. They all were small, less than adults.

"Cal," she called back.

"Yes," he said from a distance, not trusting himself to be near her now.

"When you were a kid, did they say anything about the preacher's kids?"

"Yep," he replied. "They said he killed them too and buried them around the yard to keep the good spirits away."

I think they were partly right," she called back. Then she turned to face him. "I've found a bunch of children's bones here, all neatly separated from the rock and rubble from which they must have come. Buzz probably dug them up, they were probably all in the same location, a mass grave which he hit while digging. For some reason they meant something to him because he did not just ignore them." She looked carefully at him before making her next statement. "Why don't you come take a look?"

Cal paused, then approached. "Why don't you step back," he suggested. She did so as he approached the small pile.

Whatever he had felt under the house came to him again, and he knew that she was right. This time he spoke more forcefully. "Yep, these are the bones." He looked up to her. "And Buzz knew it too, that's why he put them there, because they were sacred."

How would Buzz know? Does he know the stories?"

Cal looked back to the bones. "No. But he knows. He knows whose bones these are. And I imagine he cried when he dug them up." As Cal said this a single tear crept down his face as he felt just a portion of what Buzz must have experienced. He knew Buzz had cried, perhaps for a long time before setting the bones aside. But then he returned to his work. It was part of the insanity which Buzz shared with him, and which also had been shared with a man long since dead.

Cal felt himself slipping and this time pulled out of it. He looked up and saw Helene's hesitant eyes.

"I'm okay," he said. "I felt myself slipping that time, but I'm okay now." He looked back to the bones. "Let's go," he said. "This doesn't feel good."

She agreed and as they turned to return to the truck they saw Buzz pulling up the road with his new toy.

Seven

COMSTOCK, TEXAS – 1907

1

The sun pounded on the dry cracked soil of the small town which was just five miles northeast of the Rio Grande. The river stood as a barrier between Texas and Mexico. There were no clouds in the dusty blue sky. There had been none the day before, and there would be none the following day. Ten miles to the west the Pecos River was at its lowest level in thirty years. The same distance to the east the Devil's River was nothing more than a dry trench filled with vegetation which sought out the last source of moisture.

There was no wind to cool the members of the Comstock Baptist Church as they walked and drove their carts toward the white stone building which rested on the top of the hill near the south end of town. It was Sunday morning, and the worst of the heat was yet to come. Many members of the church had fallen into the temptation which caused them to miss the Sunday evening gatherings because of the heat. The truly faithful traced the paths they were now taking three times each week, including the trek for the midweek services.

Elizabeth Walker held tightly to her mother's hand as they walked together through the heat. As she walked her small white shoes kicked up the dirt which covered the road, and it flew into small brown puffs which did not fly away since there was no breeze. She breathed heavily and concentrated on the road before her as a drop of sweat raced quickly from under her hat and down the side of her face. It was always the hardest climbing the hill. Sometimes someone would stop in their buggy and offer to take Elizabeth and her mother the rest of the way, but today they were late, and the buggies had all climbed the hill before them. About now Brother Morris would be mounting the steps which led to the podium where he would lead the congregation in an opening prayer. If they hurried they would be able to join in the singing of the second hymn. They would easily make it in time for the sermon.

Elizabeth had to take large, fast steps to keep up with her mother who seemed to be threatening to break into a run. The little girl looked up to her mom with a pleading look on her face, but her mother did not return the glance and instead kept her eyes on the goal before her. Finally they reached the steps which lead into the building and walked to the top of them. Elizabeth stood still for a moment and watched as her mother took a few deep breaths and composed herself. The little girl did the same. It was important to at least look as if one had not just come out of a fiery oven in a race for one's life, especially when a few scrutinizing eyes would be carefully watching.

Elizabeth's mother held tightly to her hand as she pulled open one of the large wooden doors. The muffled sounds of singing became clear and loud as the door flew open, and the two entered quietly. Elizabeth saw immediately that the two back rows were taken up and that they would have to walk past them to find a seat. She felt the probing and accusing eyes of Esther Perkins on her back as she walked with her mother to their seat. The seats were long wooden benches which by the end of the hour-long service seemed to poke and prod mercilessly. Elizabeth resisted the unladylike urge to wipe her forehead as another bead of sweat ran down it and got into her eyes.

Elizabeth and her mother joined in with the singing of "Shall We Gather at the River," which sounded like a wonderful idea to Elizabeth. She wondered why they had to meet in the stuffy building when they could most certainly be closer to God outside the building, maybe even in the river. She let her mind wander into her own world while she mouthed the words to the song and those that followed. By now she knew all of the songs by heart, and this allowed her to go to other places in her mind without letting on that she was not really paying attention. It was the only way she could be certain she would not fall asleep and thereby earn the wrath of her mother, and the shame of the congregation.

Finally the singing was over, and the congregation watched as Brother Morris walked down from the small platform and took his seat in the front row next to the three elders. At the same time Brother Aldredge rose from his seat and began his walk to the podium.

Brother Jesse Aldredge was the shepherd of this particular flock. He had been so for as long as the church had been standing, which was twenty-four years. Before then there had been no churches at all, nor had there been a town. The years of serving as the shepherd showed itself plainly on Brother Aldredge's face. The smile which had seemed never to leave him twenty-four years earlier was now a rare sight. He was never satisfied with his flock, they strayed so often and so severely that he wondered what good, if any, he was doing. But he would not quit. He would never quit. It was well known that when Jesse Aldredge set his mind to a task there was nothing, including hard liquor and bawdy women, which could distract him. In all his years as the leader of the congregation he had never been accused of nor had he committed any acts which might be construed as impious. He was a hardworking, honest man. He ran a small farm, as did a large portion of the town's inhabitants. Good access to the railroad made farming a more profitable venture than many others.

Brother Aldredge was a hellfire and damnation preacher in the finest sense. He kept his flock and his family on the righteous path by instilling in them an appropriate amount of fear. It was fear of hellfire which he preached upon his people, and it was fear of a heavy hand which he used in his home.

But recently things had changed. Little Elizabeth Walker had first noticed it, as had the rest of the congregation, three weeks back. The Aldredge family consisted of one small and meek wife and eight children, six girls and two boys. The Aldredge family always sat in the second row from the front, behind the elders. Three weeks back and for the first time in anyone's remembrance there were family members missing. The wife and girls were there, the two boys were not. Brother Aldredge had announced that the boys had taken seriously ill, though in the past that had been no excuse for absence. One time the oldest girl, who was certainly old enough to have stayed at home alone, had come into church looking pale and quite sickly and had then thrown up halfway through the services. Even after that she'd been required to remain for the rest of the services while her bile smelled up the building.

Two weeks ago only the wife had shown up for services, and she appeared quite pale and nervous. Last week Brother Aldredge had come alone, as he had this week. There had been visits to his home and much praying, but as yet none of the members of the Aldredge family had been seen since two weeks ago. Visitors to his home were always met at the door, and never allowed any further than the entry way for fear of contagion, as Brother Aldredge explained it. At the same time Brother Aldredge's sermons had taken a bizarre and sometimes macabre turn. The congregation had become concerned that perhaps he, too, had caught whatever disease had struck his household. Once in a while he would break into words which were English, but which together had no meaning. He would frequently turn to talk of the "great white hawk," of the "terrors beneath the earth." Elizabeth recalled some mentions of hell being below, but she had never heard of any references to a hawk. When she had tried to discuss this with her mother, Nora Walker had dismissed her questions and told her to read her bible more diligently. Each Sunday became a little more bizarre, and the congregation's concern had continued to grow.

The weary man stood before his flock looking them over. The look was one of disapproval, as it always was. He was of average height, and though he once could have been considered portly his body had become thinner over the years. Today he looked as thin as he had ever been, and Elizabeth was sure that he was sick. His face had thinned to the point that she could clearly make out his skull. His eyes were set deep in their sockets, above them were thick black eyebrows which grew together in a 'V' over his nose. His hair was black as well, and today it looked like a poorly built dove's nest on top of his head. Until his family had taken ill he had been the best example of fine grooming. Today he was quite clearly the worst groomed and worst dressed of all present, including the very poor Nichols family who walked every Sunday from the edge of town and sat in the very back row. His clothing was dirty and torn. A razor had not touched his face since the previous Sunday. Those who sat in the rows closest to the front also observed that he smelled as if he had not bathed in as long. He stood looking out into the congregation with eyes which seemed possessed and distant. A smirk played at the corners of his mouth, but no words came forth. Sweat beaded up and ran down his face in intervals as the congregation awaited his words. The confusion and doubt that had been building within the congregation the past several weeks were building to new heights as the flock saw what had become of their shepherd. Whispers had flown about town concerning what was happening to the man, but it was all nothing but hearsay. The rumor was spread that a consumption had killed first the Aldredge boys, then had spread to the rest of the family. Visitors were eventually turned away by a more and more haggard-looking Brother Aldredge. Finally the members of the church had stopped visiting. Now they sat looking at a man who himself seemed on the very edge of death.

Yet the man was alive.

They had become even more frightened of him than before the cancer had come. His mind seemed to wander, his sermons often seemed nonsensical, but he had been their shepherd for so long that it was impossible to bring him down. It was also just as impossible to help him. So instead of doing either, the people just whispered amongst themselves or waited.

Waited to see what would happen.

Suddenly the hot silence was broken.

"I see before me a host of unworthiness!"

The words caused Elizabeth and half of the congregation to jump. They had come so suddenly after the prolonged silence, and they had come without the usual lifting of hands or raising of the head. They had simply leapt forth from the mouth of the possessed man before them.

"Hell has places waiting for all those who will come to it, and those who will come to it are many!" As he spoke he slowly nodded his head back and forth, looking over the entirety of the congregation whose eyes were locked to his. Spit dangled from his lower lip as he stood silent for another moment. Then he grabbed his head as if in pain. "I speak, and I speak, but you don't listen!" He shook his head violently back and forth, throwing the dangling spit toward the crowd. Elizabeth's eyes grew wide at the display.

He stopped and composed himself, though his eyes remained wild. He pointed into the crowd and spoke. "As the great prophet Isaiah said, 'Yea, thou knewest not; yea, from that time that thine ear was not opened: for I knew that thou wouldest deal very treacherously, and wast called a transgressor from the womb!'" He threw his hands to the ceiling as he shouted out the final word. Then he began to cackle. He laughed toward the skies for a moment then looked quickly and reproachfully back to the audience. Fear crept slowly through the congregation as it had never before. Their fears of the past few weeks refused to be buried this Sunday but instead leapt out at them in a terrifying form. Yet no one dared stop him.

"You!" he said, pointing at no one in particular, "you must beware the terrors that lie within the earth. The earth is full of unrighteousness and evil. It holds both wonders and terrors beyond your tiny imaginations." He began to waver back and forth as he spoke. "I, I can see before me, but I cannot hold to wonders which - so far from my eyes but I can - reach, reach forward to my destiny, through the fire of life, though life it is before my eyes as a, a," he began again the series of broken sentences which seemed to lead nowhere. His eyes and his focus wandered slowly from the audience as he became lost in his own confusion. The congregation stared in silence as he muttered his nonsense. At one point he began to fall but caught himself on the podium. He stood again and looked confused, as if he didn't know where he was, or what he had been doing. Then he began to speak things which they could understand.

"I can do nothing to keep you faithful. I try, but it is all to no avail. As Moses said to the children of Israel, 'I know that after my death ye will utterly corrupt yourselves and turn aside from the way which I have commanded you and evil will befall you in the latter days; because ye will do evil in the sight of the Lord, to provoke him to anger through the work of your hands.'"

His words dwindled as he spoke them and as he finished he slowly brought his own hands upwards before his eyes and began to stare into them. Elizabeth pondered the words he had said. Until now there had been no mention of either sickness of death. Now he had perhaps revealed the source of his confusion and anger. He did not want to die because he felt it would be condemning his flock to hell. She looked up at the back of the hard and worn hands of the man standing before them all. His fingers were thick with callouses, and dirt filled his nails which had grown too long. The air was thick with anticipation, and heavy with dread. The man that stood before them was the only leader they had ever known, there was no other in town who might replace him. If he were to die, then he would probably take his church with him as it too would slowly wither away.

"Remember where you came from," the words came, though the man before them still held his hands in front of himself and seemed to be speaking to them and not the congregation. "Isaiah says, 'Hearken to me, ye that follow after righteousness, ye that seek the Lord: look unto the rock whence ye are hewn, and to the, the hole of the pit whence ye are digged!" He lowered his hands, and the frantic overtones of his speech were returning. His eyes began to dart about as his mind searched for the scriptures which would redeem him.

"David says in Psalms, 'Behold, he travaileth with iniquity, and hath conceived mischief, and brought forth falsehood. He made a, a pit, and digged it, and is, is fallen into the ditch which he made!'" He lowered his hands slowly and his now pleading eyes ran from face to face about the building as he stammered his way through the scriptures.

"As the prophet Amos writes, 'I will slay the last of them with the sword: he that, he that fleeth of them shall not flee away, and he that escapeth of them not be delivered. Though they, they dig into hell, thence shall mine hand take them!'"

The madness in his eyes slowly turned to fear, and it seemed to be a deep and profound fear. He looked beyond them, as if he was seeing some terrible sight which lay beyond the physical realm. He spoke no longer to them, but to his God.

"As David has said to thee, oh God, 'My Heart is in anguish within me; the terrors of death assail me. Fear and trembling have beset me; horror has overwhelmed me!'" With this he slid to his knees, holding onto the podium before him. His body and face became hidden from the congregation, but his uplifted arms became visible as he raised his hands to the ceiling and spoke beyond the sanctuary and into the heavens. From the torn pieces of his mind came a scripture of lament which became his own cry. "'My soul is full of troubles: and my life draweth nigh unto the grave. I am counted with them that go down into the pit: I am as a man that hath no strength: Free among the dead, like the slain that lie in the grave, whom thou rememberest no more: and they are cut off from thy hand. Thou hast laid me in the lowest pit, in darkness, in the deeps. Thy wrath lieth hard upon me, and thou hast afflicted me with all thy waves. Thou hast put away mine acquaintance far from me; thou hast made me an abomination unto them: I am shut up, and I cannot come forth. Mine eyes mourneth by reason of affliction: Lord, I have called daily upon thee, I have stretched out my hands unto thee. Wilt thou show wonders to the dead? Shall the dead arise and praise thee? Shall thy loving kindness be declared in the grave, or thy faithfulness in destruction? Shall thy wonders be known in the dark, and thy righteousness in the land of forgetfulness? But unto thee have I cried, O Lord; and in the morning shall my prayer prevent thee. Lord, why castest thou off my soul? Why hidest thou thy face from me?

I am afflicted and ready to die from my youth up: while I suffer thy terrors I am distracted. Thy fierce wrath goeth over me; thy terrors have cut me off!'"

There was silence for a moment, then his arms disappeared behind the podium as he lowered them to his sides. A moment later the man slowly rose from his place and stood to face his flock. Sweat poured from his brow, and his hair lay strewn wildly across his forehead. But his eyes seemed to have returned to their normal state. For the moment he looked sane. He looked with recognition at the people before him and a serene smile began to come across his lips.

But then his eyes squinted with pain, as if he had been struck in the back of his head, and his hands went to the sides of his face. The smile became a grimace, and then his lips pursed together. He stayed this way for a few moments. His eyes returned to the crowd, and he lowered his hands.

The madness had returned and would not be subdued again.

The preacher pushed the podium to a crooked position as he walked around it. Then he stepped off the elevated stage and down to the aisle between the rows of seats. The people watched in both wonder and horror as he began to walk toward the back of the building. His eyes were fixed on the doors, or on something beyond them. As he walked he muttered meaningless words with profanities which those closest to the aisle could quite clearly hear yet could not believe. As he approached the final rows his eyes turned suddenly upon Elizabeth who sat mesmerized by the horror of the approaching monstrosity. His gaze shot through her and she suddenly felt a wet warmth between her legs as her bladder gave way to the terrible fear. She tried to look away, or even to scream out, but she could not. Instead she stared ahead into those insane eyes until a piece of that insanity had lodged itself in her brain. The moment seemed to last for several minutes, but it all happened in just a glance. Moments later the doors closed with a resounding noise which exclaimed a finality upon the scene.

The church was silent as the congregation sat waiting. After a little while Brother Morris stood and walked to the front of the church where he stood looking into the hundred glazed eyes which begged him to bridge the silence. For a moment he stood speechless. Then he began singing a familiar song. A few members joined in, but most remained silent. Elizabeth looked down at the wetness in which she sat, and tears of shame began to well up within her.

Finally the singing suddenly died out as the elder abandoned his attempt to return some normalcy to the services. He looked again over the lost and questioning eyes before him and announced that the next gathering would not be held until the following Sunday morning. There would be no services this evening, nor would there be any next Wednesday. He then walked back to the first row where he spoke under his breath to the three other men who occupied that row. Then all four of the elders rose and left the building together.

Elizabeth looked to her mother who did not return the glance and seemed to be oblivious to her own daughter.

Then the Nichols, who sat in the back row, stood and left the oppressive room. Gradually more and more people stood and filed out. Finally Nora Walker stood and took Elizabeth by the hand, leading her out the door and into the hot morning sun.

The walk home was a long and silent one.

2

Brother Jesse Aldredge walked slowly through the Lechuguilla and Yucca which grew from the rocky white soil beneath his feet. Witchgrass scratched at his pants as he walked. Its dead cousins, the tumbleweeds, lay strewn across the land before him. But the weeds did not tumble today as there was no wind to push them on their journeys.

He stared ahead and mumbled to himself as he made the hour-long walk to his home. He owned a buggy, and until today had used it to get to and from the church. Today, however, he had found that the buggy was gone, and he knew that he had been responsible for its disappearance, though he did not remember just how.

Jesse stopped suddenly and fell weeping to his knees. He dropped his hands and grabbed onto the white earth beneath him as he spoke the last words of Christ on the cross, "Eli, Eli, lama sabachthani? My God, my God, why hast thou forsaken me?" He took a handful of the earth in each hand and lowered his head in his lament. He remained this way for a few minutes until his bitterness and remorse had left him. Then he returned again to his feet and resumed his walking and grumbling.

It was an hour past noon when he arrived at the old wooden framed house which stood near the top of a small hill. The land near the house had been cleared of trees to make a yard, and a grove of mesquite and scrub oak trees surrounded the yard. Though the majority of the acreage on which the house sat had been cleared for farming, the small grove of trees had been left at the request of his now dead wife. The trees had served as a reminder of what the land all around them had been, and it had allowed her to feel as if she were a greater part of nature.

Jesse walked up the hill to the house and entered through the front door. The house was dark despite the piercing light outside. The windows were all closed, and the shades all drawn. The still heat inside the house was only slightly less than that which had pounded him outside. Jesse seemed to be oblivious to all of this as he climbed the stairs which led to his bedroom. Below him the living room lay in disarray. Furniture lay overturned and strewn about. Some of it had been shattered to kindling. A few of the paintings which had once hung straight and proud across the walls of their home now hung at odd angles. Several had been removed and flung into the fireplace, though no fire had been lit to complete their destruction. He walked up the stairs and then down the small hall to his room and opened its door. Inside the room lay further evidence of his distraught mind. Most noticeable were the hundreds of sheets of thin paper strewn about the floor of the room. Once these sheets had composed the family bible, now they were nothing more than reminders of what had become of his own sanctity. The bedsheets lay piled in one corner of the room while the canopy lay mangled and useless by their side. The dresser lay on its front, fragments of its once ornate mirror scattered across the floor like pieces of an unsolvable puzzle. Drops of blood where he had cut himself were dried to the wooden floor near them.

The scene once again moved the man to tears and he stumbled to the bed where he knelt with his hands before him. He cried and lamented the curse which had come to him. He prayed to his God that he too could die and be rid of it. But he could feel the curse like a disease in the back of his mind, waiting for its time. He had tried more than once to kill himself but had always been stopped by fits of insanity. During these fits he was nothing more than an observer. He watched in horror as his body did unspeakable things over which he had no control. He had not noticed it until it was too late. Prayer had failed him, and the madness took his children from him, then his wife. Somewhere to the west of his house lay all but one of his eight children, buried in unmarked graves. His wife had been taken only days ago, and the pain was still quite fresh.

Jesse groped amongst the paper on the floor, looking for inspiration in the torn pieces of the old book he had ravaged soon after his wife's death. The words all looked foreign, and the ink seemed smeared to the point of illegibility. He threw the paper into the air and cried out again, searching his mind for the scriptures which might save him.

But the scriptures were gone now. He had felt them slowly slipping away from him over the past two months. At first he had merely needed to look up the scriptures he wished to quote as a reminder of their content. This morning at church he had spoken as a man possessed. Half of the scriptures came from his own storehouse of knowledge, the other half from some bizarre and evil force which had fed them to him cruelly, as if to give him one last glimpse of what he might never see again. Now he could call forth no scriptures save the very simplest which he had known since childhood, and he began to speak these.

"'For God so loved the world," he began, "that he," he paused for a moment, trying to remember. His hands shook feverishly as he held them together. "...that he gave his only begotten son, that whosoever believeth on him might not perish, but shall have everlasting life." He knew this was close, but he also knew it was imperfect. "The lord is my shepherd, I shall not want." He spoke the first verses, then the remainder of the Psalm. At some points he stumbled badly, reversing sentences and using words which were close, but not exact. He fought his way through the scripture and began his imperfect version of the sermon on the mount. As he stumbled along he remembered his youngest son's similar struggle as he learned these very verses and tears once again assaulted his cheeks.

He stopped his prayers and rose to his feet, using the bed for support. He walked slowly across the room to the one mirror which remained intact despite his fits of fury. He looked into it at the thing he had become. He was merely the frame of the man he had once been. His cheeks sank deeply into his face, and his eyes seemed to be disappearing into his head. He studied the monster before him and again he felt despair rise within him.

Then he walked slowly to the window by the bed. He stood before the closed curtains for a moment, then he reached forward and parted the right curtain slowly. The sunlight burned his darkened eyes as he looked out upon the bright land before him. He looked down the hillside which lay a hundred feet from the eastern side of the house. At the base of the small hill was a pit. Piles of white rocks lay near the pit, and there were various picks and shovels lying near its mouth, as well as his two wheelbarrows. He looked down into the pit which disappeared into the earth. Though the sun did not light the bottom, he knew where it was.

And still he could hear it call to him.

He let the curtain drop and he raised his hand before him once again. They were calloused and bruised from the Devil's labor which had forced itself upon him.

"Oh, accursed hands!" he called out. "Why have you betrayed me? Why have you brought the abomination of Beelzebub upon my house?" He fled from the image before him and ran back down the stairs, through the living room and into the kitchen. He groped through the drawers for the carving knife which he soon found. The blood of his family already stained the steel blade. He felt the pain again as the madness began to overtake him. He pulled the knife from its drawer and quickly raised it over his head. He placed his left hand out on the counter before him and concentrated upon it. The pain in his head grew quickly and he knew that he would probably fail, but he brought the knife toward his hand with force, nonetheless.

Blackness covered his vision as the blade swerved from its course. The knife sank into his small finger, slicing through it, but not completely severing it. He released the handle of the blade and the knife continued to stand in the wood counter before him. The blade pinned his hand down by what little of his finger remained attached.

His now fiery eyes returned to the counter and a crazy smile slowly came to his face. Jesse pulled his hand firmly from the counter, tearing away what remaining bone and tendons held the finger to his hand. Blood raced from the wound and dripped to the floor as he held the hand before him, looking with a madness upon his newest deformity.

But in a way he was glad he had failed. In a way he felt good that he would still be able to use this hand for the work for which he had been chosen.

Then there was a pounding upon the door which startled him to near sanity. He looked down at his hand and now he again lamented at this failure. He looked for something to cover his hand with and found a good kitchen rag which would have to do. The pounding continued and he walked slowly to the door. The visitors had stopped coming a little while back so he could only guess who it might be. He made as if he was drying his hands when he opened the door. Before him stood the four elders.

Jim Pearson looked at the ragged man who stood before him. Jesse Aldredge looked as sane as he had seen him in weeks, though hints of insanity remained deep in his eyes. Jim noticed that Jesse seemed to be drying his hands off, but something didn't quite look right about how he was doing it. Jesse did not greet him, he merely stood holding onto the rag and staring into Jim's eyes.

"May we come in?" Jim asked.

Jesse almost said yes, then remembered the state of the house. "I'd rather you didn't," he replied. "The house is not in order."

"This is a very serious issue which should be dealt with inside," Jim suggested.

Jesse did not agree. "I don't mind dealing with it here." He knew that he should be able to figure out what it was Brother Pearson was going to tell him, but he waited for the words since his clouded mind could not decide for sure what it might be.

Jim watched Jesse Aldredge as his eyes wavered between the world of the sane and the insane. He looked quickly back at the three other men for some support. Fred McKee cleared his throat but said nothing.

"Your lesson today was quite disturbing." He waited for a response, but Jesse simply stood staring ahead at him, holding the rag firmly over his left hand. "We, uh, we think that perhaps you should take a break from preaching until you are feeling better." Still the preacher showed no reaction, said nothing.

Fred McKee finally spoke. "Only until you're feeling better, then we need you back."

A silence followed in which an uneasy look crept onto each of the four men's faces. Jesse stood staring beyond them, as he had stared beyond the congregation earlier that day.

"There are many folks who are very concerned about you and your family," J. Alvis said. "The church sends its prayers and hopes that you will soon be well. Doctor Hamilton would still very much like to visit with any sick members of your household."

Behind a grove of trees sat the cart which the four men had used to travel to Jesse Aldredge's home. In the cart sat Doctor Ben Hamilton. It was hoped that Jesse would be persuaded to let the doctor have a look at the surviving members of his household. It was fairly certain from the preacher's ramblings in the church that morning that at least one member had perhaps died.

"Doctor Hamilton," Jesse said, his eyes darting about beyond them. It wasn't a question, just a statement.

Silence again ruled as the men stood in the sweltering heat, trying to communicate to the man who had at once meant so much to them, but who now seemed to be slipping away from them forever.

"How's Amanda doing?" Wayne Sumner asked.

"Amanda," Jesse muttered. Then his eyes calmed but continued to stare beyond them. Then his eyes began to glaze over, and a look of anguish crept into them. "Amanda," he said again, this time wistfully.

Jesse suddenly fell to his knees again and brought his hands to his head. "Amanda!" he cried out, the torment of his loss coming through to his conscious self once again. The blood of his wife rose to accuse him again. "My Amanda!" he cried. The cloth slipped from his hand and blood began to flow from his severed finger and over his left cheek as held his hands to his face. "Oh, my sweet Amanda, what have I done?" he cried.

The four men stood staring at the hand from which blood flowed. Once again they feared the great insanity which was prostrate before them, looking now into the heavens. They had hoped somehow that they would be able to talk with him, to speak rationally of what had to be done. Now they could each see that this would not come to pass. They did not wish to bring down their beloved shepherd, but he was leaving them no choice.

As Jesse stood on his knees lamenting the passing of his wife, Jim walked away from the door. The three remaining men stepped back and looked at each other, then to the babbling man before them. Jesse raised his hands again to the skies and the blood from his wounded hand began to run along his arm.

Jim walked back to the cart where he informed Doctor Hamilton that Jesse would have to be sedated, then carted into town where he could be treated. The living members of his home would also have to be retrieved and treated. Ben hopped from the cart, carrying his bag with him.

Jesse looked down from the heavens and saw Jim and Doctor Hamilton approaching his house. His eyes grew wild again and he stood, facing the three men.

"You Damned fools shall not stop me from my task," he muttered. Then he stepped back into this home and closed the door.

The three men waited for the arrival of the doctor as they listened to the banging and smashing noises which came from inside the house. When Jim and Doctor Hamilton arrived the men stood looking at each other until Jim suggested that they enter the house.

Jim reached forward and opened the door. He and Ben Hamilton walked together into the entry of the home. From where they stood they could see the chaos which the living room and kitchen had become. Noises came from the back room, on the other side of the living room. The two men entered and began walking toward that room, followed by the three elders. Suddenly Jesse appeared out of the room clumsily carrying something long and black. As Jim realized what it was the first shot rang out, catching Ben Hamilton in the shoulder and throwing him back into Fred McKee. Jim turned and faced the three standing men who stood staring in shock at him. Then there was the sound of another bullet being chambered in the Winchester Model 73 rifle.

"Get out!" came the shout. It was Jim, not Jesse who shouted.

A second shot rang out and the window near the front door shattered as the bullet missed Jim's head by less than an inch. Fred grabbed Ben's shoulders and dragged him back out the door as the three other men made their own escape. Ben was conscious and trying to get to his feet, but Fred was pulling backwards too fast. Once outside Fred looked at Ben who then stood on his own.

"It's just superficial," Ben said, "I'll be all right."

"Let's go then," Fred answered and turned to run.

Another shot rang out, though Jesse was still inside the house and the five men had all left it. Chips of wood flew from the edge of the open door and Jesse's steps could be heard approaching.

The men outside Jesse Aldredge's house took flight as the crazed preacher appeared at the door and fired two more shots in their direction. He had never hunted much and was not a very good shot, so the men were able to make it around the trees and to their cart with no further harm.

They slapped the reins on the horses who jumped and then headed toward the road away from the house. Jim drove and listened to the indistinct ravings of the lunatic behind them as they rode off. He heard two more shots ring out, though they were no longer in the line of sight of the house.

They had waited too long.

Now they would simply have to let him die alone.

3

Jesse sat on the front porch with the rifle in his hands until nightfall. He waited patiently for anyone who dared to come up the road. As the sun set deep dark clouds appeared on the horizon. A breeze finally stirred and grew gradually into a hot summer wind as the last of the sun dipped below the horizon. An occasional flash of lightning illuminated the approaching clouds.

When the sun finally set Jesse walked into the house and retrieved his lantern. He lit it and walked across the yard to its eastern side. He carried the gun with him, in case any other unwanted visitors came to disturb him as he worked. He walked across the hard ground to the base of the hill where he had spent many of his recent nights. Then he put the gun on the ground and picked up the rope which lay coiled near his feet. One end of it was tied firmly to a tree which grew about ten feet south, slightly up the small hill. He tossed the rope down into the hole. It uncoiled and slapped the bottom of the hole with a thud. Knots were tied every two feet to make it easier for him to climb down. Jesse walked to one side of the pit where a small pile of stones had accumulated. Next to the pile rested a now empty bucket, waiting to be filled. The bucket had a rope tied around the handle, and the rope went through a pulley which was attached to a small A-frame he had constructed. He tilted the frame upright and pulled on the rope. The bucket lifted from the ground and swung out over the hole. Gradually he let the bucket down until the rope slackened. Finally he climbed down the rope ladder. The first time he took only the lamp, and he used it to light two other lamps which he kept on ledges near the bottom of the pit. On the second trip he took the pick. He left the rifle at the top of the hole where he could get to it quickly.

Jesse took the pick into his hands. The magic of it took hold of him again. He could feel the energy surging from the ground below him and once again he forgot his worries and his pains. He was not hungry, nor did he feel any discomfort. Power surged through his body, beginning with his feet and working upward until he felt like a new man. The further down he got, the better this feeling became.

He lifted the pick over his head and brought it down forcefully. The clink of the metal on limestone resounded in the night. A flash of lightning from the approaching storm lit in unison with the strike as pieces of the white rock flew from its one-hundred-million-year-old resting place. He raised the pick again, and again he brought it down with more strength than he could possibly have possessed.

Above him the air grew more restless as the remnants of the tropical storm which earlier had pounded the coast of Mexico flowed northeastward through the night sky.

4

A flash of lightning brought Elizabeth suddenly out of her deep sleep. Her windows were open and the breeze coming through them dried the sweat which had been brought forth not only by the heat of the night. Tonight sleep had brought to her bizarre and horrifying dreams which taunted and terrified her continuously. She awoke with a start and her heart raced until another flash of light brought to her the realization that she was awake. How she had longed to be awake, but the dreams would not let her go. Not until now.

The dreams had been full of terrible images. There was fire, and strange music. There were naked men dancing about and she could see all of them; their muscular chests, their bony legs, even their dangling penises, and it frightened her. Then there had been a large white bird which had chased her through the woods. It clawed and pecked at her, and everywhere it broke the skin her flesh renewed itself to be torn again. There were other things, things which even now faded back into her subconscious from which they had come.

Her curtains fluttered and she watched as the lightning turned their shadows into giant bats on the opposite wall. For now there was lightning, but no thunder. The storm was approaching, but it had not yet arrived. Perhaps it would bring some coolness. Perhaps it would bring some rain so that a portion of her father's crops might yet be saved.

Then she heard a noise outside her window. Her curiosity overpowered her fear as it was a more curious than frightful sound which she heard. She rose from her bed and walked slowly to the window. As she neared it, the curtains reached out and petted her, beckoning her to come closer, and she did. The wind blew her little night gown around her small body, and the coolness it brought to her felt wonderful. She pushed aside the curtains and looked out into the night sky. Just above the house the full moon shone brightly, bringing an eerie glow to the ground and trees in the yard. The stars lit the sky, though there weren't as many as there were when the moon was not full or was not in the sky at all. To the west the stars disappeared suddenly behind a wall of thick blackness which rolled toward her and her parents' house. It was an ominous and threatening darkness which seemed not to cover the stars but swallow them as it approached.

The foreboding nature of the approaching storm did not frighten her. Instead it seemed to call to her. It seemed to promise a salvation which her dreams had threatened. But it was not only the sky which called to her, it was the earth as well. And as she remembered what had happened the previous morning in the church, she knew where the call was coming from.

Elizabeth walked to her bed and put on her slippers. Then she returned to the window and climbed through it. Now the curtains wrapped around her and seemed to be trying to hold her back, but she made her way through them and to the ground below.

A part of her wanted to stay home. That part knew that this was all wrong, that she was doing something that she would never have dreamed of doing before this night, before her dreams.

But another part of her urged her on. This part of her promised rewards and fulfillment which her young mind did not even understand. This was part of the madness which had been given to her that morning as Brother Aldredge had stared into her then innocent eyes.

Elizabeth stood in the warm breeze and for a moment she fully intended to return to her bed and forget this wild notion. But it only lasted a moment and then she began to walk to the northeast.

She crossed the dirt road and walked to the fence which separated the road from the Dunn's ranch. Then she walked to a part of the fence which sagged and climbed over it. It was a feat she had performed many times, but in the past it had been for the purpose of sneaking to the back of their small apple orchard and stealing a sweet summer snack. The edge of her gown caught on the barbed wire as she climbed down. She felt the firm tug and simply pulled the gown with her hand, tearing away the portion which was snagged. The full moon still lit the night well enough for her to make out the narrow paths which would take her through the Dunn ranch and eventually to the Brotherton ranch. Occasional flashes of light would suddenly reveal portions of the landscape which had remained hidden in the dark. Now she could hear the thunder as the storm approached.

She walked and felt her way through the brush and rocks which predominated in this part of the country. The ground was hard, and trees were a rare sight. She continued on her journey until the land suddenly acquired a more varied terrain. She felt that she was walking up a slight incline, and trees began to appear within her range of sight. As she walked toward them they disappeared. Everything did. One moment the world was a dark silhouette of itself around her, then it all slowly faded to darkness. Then she realized what had happened. She looked upward into the skies and saw that the moon had been overtaken by the rolling black clouds. There was a brilliant flash of light, followed almost immediately by a clap of thunder. She felt the first drops of rain as they fell onto her uplifted face.

Then she heard a voice speaking to her. She did not understand the language, but the meaning tugged at the edge of her consciousness. She looked back to the darkness before her and resumed her walk. As she continued slowly through the wooded area the wind became fiercer and the rain began to fall heavily upon her. It was a warm and refreshing rain, though it did turn the topsoil to a mud which soaked her slippers and caked onto their bottoms. Her left slipper got stuck in the mud, so she left it behind. She paused for a moment, then kicked off the other slipper. Elizabeth resumed her walk through the mud which squished through her toes and gathered on the tops of her feet. As she closed in on her goal the world around her became less and less important and the voice equally more important. She became almost oblivious to her tender feet which were being abused by the jagged rocks on which she walked, and her legs which were becoming scratched from the underbrush which grew thickly in places.

Finally she crested a small hill and saw a light below her. With the light came a sound, the sound of metal on stone. A brilliant flash lit her surroundings and then she saw the old wooden house, and she knew where she was. For the first time since she had climbed from her window she became frightened. For the second time she was resolved to return to her house and her bed. She felt as if she had awoken from a dream yet had failed to appear in her bed. Dream mixed with reality as the unreality of her situation closed in on her.

Then she saw a form moving at the base of the hill below her. It crawled from the earth and stood. The rain blurred her vision, and she could not make out the creature. Elizabeth was frozen by fear which came to her with the vision. She watched as the creature put itself to some sort of task. Then another flash of light revealed that the creature was in fact a man, and one with whom she was familiar. In an instant an image of Brother Aldredge lifting a bucket filled with white rock from a pit in the earth became impressed upon her mind.

The next moment the ground beneath her gave and she felt herself sliding. She put her hands behind her to soften the fall. Thick and moving mud filled her small hands. She slid a few feet then struck a rock which pushed her sideways and she began to roll. She felt the pushing and scraping of the ground and its growths as she tumbled down the hill. Her foot struck the trunk of an old tree, and she felt the sting of it as she rolled over a large stone. The world was all black except for the small light which went around her again and again and seemed to become brighter with each pass. This continued until the light became everything. There was nothing but brightness before her and she looked away from it.

Then her eyes began to focus, but the world still seemed to be spinning around her. She realized that the light was a lantern with a small tin cover to keep the rain away from the flame. Still the flame bent and danced with the wind. Her right arm was pinned under her as she lay on her side trying to decide if she was injured or just terrified.

Then her terror overtook her as she saw a shadowy figure looming over her. Eerie shadows leapt on its face as the flame of the lantern danced about. She could make out an evil grin which seemed to contain too many teeth. She looked into the wild eyes of the hovering creature, and then she knew what this creature was. The previous morning a part of this thing had reached out and planted itself in her brain. But now it did not seem to recognize the kinship for she distinctly saw murder in its eyes. As she lay watching this thing it leaned over and put down the bucket of stones which it held in one hand and began reaching for a pick with the other.

The madness which had nestled in a corner of Elizabeth's mind fled as a misty reality set in. She shook off her paralysis and got to her feet. Dozens of needles pricked her right arm as she stood and turned to run. She ran away from the pit, away from the madness which seemed to emanate from it. Behind her she heard the indistinct ravings of a man with murder in the forefront of his mind. The rain and thunder drowned out the curses and rebukes he flung at her as he chased after her. He limped and he followed, favoring the leg which had not had its kneecap crushed by falling stones an hour before. She was not gaining any distance as she ran toward the big house, but she was not losing any either. She ran through the muddy soil, afraid that she would slip. If she did he would be on her in a matter of seconds. She ran forward until she reached the side of the house, then she ran around to the back of it. A brilliant flash of light suddenly revealed to her a means of escape.

For the few seconds in which she remained out of his sight Elizabeth pulled open the cellar door and disappeared down into the earth underneath the house. The door slammed shut behind her, its sound muffled by a loud explosion of thunder. She listened as Jesse rounded the corner of the house and began shouting for her again. He threatened her with violent descriptions of dismemberment, then teased her with promises of sweetness. Finally he cursed the Lord's name as he ran just past the cellar doors and entered the house. Elizabeth listened as his feet pounded frantically on the floor above her. The ground below her was a moist dirt and the air was heavy and stale. She stood staring through the darkness at where she knew the door was when she became aware of the rancid odor which assaulted her. It was strong and came to her so suddenly that she coughed loudly and almost threw up. But she did not throw up. Instead she considered her chances of making it into the woods from the cellar before he saw her.

Then she noticed that she could no longer hear the pounding of his boots above her. She listened through the sounds of the storm as she strained to hear the pounding which might tell her where he was. Then she heard a creaking sound coming from before her and saw a slice of light break into the darkness.

"Are you down here, you little squirrel, you silly little girl?" she heard his voice taunting her from ahead. He had gotten a lantern inside the house and was coming down into the cellar with her.

She backed slowly from the entrance, just out of reach of the light which glowed in an indistinct circle around the madman who walked slowly toward her. The light illuminated his face, his eyes stared wildly in her direction, as if he knew where she was, but meant to torment her further before driving the knife he held in his left hand through her skull.

She backed further away from him and hoped that she did not run into something or knock something over, though she knew that it was only a matter of time before this did happen.

But before she hit any of the storage shelves which contained rows and rows of preserves, before she hit any of the crates stored in the dark cavern, she ran into a hard wall. She backed up against it as a dim flash of light seemed to come from somewhere to her left. She realized that the flash had come through a window, and she headed toward it, her back to the wall as she kept an eye on the approaching horror. She watched as he sensed proximity to the same wall she had found and began to turn his search the other way. Then, as she turned to her left and began to hurry toward the direction where the light had come from she did hit one of the shelves. No jars fell, but the soft thud was just enough. Jesse's face turned suddenly toward her again and the sinister toothy grin returned to his wild countenance. He began to walk quickly toward her.

Elizabeth put her hands out in front of her and moved quickly as she darted toward the window she knew must be there. Another flash of light confirmed its location. Behind her Jesse again began to mutter about the horrible things he planned to do to her, some of which she did not understand. He had the advantage here. This was his cellar. To her the darkness held surprises and dangers which she could imagine quite clearly. One time when she had been at a friend's house they had sneaked into a neighbor's cellar and found a den of rattlesnakes. This image teased her as she stumbled to one knee. She stood and continued, without looking back. She could tell from the brightness of the approaching light how close he was, and she was afraid that if she looked back she would freeze with fright. She ran into another shelf and felt her way around it as the grumbling man and his shiny knife approached. He seemed to be in no hurry, as if he knew she were walking into a dead end. Indeed the window was near the ceiling of the cellar and was only half a window. Maybe it wouldn't open, or maybe there would be no way for her to reach it. Perhaps he knew these things and was letting her fear escalate while he reveled in the power it made him feel.

Jesse limped toward his prey. His mind was foggy, and his leg was screaming out as the fractured kneecap ground against muscle and tendon. He wanted badly to get her, to tear and rend her with the blade he held in his hand. But he would have to work slowly and trap her into the corner where she was headed. When he had her trapped, then he could move in. Then he would cut her heart out and toss it into the pit as an offering.

Elizabeth rushed through the darkness toward the back wall. As she ran her foot struck something solid and she tumbled forward into the darkness. She fell into the shelves which covered the back wall and rolled to her right where she came to rest against a floor which seemed too soft. She felt the arms of her pursuer suddenly around her and his breath smelled like death.

Then a bright flash of lightning illuminated the window seven feet above her, and the thing which had hold of her. She looked with terror into the dead and bloody eyes of Amanda Aldredge. The eyes were black sockets, and her shirt was torn open. A gigantic hole in the woman's chest revealed rotten guts and flesh, and something alive and squirming was in there.

Elizabeth was hurled again into darkness as she jumped up and backed away from the dead body. She tried not to gag. Her head felt light, but she knew that if she passed out that she would become like

Amanda. She looked toward the front of the cellar and saw that Jesse was very close now, and the light from his lantern faintly illuminated her. His gruesome smile increased as she became visible to him.

Elizabeth turned and began quickly to climb the shelving. She hurried up the shelves which were nailed in place. Jars and tools fell as she climbed. She quickly reached the top and pushed up on the window. It was not opening. She could hear the cackling of her pursuer as she pushed harder. There was no lock, but the window had remained shut for some time, and now the moist weather has caused the frame to expand slightly. Then she felt a hand on her left ankle. She screamed out as another flash of light lit the sky. She pushed one last time and the window flew upward, breaking the glass as it struck the top of the frame. Jagged pieces of shattered glass fell to the top of the shelf before her. She reached for the window to climb out, but she could not. Instead she began to slide across the shelf and back toward the ground. She tried to hold onto the lower frame of the window, but her grip was no match for the crazed man below her. First her right hand slipped. As her left came loose she grabbed for a piece of glass with her right. She sliced one of her fingers but found a piece sufficient for her cause. Her left hand came free of the window frame, and she slid back off of the top shelf and fell again to her right. She fell to the floor, but the impact was softened as she again fell onto Amanda. As she lay in the stench and rot she could see the youngest Aldredge daughter stuffed into the shelf just above the ground. It was the only other body she could see in the light of the lantern which Jesse held onto, but she was sure this had been the fate of his entire family. She looked up into the killing eyes of the man above her. He placed the lantern on the second shelf, where it illuminated the corner they were in. With his left hand he reached forward and grabbed hold of Elizabeth's neck. She gasped for air as her breath seemed to be leaving her. His eyes bulged out of their disappearing sockets, and she could feel the bones of his thin hand pressed against her neck.

"Now you too shall become an offering," he said.

Another flash of lightning lit the night sky as he leaned toward her, bringing the knife back next to his ear, the blade pointing toward the top of her head.

Quickly she brought the glass forward from its hiding place. She thrust it toward his face where it stuck in near the mouth and ran a slice toward his right eye. At first she thought no damage had been inflicted, then suddenly the blood began to course across his face from the wound. He released his grip on her neck as he instinctively grabbed his wounded face. He cried out holding his face together, forgetting for the moment his goal. Elizabeth used that second to get to her feet and knock the lantern to the floor. The glass bottom which held the kerosene burst and the pink liquid ran across the man's feet. Elizabeth resumed her climb as the flame followed the liquid and his boots began to burn. She climbed quickly upward, leaving spots of blood on the shelves from her wounded hand. She pulled her head and shoulders through the window and into the rain. As she moved her hands to get another grip a hot pain tore her right leg. She ignored the pain and pulled herself the rest of the way out of the window. She tried to stand and run toward the woods which lay just beyond the pit, but she fell quickly to the ground. She felt the pain near the base of her leg where Jesse had cut through her Achilles tendon. She could not run. She got to her knees and began to crawl instead.

She made it halfway to the woods when she heard the loud cries of the madman who had resumed his pursuit. Her hands splashed in the mud as the rain fell down about her, washing off the blood that was draining from her too quickly. As she approached the pit she heard a laughter, and she knew that it was triumphant laughter. As she came to the first tree near the base of the small hill she felt the boot in her side and fell forward to the ground. She lay still for a moment, waiting for death. When it did not come for what seemed a long time she rolled over slowly to see why.

She lay on her back, staring up at a terrifying creature. The lighting which flashed almost constantly lit his gruesome and bloody features.

His pants were cooked to the flesh of his legs by the fire which she sent upon them. He was the very image of death. He stood waiting for her to turn toward him. He wanted to see her eyes when she died, and he wanted to pierce her heart. She stared up at the terror who had dropped his knife and had again grabbed his pick from the ground. The pick was more symbolic, the death would be a purer one. He held the pick high over his head as he stood over the girl who lay limp, resigned to her fate.

"To the earth," he shouted, "I commit this body. To the pit I commit this soul!"

She saw the loose and bloody flesh which dangled from his face as he spoke. She watched in terror when his worn muscles tensed as he brought the pick over his head, aiming at her soft chest.

But he stopped at the apex of his swing as a great white fire lit the skies and a thunderous explosion tore the air. Elizabeth watched, waiting for death's arrival. She watched as the white fire reached out of the sky and grabbed hold of the pick, not allowing it to come toward her. She watched as in a split second the man above her sizzled and smoked before falling back to the ground.

Just before she fell unconscious from the shock, she smelled the odor of cooked flesh which the lightning had left behind. There was a bitter taste in her mouth, and she knew it was the taste of death. Then a darkness, which wouldn't rise for three days, fell upon her brain.

The storm raged on for another half hour before finally moving on to the east.

Eight

1

Margaret Shaw drove into Del Rio around noon. She had been unable to get a hold of her husband, Buzz, for several days now. His office kept saying he was in the field, and that they would get him the message. He didn't answer the messages she left him at home. So she had driven to Del Rio to look for him.

She headed first to the house and found it in terrible disarray. Buzz had always been messy, but this was much worse than that. Dirty clothes lay strewn about the house, some of them reeked of human waste. The air conditioner was not running, and the hot house was full of pungent, rotten odors. Food lay spoiled on the kitchen counter, and on the kitchen floor. The television in the bedroom was broadcasting only static, and very loudly.

Margaret could tell that her husband had not been in this house for some time, though she couldn't be sure exactly how long. She picked up his phone and called his office to ask again where her husband was. Betty was giving her the runaround, so she asked for Dave Ostrand. Dave was very blunt about the situation. Buzz had gone loony and disappeared. He had last been seen by one of the crew at the site near Comstock. Wherever he was, he probably wouldn't have a job when he did return.

Margaret hung up the phone. Buzz had done some odd and thoughtless things in his life, but nothing quite like this. She looked around the room and had the urge to clean it all up, but her urge to find Buzz and get to the bottom of all this was stronger, so she left.

2

Joe Payne looked with astonishment at the big junction box which lay outside the telephone switching station. There was melted plastic everywhere, like the wires had all overheated and melted off their contacts. But telephone wire didn't get that hot, not without help anyway. This was a mess, and he didn't have all of the tools and equipment he would need to fix it.

The station was small and unmanned. There were only a thousand phones in Comstock, and usually the problems could be fixed with a quick trip. Most of the folks in Comstock had grown used to the static and the interrupted calls, however, and it was rare that anyone ever reported trouble. But the office in Del Rio had gotten a call from a couple of operators yesterday about the lines. When they tested them nothing had worked. Now Joe knew why. They weren't going to be happy back in Del Rio when they heard about this.

Joe walked back to his van and took out some of his testing equipment. He didn't have what he needed to correct the whole problem, but he would be able to get a few lines up. He would start with the sheriff's office, then the diner. Those were the two places that people would go with trouble anyway. Then he would have to make a trip back to Del Rio to get more tools and a helper.

As Joe gathered his test box and a large roll of telephone wire he heard the side of his van pop, then he heard a distant explosion. Before he understood what the sound was he felt something hit his shoulder, and there was another distant explosion.

Joe turned around quickly, still confused. He finally understood that he was being shot at when the third bullet took him in the chest and threw him back against the side of the van. The bullet tore through his body and took pieces of his liver out through his back.

On the rocky hillside overlooking the switching station Jim Dewey watched as Joe slid down the side of the van and crumpled into a lifeless pile. He grinned slightly. Then the voice told him to head back to the highway. Tommy Bonner had been watching the telephone man from a distance. He'd wanted to see how they got into those big gray boxes, so he'd watched from a place where he couldn't be seen. As the echoes of the last shot faded away, Tommy ran as fast as he could to see the sheriff.

3

The old albino woman sat in her dark room singing her ancient songs and swaying to their timbre. They sounded almost like old Native American chants, but they were different in many ways.

She, too, had seen the hawk. But she had seen it all her life, as had her mother and her mother's mother. The hawk which had taken their land and scattered their people.

Finally the time had come again, as it had come only once every hundred years or so. She was called northward to help the great warriors, and so she sat amidst her candles and her simmering sweet herbs, singing.

She picked up the small doll with the badge on its chest and began singing into its ears. She sang of the past, and of the future. And she could see into the man's mind and his soul.

4

The Val Verde sheriff's office was a small two-man office which stood alone near the edge of the city limits. There were only two jail cells inside, and they were used only to hold drunks and occasionally crooks who were being transferred to Del Rio. The building was old and worn down and didn't come close to meeting the electrical and plumbing codes which no one enforced anymore.

Sheriff Clark Rodriguez sat in the office with the fan on high. It was too hot to patrol the streets, and all of the crooks were waiting for cooler weather too. At night a few tempers flared, and recently there had been a series of problems. In the past three nights there had been four domestic disturbances. Nobody had really gotten hurt in those, except for Tom Crownover. Tom's wife had decided to go after Tom for cheating on her and had split his skull with a Tequila bottle. It wouldn't have been so bad if the bottle hadn't been almost full. But a few other things had happened, and they hadn't been so harmless. Rusty Crawley had hanged himself in his closet, Alice DeLagarza had shot her husband in the stomach (all the while raving about a big Indian man), and Jimmy Escue had burnt his house down. They'd found Jimmy's burnt body in the middle of the couch, still sitting up like he'd just watched the fire as it consumed first his living room, then him. It was strange. Then there were the deaths on the Walker ranch, in that old cave. And of course there had been the dreams.

Since the crazy stuff had started Sheriff Rodriguez had been fighting the strangest dreams. When he awoke most of the dreams had faded from memory, but he could remember bits and pieces about the old house and the big bird. He also had dreamt that the sky was falling on him, and that it was red, just like it had recently become late in the night.

The phones only worked inside Comstock now. But his radio could still reach out to Langtree and Del Rio, though its reception had grown steadily worse. He had spoken to Bob at the sheriff's office in Del Rio about the skies, but Bob only answered that the night skies in Del Rio were just like they'd always been.

Clark had been born across the border where his parents had been raised. He remembered the childhood stories of the ghosts and spirits which wreaked havoc and tormented the small Mexico towns. The stories seemed so vivid now, and now they spooked him as they had then. On the surface he dealt with it on a day-to-day basis. The people in town seemed to be affected by it all. But they, too, seemed to be simply living with it for now. But inside, Clark was frightened. It was as if something had come to his small town and was determined to push its way into its inhabitants. He felt threatened, even though there was really nothing solid to fear. There had been no ghostly sightings, no sightings of anything, just bad dreams and bad feelings.

Then he heard the ringing sound, and he suddenly remembered all of his dreams. He remembered the hawk, and the claws, and the men dancing naked. He knew what it meant; he grasped the symbolism.

But the ringing grew louder inside his head, and with it the pain.

Sheriff Rodriguez grabbed his ears as the pain grew. It felt as if a hot iron were being pushed through the top of his head. There were awful smells, and sweet smells, and he saw stars at the periphery of his vision.

When he opened his eyes the ringing stopped.

The room was different now. Something had changed.

Then he heard someone coming to the door and knew who it was going to be.

In 1984 Sheriff Rodriguez made the biggest arrest of his life. The man had been running a secret route across the river, bringing cocaine and other drugs into the country. The man's path cut through Comstock, and Sheriff Rodriguez had caught him one night, on one of his runs.

The man had been a Mexican national. He had pretended that he could not speak English, but it was futile since the Sheriff spoke the language of northern Mexico quite fluently. It had been a somewhat routine stop, one made more from a hunch than anything else. The man had tried to flee, but Rodriguez had chased him down. It was dramatic, something talked about in the coffee shops of Comstock for years afterwards. It had made the already popular Sheriff a hero of sorts.

The man had been sent back to Mexico. Less than a month later there was a phone call. The sheriff was to expect company.

That call had been over eight years ago. But somehow, inside, the sheriff knew that the time had finally come.

He lowered his hand to his gun as the door opened slowly inward.

5

Helene watched Cal as he dialed out on his mobile phone. She had told him that she had been unable to make any calls outside of Comstock, and he had offered to make those calls for her. But now, as they drove away from the Aldredge ranch, it became clear that the problem was not isolated to Helene's hotel.

"What's happening?" she asked.

"Nothing. It's like I didn't even dial the number. There's some clicking noises, then it's just dead."

"Could it be your phone?" she asked.

He looked at the signal reading on the handset. "It could be. But I doubt it." He dialed the number of the gas station where he got his truck worked on. The call went through, but no one answered. "It's working on local calls; I just can't call any numbers outside of Comstock."

Was this related to the cave and Buzz's pit? It seemed too odd a coincidence. "How can we get a message out of town?" she asked him.

"By driving, I guess." Then another idea came to him. "They've got a radio over at the police station which can reach Del Rio. Maybe Clark can get a call out."

Helene nodded and watched as Cal dialed the emergency number and waited.

After several rings Clark Rodriguez picked up the phone. "Sheriff's office. Clark here."

"Hey Sheriff, this is Cal Price."

There was a hesitation. "Sure, Cal. What can I do for you?"

"Have you heard anything about the phones in town? I can't seem to get a call out."

The pauses between the questions and the answers seemed too long. "The lines running out of town were dug up by someone with a Ditch Witch. The phone company can't get a crew out here till tomorrow."

That made sense, though it seemed like an awful long time for repair. "Can you get a message out for us on your radio?" he asked.

"Come on down and send it yourself," Clark offered. "I'll patch you in to Del Rio, they should be able to put you on a mobile line."

"Great. I'll be there in ten minutes."

Cal hung up and explained the conversation to Helene. Then he turned onto the main highway and headed back toward town.

6

Margaret closed the gate which led to the Aldredge ranch and got back into her car. She had found her husband, or at least she had found where he was supposed to be. Apparently there hadn't been any drilling activity in the Comstock area in years, so just about everyone at the coffee shop knew about the new well, or what was supposed to have been the new well. The rumors had persisted that they were still up there, even though the heavy drilling equipment had been seen leaving town three days earlier. There were only two small hotels in town, and Buzz had checked-in to neither. So he had to be at the site. He had probably had a trailer set up to stay in, and he was probably still working the site. She figured that the people in town had seen somebody else's rig leaving the city limits, perhaps passing through town. Buzz was probably still up there with a small crew trying to get something out of the new site. He had told her how important this all was, how it could mean more money and a better title. She knew Buzz too well to think he would give up before drilling through a mile of rock, if that's what it took. He was willing to take that risk. And he said something one night about Comstock, how he was sure this was the one. Once he had committed himself to that level he wasn't likely to let up until he had to.

But it was approaching that point, if it hadn't already passed it. The home office couldn't get a hold of him and had decided not to send anyone after him. They had given Margaret a message to pass on, and it was not good. Unless Buzz was dancing underneath the shower of a black gusher, she intended to give him an earful and send him back to Del Rio, before he succeeded in losing his job. Her teacher's salary was not enough for them to live as they had grown accustomed to living.

As she topped the hill she saw the tremendous pile of rocks and the big yellow steam shovel. The monster was not moving, but she could hear the rattling sounds of construction. This was all wrong. There was no oil field equipment here at all. This looked more like an excavation than a drill site. She pulled up to the side of the rock pile and stopped the car. The sounds of a gas-powered jack hammer became clear as she climbed out of her car. She walked to the edge of the pit and looked down into it.

Buzz was at the bottom, hammering away at the white rock. It was too hard to shovel out like dirt, but it broke apart easily and he was already standing ankle deep in a pile of rubble. He was almost seventy feet down, and the afternoon shadows cast off lines across the wall beside him. She stood and watched, knowing he would not hear if she called. But then he suddenly let off the hammer and looked up at her.

She couldn't believe what she saw. Even from here she could see that he had lost weight, a lot of it. How could he have lost so much so quickly? His face looked thin compared to what it had been just weeks earlier, and even from this distance she could see something in his eyes, something which added to his foreign look.

"Buzz? Are you alright?"

He stared for a moment. At first he had not recognized the woman. But then she had spoken, and something in his head told him who it was. The thought alarmed him. She was not supposed to be here. This was not good. This could be a threat to his work. He had to diffuse the situation or there could be trouble.

She called his name again.

"I'm okay. What do you want?"

He didn't sound right. His voice was flat, not irritated as it usually was. He looked at her with an emotionless face.

"No one seems to know where you are for sure. Your office is worried. I was worried." He continued to stare blankly up at her. "Why don't you come up here and we'll go get some lunch. We can talk about this."

He finally looked away from her and back to the rocks around his ankles. The call was strong, very strong. He found it difficult even to consider climbing out of the pit, getting further away from the wonderful thing which called to him from below. But he had to do it.

Margaret watched as Buzz put his jackhammer down and began climbing out of the pit. He used a rope which lay on the most gradual slope of the pit and was tied off to an old stump which stuck two feet out of the ground. His arms were weary from the work, and they shook as he climbed. Perhaps he did need some food. But that would mean going away from the pit. In the back of his mind he knew that if he left, the pit might fill back up again, or someone else might take up the work, someone like that one-armed rig manager that had knocked him down. Cal knew about the voices under the ground, Buzz had seen it in his eyes. No one but Buzz was going to get the reward.

Buzz reached the top of the pit and Margaret almost gasped at what she saw. His arms were burned, and so was the top of his head. He had lost maybe a hundred pounds. His eyes were dead looking, and skin hung loosely from his face. His head was slightly lowered, and this made him look almost sinister.

"God, Buzz. You look awful."

Buzz didn't answer. Instead he just looked at her with those dead eyes and breathed that stale breath on her face.

And she felt something else, something which made her eyes and the back of her head tingle. It made her want to run away, and it made her want to jump into the pit. It confused her, and she began to wonder what it was that had taken her husband.

"Food would be good," Buzz finally said. "I think I need some food."

"When did you eat last?" she asked.

His clothes were baggy, and he had cut new holes in his belt to keep his pants up. He had just taken them off completely for a while but then his legs too had burned. And the rocks had worked them over. He needed the pants on, so he had to put them back on.

Buzz thought. He didn't know when he had eaten last. He knew he had taken water not long ago, but he knew he had not taken food in a long time. He had thought that he would be able to go a few days without it, but now there was an opportunity to get some, and he was beginning to doubt whether or not his work would be done in a few more days.

"You will get me some food, and bring it back?"

She looked at him closely. His speech wasn't even normal. But it was definitely still Buzz that stood before her. "I'll take you to town, and we'll grab some lunch."

"I can't leave here."

"Why not?"

Buzz looked back into the pit. "I can't leave," he said again. "I'm not finished yet."

Margaret looked down into the pit too. Again she could feel its pull. "Just what are you doing here anyway?"

Buzz's dead eyes returned to hers. "I'm digging."

"For what?"

His eyes darted about as he looked for the right answer, the answer that would get him food. "Oil?"

"What?" Margaret had been married to Buzz too long not to know this was not how oil was extracted from the ground, not these days.

"I mean there was oil. But I'm digging now." He couldn't say what he wanted to say. The thoughts and the words were elusive. He knew his chances of getting food were getting worse.

Then she surprised him. "I'll go get some food and bring it here. Then we'll talk. Okay?"

Buzz's eyes showed distant pleasure. "Yes. Get the food, then we'll talk."

They stood there looking at each other for a moment. Then Buzz turned away from his wife and headed for the big steam shovel. She backed away as he started it up and began moving the loose rock out of the pit. The steam shovel wouldn't reach much deeper than it was now, and somehow she knew he had much further to go.

Before what?

Her thoughts were confused, and she knew she had to get away from this place to sort them out. Margaret turned her back on her husband and his machine and his madness. She got back into her car and headed for town where she hoped to clear her head and decide what to do.

7

Cal knew as soon as they entered the police station that something was wrong.

Clark rose from his desk with his hand on his gun. Then he relaxed when he recognized who it was. "Hey, Cal, what can I help you with today?"

Cal looked around the room. It was not as neat and tidy as it usually was. The sheriff's desk was a mess. The floor had pencils and handcuffs and overturned chairs scattered across it.

"I came by to use the radio, Clark. I can't seem to get a call out of this town."

"It's like I said," the sheriff reminded Cal, "a guy with a backhoe dug up the lines. Phone company won't be able to get the cable in 'till next week."

"I thought you said he was using a Ditch Witch." Cal saw immediately that his point irritated his friend.

"I meant a backhoe. It was a backhoe, not a Ditch Witch. He was digging a sewer line, and you can't very well dig sewer line with a Ditch Witch, now can you?"

Clark was agitated beyond what might be normal. "Of course not, Clark." Cal looked around nervously. Helene kept her eyes on the sheriff. "Do you think we could get a call out on the radio?"

"I'm afraid not."

The surprise appeared on Cal's face as the disappointment came to Helene's. Clark's face didn't waver.

"Why not?" Cal asked, afraid of what the answer might be.

"It's gone out. It's not working."

Cal knew a little about radios and even had his short-wave operator's license. "Why don't you let me take a look at it?"

At first the sheriff looked agitated. Then his face went blank. "Sure. But you're not going to be able to fix it. I'm not so bad with a radio myself."

Clark stood from his desk and led Cal and Helene to the back of the station house. Cal could see as they approached the radio that it had been smashed. It looked like someone had taken a board to it, and then he saw the night stick lying on the floor and knew what had been done.

Clark Rodriguez picked up a stapler which rested next to the broken radio and began talking into it. "This is the sheriff's office in Comstock, does anybody copy?" He let the stapler open up and a spent staple fell to the floor. Then he pressed it together again. "This is the sheriff's office in Comstock, does anybody hear me?" He let up again and listened with an intent face. Cal and Helene watched in both astonishment and fear. Then the sheriff turned to Cal and held the stapler out to him. "See, I told you it was broken. You're welcome to give it a try yourself."

Cal looked at Clark closely. The man wasn't pulling a joke. Then he heard a shuffling noise coming from the holding cells down the small corridor behind the sheriff. He glanced and saw that there was someone in one of the cells. The man looked beat and bloody, and his right arm was bent oddly. Then the mess of a man called out to Cal, and he knew who it was.

It was Deputy Barnes.

The sheriff drew his gun and turned around suddenly. "You shut up, you filthy shit!"

Cal jumped. Helene took a step back.

"Say another word and I'll shoot you again, you stinking drug dealer, and not in the leg this time!"

Cal looked into the cell at the bloody deputy and knew something had gone very wrong with the sheriff. Then he began to wonder if it was more than this. There was too much here, unlikely that it was all just a coincidence. It was Buzz, it was the cave, it was the dreams. Now it was the sheriff. What else was it? What else was happening in Comstock, and where was it all leading?

The sheriff turned slowly and faced Cal and Helene. He did not lower his gun. "Do you think you can fix it?"

"What?" The question confused Cal.

The gun was still pointing at Cal. "The radio. Do you think you can fix it?"

"No," Cal answered quickly.

"That's too bad. Do you have to leave now?"

"Of course," Cal answered.

The sheriff smiled, then looked down at his gun which was still pointed at Cal's chest. "Oops!" he cried out. "I forgot, sorry."

Cal backed away as Sheriff Rodriguez holstered his gun. "Thanks anyway, Clark. We'll just pass on the radio for now."

The sheriff watched uneasily as the two of them walked toward the door, his hand still twitching anxiously near his gun. "Where are you two going? Are you leaving town?"

Helene watched Cal nervously, hoping he did not give the wrong answer.

"No, Clark. We're just going to get a bite to eat."

The sheriff smiled and returned to his desk. "You two be careful out there. It's getting dangerous, you know."

Cal wanted to ask what he meant by this, but he also wanted to just get out of the station, so he nodded as he opened the front door and let Helene out. The sheriff just grinned as he watched them go.

In the cells behind the sheriff Deputy Sam Barnes crawled back to the bed he had been resting on when he had heard Cal come in. He had hoped to get a message out, and he thought Cal had seen enough, but he wasn't sure. He lifted himself slowly to the blood-stained mattress and laid his sore head down once again.

8

Margaret pulled up to the pit again. Buzz had made the pile of rocks larger and now he was busting up more of the hard rock below. Margaret didn't know exactly what he was doing, but she knew that there was something down there, under all that rock. One part of her told her that it was something redemptive, something which would bring a sort of salvation. Another part told her that it was a terrible evil, something which sought to destroy. She was right on both counts.

Margaret got out of her car and approached the edge of the pit with the bag of food. It was hamburgers. It had taken her almost an hour to get them. The lady cooking them didn't seem to be in a hurry, and there had been only one other customer in the dirty burger joint, which was also the gas station.

As Margaret looked down into the pit she felt something tingling in the back of her head. Then Buzz stopped working and turned around.

At first his eyes strained, and he didn't seem to recognize her. Then he remembered, and he put down the jackhammer.

He climbed up out of the pit. His arms felt like rubber, and they were losing much strength. The food should help. Sleep would probably have helped too, but he didn't have time for that. He could go without sleep and still finish the job. The food, however, was becoming important.

As he reached the top of the pit the smell of burgers caused his stomach to tighten and his mouth to water. He snatched the bag from his wife and tore it open. The burgers fell to the ground, and he greedily picked two of them up and began shoving one in his mouth. In seconds it was gone, and he began working on the second. Margaret just watched, and decided she would let him have her burger too.

"I think you should come back with me."

Buzz looked at her but did not answer.

"You need to come back to San Antonio with me where we can sit and talk. You need to get some perspective on what you're doing."

Buzz finished off the second burger and then picked up the third, along with the fries which had not spilled out of the bag.

"You need to come back with me, at least for a day or two. Get away from this and think about it. If you still think you need to come back here, then you can."

Buzz's eyes betrayed him. He wasn't going back. He had made up his mind, and he wasn't even going to discuss it.

She knew now he was crazy. The way he looked, the way he ate, the thing he was doing here. None of it made sense. Something had snapped in Buzz's head, and he was nuts. That thing under the ground had pushed him over the edge, and he wasn't going to leave here. She knew then she was going to have to either leave him to his madness or get someone else to help her take him away from here before it killed him. If she thought he would stop before it did kill him she would have left him to his own devices. But she could see that he would not. He was going to stay here and work himself to death.

"You need help, Buzz."

Buzz looked into the pit. In a way she was right. He looked back into her eyes and this time felt something slipping from his brain. "You're right. I could get this done much faster if I had help."

For a moment Margaret agreed to stay and help him with his work. She could run the steam shovel while he loosened the rock.

But then she shook her head loose from the thought and turned away from her husband. She had to leave now. Something was happening to her. She began to fear that if she did not leave immediately she would become like Buzz.

"Honey," Buzz said. "Look at me."

She refused. "I have to go now. You need help."

"Don't go," he suggested. But without eye contact his suggestions were impotent.

Margaret took a step away from her husband, then she felt his hand around her arm. Buzz spun her around, trying to force her to look into his eyes. But her eyes were closed.

"Look at 'em, Margaret."

No matter how irrational it seemed, she knew that if she looked she would never be the same. Something was waiting for her, something which had nested in Buzz's brain. A piece of it was waiting to jump out of his eyes and into hers, but only if she looked.

Then she felt her feet slipping as Buzz turned suddenly toward the pit. She opened her eyes and turned her head away. She cried out as they approached the pit, Buzz's strength suddenly returning as something else took control of his weary muscles.

"You have to stay and help me Margaret."

He held her over the edge of the pit. Without the rope she would tumble down the rocks. If it did not kill her it would break too many bones. She looked down into the pit, away from her husband's eyes.

Buzz grabbed her face with his free hand and tried to turn it toward his, but she fought against him. He pressed hard, smashing her cheeks. Then she cried out and brought her hands across his face. He felt the sting of the slap, then the hands were back, slapping and clawing. There was burning, but not pain, not as he had known it before.

It was obvious she would not look. She would not help.

He let go.

Margaret grabbed onto Buzz's neck and screamed as she stumbled back, her feet slipping into the pit. She kicked at the ground, trying to regain her footing, but the rocks were breaking away and rolling down the sloping wall of the pit. She felt her hand slipping and she realized that he was going to let her fall. This was really it. It was over.

As she felt her hand slipping she looked up at Buzz. "Please."

His eyes were cold and in that instant she knew that the man she had married was not there. She was ready to give up, ready to help him now. It was better than what was happening, it was certainly better than death.

Buzz didn't answer. No power leapt from his eyes. Instead his hand came up swiftly and slapped her hand from his neck. Her eyes grew wide as her grip disappeared. For that instant she was frozen in space and time, knowing it would be her last sane moment alive.

Then she slipped away.

At first she just slid on her front, her clothes untucking and tearing, rocks biting at her stomach and legs, tearing at her bra. Then her foot struck a large rock which was still embedded in the wall of the pit, and she began to roll. The wall was steep, and it was a few seconds before her rear hit the ground, then her head snapped back and folded as her legs again looped over her head. Halfway down she was knocked unconscious, struck on the temple by another protruding piece of limestone. The rocks tore at her clothes and her flesh as she bounced to the bottom of the pit and finally came to rest in a pile of white dust next to the jackhammer.

Buzz used the rope to descend carefully into the pit. His wife was a mess and only wearing half the clothing she had started the trip with. He saw that her naked back was still moving, rising and falling slowly with her shallow breaths. That didn't matter. She was probably in a coma, or at least unconscious enough she wouldn't realize what was happening.

Buzz fired up the jackhammer and began working on her right shoulder.

There was no way he could put her down that hole in one piece.

Nine

The Great Lands - 1648

1

These were the Great Lands. The wandering peoples had found a place where they could remain and wander no more. The buffalo were plentiful, the land bore crops which could sustain them. There had been peoples here before, peoples like them who had left paintings on the walls of these caves since before the time when the great pyramids were built in Egypt.

But already the thing which would destroy them had landed in the east. It grew there like a blight and its disease and its vices were seeping westward ahead of it. It was still far away, but in the greater picture of time it was almost here. Within a hundred years the Native Americans which roamed the plains to the north and the wooded lands to the east would begin carrying tools and weapons which came from this faraway place. Within two hundred years something else would come. Something terrible.

He knew because he had seen the vision.

His people were not the Native Americans. They had seen these people, and they had learned some things from them, but they were not them. These people had wandered across the trans Pecos area they called the Great Lands for thousands of years, isolated in their own places. Sometimes they wandered. Sometimes, when the land was good to them, they settled. Here the land had been good for many, many years. He was born here. His mother and father had both been born here. In a few months his ninth son could have been born here.

But he had seen the vision, and he knew that they would have to leave. He had gone onto the top of the hill and looked into the sun. There the sun had helped him to see more clearly. The great white bird, the hawk, was flying in on his people. In his vision it swept down out of the skies and gathered his people like so many mice as they fled and scattered. Some escaped, many were consumed and became a part of the white hawk. Then the hawk took their land. It possessed it as no one ever had. It mastered the land and put it into chains. The land would never be free again. And his people would never exist again. And in its captivity the land would die.

But he had decided on a course of action. He was their shaman, and they would listen to him. They were not a warring people, but they had the tools of war, and they knew the hunt well. He would take the women and the children southward, leaving behind men to fight the hawk. Then, after they had defeated it, he would return with the women and children, and they would feast on the bird.

And they would live again in the Great Lands.

Tonight the men would prepare for the battle. They would meet in the deep cave which was both ancient and mystical. They would sing and dance.

And then they would wait.

He gathered his ceremonial objects and regarded them closely again for their secrets. Then he closed his eyes and began to chant.

2

It was nighttime and the men gathered in the large ceremonial chamber deep within the earth. The word had been spread and men from over a hundred encampments had come, prepared for the battle. The shaman was there too, and his grown sons were there to help him. His wife was the only woman present, but she was the shaman's wife, and she would be responsible for a part of the ceremonies too.

Small fires lit up the inside of the cavern. The smoke drifted to the high ceiling then was sucked out through small holes which lead to the surface. It was hot on the surface, but down here it was very cold. Neither the heat nor the cold mattered. It was time for something greater than these things. It was time to prepare for a battle which would either save the land, or see it lost.

The shaman began the chant, and the men joined. He led the dance and they followed. Ten of the men carried torches and it made their shadows dance wildly across the cavern walls. They shed their clothes and danced naked, singing to the land for her protection, for her help. They sang to the skies and to the waters which flowed to their east, west and south. They could not fight the battle without their help. They could not win on their own.

The cold air swirled about their naked bodies and the shadows melted and reformed. The shaman danced to the center of the cavern and three of the men came with him. They were the leaders. The rest formed a circle, each man dancing in place as the shaman made the preparations.

To the first leader he gave a pouch filled with sand. This was to throw into the eyes of the hawk, to confuse it and make its vision false. It would see things not there, and things which were real would seem like a dream. To the second leader he gave a pouch with coals and flint. These would be for the fire which they would set for the hawk on the earth so that it could not land. To the third leader he gave a pouch filled with dried red clay mixed with blood. This they would cast into the skies so that the clouds would fight against the hawk and bring it down to the earth and into the fire.

The three leaders put their hands together and the shaman sliced their wrists. Their blood mingled and dripped into a bowl which lay at their feet. They bled until the bowl was filled, then their wounds were covered with cloth. The shaman drank first, then passed the bowl to each of the three leaders who also drank. Then the bowl was passed around the circle. Those who were to remain drank of the blood. Those who would leave the cavern did not drink.

Then each man took his warriors and lay down in pits which had been dug earlier that day. There were three pits, and twenty men lay down in each. Then the other men began filling the pits with the dirt and the rocks which had come from them. The men who were being buried continued to chant as the dirt and rocks covered them, the leaders of each group looking upward while his men closed their eyes.

Then they were buried and ready.

It would be a long wait, and the battle would be fierce. But they would be ready. First they would have to cross into the spiritual plain. As they did, their screams rose from the piles of dirt. In that realm they would wait for the hawk. Then they would defeat it. Then their sons and their wives and their brothers would return to the land.

Forty men waited for the screams which came from the earth to die out. Then they began to seal the cavern off. They built a wall at the entrance. Two of the men stayed on the inside to reinforce it from there, and then to guard the souls of the men who waited. When they had finished the shaman led the remaining men to the surface where the women and children waited. Their belongings were stuffed into their carrying bags and all that remained was for them to be led away.

It was daybreak already. The ceremony had only lasted two hours, but the entire night had passed. The shaman knew that this was because the cavern was either sacred or evil. He hoped its powers would work for them and not against them.

His body ached and his soul was weary, but he and his wife led the way, nonetheless. He led them all across the river to the south, then on from there. They would go far from this place. They would wander until they heard the voices of their brothers calling them to return. He would know when the hawk had come, and when it was dead.

If it could even be killed.

Then he would bring his people back.

And the Great Lands would sustain them once again.

Ten

1

Michael Powell drove westward on Highway 90. He hadn't heard from Helene since their telephone discussion the day before. He had lost her to the static and been unable to call her back. She hadn't called him either. The operator couldn't get through to anyone in Comstock, and she said she had reported it to the phone company.

It had been a long drive. His concern for Helene had dogged him the entire trip. He had stopped once, about three hours ago, to try and call again from a pay phone. But the lines were still down. Now he was ten minutes away from the small town, and he was growing more anxious. He was driving faster than he normally did, but his radar detector said it was safe to do so, and he couldn't make himself drive any slower.

Highway 90 had been cut through the hills of Val Verde County. Limestone walls rose and fell on either side of the fairly level road. But now the walls were growing tall, and it was like driving through a desolate canyon. Desolate because there was no life, no plants or trees on the limestone walls, just the dirty white stone rising toward the sky. He felt as if the walls had opened up for him, images of the red sea parting flashed through his mind.

And when the walls were their highest, as he came around a gradual corner, he saw the wreck.

A big truck lay all of the way across the road. It was a tanker of some kind. Then Michael saw the thick black fluid oozing slowly from the hole in the back of the tanker that had been opened by a small Volkswagen. It was a thick black oil, and it stretched in a slick puddle toward him. He hit his brakes and was almost stopped before he hit the slick oil.

His car began to turn sideways as he slowly lost control of it. He fought against it, but it was useless, and he slid trunk first into the tanker.

He had slowed considerably before hitting the oil, so the impact only confused him for a few moments. Then he realized that his engine was still running, though he was not moving. Michael cut the engine and got out of the car, stepping into the black mess which covered the road.

Then he realized that there was no one here. There were no police. There were no people. The wreck was fairly fresh. Could there be people inside the wrecked vehicles?

He could see inside the bug from where he stood, and it was empty. He hurried to the front of the truck and saw a man hanging halfway out of the truck's cab, his head pointing toward town. The front of the truck was compressed against the stone wall, and Michael had to climb onto the truck to even get close enough to see if the man was alive.

But before he even got to the man he knew that he was dead. There was too much blood. It had gathered in a puddle on the road beneath the man's head. The top of his head had been cracked open, probably on the road or against the windshield which lay in pieces. The glass lay mixed with the blood and the oil.

Michael looked back to his car. The rear end was compressed, but it looked like it would still run. He could get in and drive it to Del Rio. If the car was still in good shape he would be in Del Rio in thirty minutes. If not, he would be broken down somewhere between here and there. And Helene was just a few more miles down this road, maybe in trouble.

He decided he would walk to Comstock. Something bad was happening. The phones had been cut off, and now the only road in from the east, and out for that matter, had been completely blocked. He had the feeling that someone was trying to keep him out. But why? Was it just Helene who was in danger, or was something bigger going on?

Michael climbed down onto the pavement on the Comstock side of the big truck and began his walk toward town. Less than a hundred yards from the wreck he found the body of a young woman. She must have been the occupant of the Volkswagen. She was lying in the center of the road, face down. As he approached he could see the blood and the hole in her back. He knew that this was where the bullet had come out. He could see from the drops of blood which led to the body that she had run for at least a hundred feet before going down. Her left leg was torn, probably by the first shot. She had not only died, but she had also died terrified. The blood was dry, but the body was not yet stiff. This had happened recently, perhaps only minutes ago.

But where had the shot come from?

He looked up to the top of the limestone walls for his answer. At first he saw nothing. Then he saw a man's figure appear at the northern wall. He saw the man raise a rifle and take aim. Then Michael turned and ran.

Pavement flew up at his feet as the first shot exploded. Michael ran fast and straight, forgetting that running straight made him an easier target, hoping that simply putting more distance between him and the man with the rifle would save him. The man had shot many deer, many from farther away than this. But the deer had been standing still. Michael flinched as the second shot hit the road about ten feet in front of him. He had to be at least two hundred yards from him now. In another fifteen seconds it would be three hundred. But the old man on the hill could fire his entire clip in those fifteen seconds, and Michael knew it was simply his speed and luck against the man's skill.

In an earlier day the man would have the trespasser down by now. But his eyes were getting old, and he could not hold the gun as steady as he once had. His shots were close, but off the mark. The woman had been walking when he had gotten to her, and she hadn't been able to run very fast or very far once he had wounded her. But this one was getting away, and it would be a lucky shot that brought him down. But he had made lucky shots before, so he put another live round in the chamber. He held the gun as steadily as he could and aimed. He didn't have to kill him in one shot, just put him down, or maybe even just slow him down. Then he could walk along the edge of the cliff until he got a good, easy shot. Then it would be over. He squeezed the trigger slowly, concentrating on keeping the gun steady, aiming just a few feet ahead of the running man.

Michael came to the top of a gradual hill and could see the worn-down buildings of Comstock. There was something like relief which passed through his body moments before the bullet did. It passed through him suddenly and quickly, and he grabbed the side of his leg as he went down to the hot pavement.

Get up and run. Get up and run now.

He stumbled to his feet as another shot just missed his head. The wound burned, but it was not deep. He ran with a limp. Not as fast as before, but fast enough. He took in deep breaths of the hot south Texas air as he hurried toward town.

There were two more shots, though now they were hitting the pavement around him, and one ricocheted off the limestone wall to his left.

Then the shots stopped.

He had gotten through.

But he didn't think that there would be many who did.

He was exhausted from running, but he kept going toward town at a jog. His wound was bleeding only lightly, and he needed to keep moving at a good pace, in case the man had a vehicle and could appear at the top of the limestone wall again.

But Jim Dewey just watched as Michael ran toward town. Jim was upset that he had missed. If he had been there when the man had gotten out of his car it would have been easy. But he had gone back to his truck to reload, and now he would have to go back again. He decided that he would just bring the whole box of shells with him to the edge of the cliff. Then he could get behind that big rock, where he'd been waiting all day for that oil truck. Then he wouldn't miss anyone else.

But this man had gotten away, and it bothered Jim as if he had failed at the only job he had ever been meant to do. And for now it was all that he was. He did not remember what he had been before this task, and there was no future. Only this task. Then they would be here.

Jim smirked as he hurried back to his truck for his ammunition and his water. He only had to last for a few more hours. Then it would all be out of his hands.

2

The town looked all wrong.

Comstock was small, and there never was much activity in the area which was considered 'town.' But today it was quieter than usual. The phones were still out, and it was becoming clear that they were going to stay that way for a while. Cal had not been the first one to visit the sheriff. Word had gotten around that Sheriff Rodriguez had gone batty, and nobody but Cal had seen the deputy. There were still a good number of trucks parked at the gas station that also served sandwiches and burgers. It was the central meeting point for the people of the small town, and now there was something very important to meet about. There had been some strange accidents, and too many people had disappeared. Jim Dewey hadn't been seen in days, and Marge Wilson had last been seen running naked into the dry ranch lands. A few of the men who had gathered in the cafe had spotted a mysterious Albino woman lurking around odd places at indecent hours. And of course there was the matter of Sheriff Rodriguez.

It was decided that Dub Watson and Ben Hurst would drive to Del Rio to see if they could get some help on the phones and maybe get a hold of the sheriff's office there. It was clear that outside help was needed now, even if it meant sacrificing what little pride the town members had in their small community.

The two men didn't make it very far past the city limits. When they stopped to inspect the wreck that was blocking the road Jim Dewey shot both of them in the head before either one knew what was going on.

Nancy Ferrel needed to make her weekly trip to the podiatrist in Del Rio phone service or no. Nancy was approaching the scene in her dirty brown Subaru when she saw Dub Watson's head explode. She screamed and stopped her car, then turned back toward town. As she drove away from the growing pile of vehicles her back windshield exploded.

Ten minutes later she was telling her story to Sheriff Rodriguez. He promised he would take care of it, and then clubbed her over the head with his nightstick when she turned to leave. Her head made a funny popping noise, and something flew out of her ear and made an odd stain on the vinyl tiles.

The sheriff dragged Nancy's body to the back cell where he threw it in with the two others he'd had to store there. The deputy was still handcuffed to the bed at the back of the cell and just watched, wondering what was going on and why he was still alive.

Sheriff Rodriguez returned to his chair to await the next unsuspecting meddler. It was good these people trusted him. When they found trouble, this is where they came. The Bonner boy had showed up to report seeing someone shoot the man who had come to fix the phones. He, too, was crumpled in one corner of that cell.

Pretty soon they would catch on to Jim up on that ridge. But by then it might all be over. It wasn't so important that the inhabitants of Comstock be kept in, but if word got out now about all that was going on there might be too many people coming in. It was going to be hard enough working with the minds of the people who were trapped here. It would be almost impossible if new minds kept coming into the mix, changing the images and forces surrounding the place. Then the clouds wouldn't be able to descend.

The sheriff knew this was true, but he didn't understand what it meant. He could not conceive that he had become a part of a larger consciousness, which included an old albino woman who sat in a dark room singing her chants, surrounded by images of people the sheriff had known for years. And of course there was the doll with a small badge pinned to its chest.

There was a deep rumble, and the floor shook softly under the sheriff's feet. Then he knew that no one else would be leaving Comstock.

3

Cal had given Helene one last chance to leave town, but she had refused again. The people here were acting oddly, and she knew that it had something to do with that cave on the Walker ranch. She had lost a friend in that cave, and she feared what power might now be leaking from it. She agreed with Cal that they needed to seal the cave then take care of Buzz. Helene didn't want to think much about what that meant, but Cal knew in the back of his mind that it was going to come down to murder. He hadn't fired a rifle at a human in over thirty years, and he wasn't looking forward to it. But he had no doubt that Buzz was in on this thing, that this strange feeling which was in his own head was buried deeply within Buzz's. He knew from his own feelings what Buzz wanted, and that nothing would stop him short of death. Cal also sensed that Buzz had already taken at least one life, though how he knew was a mystery even to himself.

Cal knew the people and places of Comstock quite well. This was going to come in quite handy now. Three years ago the state had blasted through a hundred feet of limestone to finish out the widening of the highway. Not all of the dynamite had been used, and Cal knew where it was being stored. He drove down the gravel road which led from the highway to a metal storage shed which had been rusting in place since the highway project had started. The doors were around back, and Cal had the tools he needed to cut the lock.

But as he drove around the side of the shed he could see that the doors were open. He pulled up to the back of the shed anyway and got out of his truck. Helene came with him. She could see that something was bothering the man.

"What's wrong?" she asked him.

"This should be closed. The state locked it up three years ago, and no one in town has the key."

Cal inspected the lock and saw that he was not the only one with a set of bolt cutters.

Helene wiped her wet forehead and looked to the west. The sun was beginning to set, and the sunset was a deep red which reminded her of blood. Then she noticed that there were clouds on the horizon, clouds which seemed to me moving slowly in their direction.

She turned back to Cal who was walking into the stifling air of the shed. He stopped after a few steps and put his hand on his hip. Someone had been here and some of the dynamite was already missing.

Then the ground shook under their feet and there was a deep rumbling which seemed to come from the earth. The sound followed closely behind the shaking and even Helene's untrained ears could tell that there had been an explosion.

Cal looked at Helene with his eyebrows raised. "I guess that's what happened to the missing dynamite."

"What was it?" she asked. "What got blown up?"

"I'm not sure."

Cal stepped out of the shed and looked in the direction from which the sound had come. Smoke was rising in a puff about two miles to the west. He could tell from the distance and direction what had happened.

Helene followed him out and regarded his westward gaze. "Can you tell what it is?"

"It's just outside of town. It looks like the hillside has been blasted. I'd say there's about fifty tons of limestone lying across the highway leading to Langtree. That means the only way out is to the east, toward Del Rio, if that hasn't been blocked somehow."

"I don't understand," Helene stated.

"I don't get it all either, but I think that no one is supposed to leave now. And no one is supposed to come in either. I think it has something to do with keeping a constant force, but I don't really know what that means either."

Helene looked at Cal. He was still watching the rising cloud in the west. As it gained altitude it, too, seemed to take on a red hue. Cal looked okay now. He hadn't said or done anything too bizarre since they had been in the house on the Aldredge ranch. There was something about that place which brought it out in him. Out here he seemed safe, and now she didn't want to be without him. He turned to her slowly and saw these things in her eyes. It made him feel warm, but only for a second. She smiled, and then his mind returned to the business at hand.

"Help me load a few of these crates. It won't take much to do what we need to do."

Helene nodded her head and followed Cal into the shed.

Fifteen minutes later the truck was loaded, and they were heading to the Walker ranch.

4

Jim Dewey watched as the boulders tumbled down the hillside and onto the highway. He had done a good job of placing the explosives. He knew where the big, loose boulders had been, and now they, along with all of the rubble they had been able to gather, were piled across highway 90. The cars had piled up pretty good on the east end of town. No one would be passing anytime soon. No one would be passing either barrier tonight, which was all he needed.

Now the sun was setting, and the red clouds were beginning to form in the sky above town. There was still danger, and now it was back at the cave. Jim returned to his truck and headed for the Walker ranch, driving as fast as he could across the rough wilderness toward the old ranch roads.

5

As they approached the ranch the skies grew an even deeper red. The sun was beginning to dip below the horizon, and the clouds seemed to be casting a flow of their own. The ground around them was starting to reflect the red hue, and Helene sat on the edge of the passenger's seat, praying that they would get there in time, and that what they were going to do would put a stop to this terrible thing.

Cal turned onto the ranch road and headed for the cave. The truck slid back and forth across the rocks as he drove a little too fast, understanding some of what awaited them inside the red skies. They turned the last corner, and the cave came into sight.

Something was coming out of the cave entrance. It was a light, red mist which seeped slowly from the hole in the ground and seemed to dissipate into the air. Suddenly they both understood that this was what was causing the skies to turn red. Cal knew this was the source of the town's doom. Now it was time to put a stop to it.

Cal pulled the truck as close to the cave as he could. Then the two of them got out and began unloading the crates.

A minute later Cal stood and turned toward the cave. Something that sounded like another vehicle was driving just out of sight on the ground above the cave. Then he heard a truck door slam and knew someone else had come here, but for a different reason. The madness which had seeped from Buzz's eyes into his own let the secret loose, and the rest of his mind screamed out a warning.

Helene was looking up at the top of the cave to see who had come when Cal shouted at her to get behind the truck. A moment later as she ran to the vehicle there was the sound of a gunshot. She rounded the back of the truck as the second shot rang out and she met Cal there. He was looking at his arm and blood was soaking into the sleeve of his shirt. The blood startled her, but she did not panic.

"Are you all right?"

"He just caught the flesh above my wrist. It may bleed a lot, but I'll be okay."

"Who is it?" she asked him.

"I didn't stop to look."

There was another shot, and one of the wooden crates they had left on the ground near the truck burst open, spilling the small round sticks of dynamite.

Helene turned to Cal. "He's shooting the dynamite."

"That won't do any good," Cal answered. Then he opened the door to his truck and reached in behind the seat. He slowly pulled out his old rifle that was only used these days for coyotes and jackrabbits. He knew it was loaded and he clicked off the safety as he slipped back down to the ground.

Helene watched as Cal rested the barrel of the gun on the hood of the truck and got slowly to his feet. Blood continued to soak into his shirt, but his arm seemed steady, and the truck was providing a good brace.

Jim fired a few more shots at the dynamite, then he began firing at the truck's gas tank. The first shot was only two inches high. The bullet went through the bed of the truck and exited the other side just inches from Helene's head. Jim lowered his aim slightly and prepared to fire again when there was a sharp 'crack' of Cal's .223. Then the top of Jim's head spewed a powdery red. Then the man went down.

Cal lowered himself back to the ground and looked at Helene. "Can you help me dress this?"

Helene scooted over to Cal and looked at the wound. "Do you have clean rags?"

"Sure, there should be a bag of them in my toolbox, in the lower right-hand side."

Helene got a couple of rags and made a bandage for the wound. The bullet had caught a vein and though there was a lot of blood, the wound was not serious. Minutes later she was carrying the good boxes of dynamite, one at a time, inside the cave. Cal directed her where to place each box and told her how to set the blasting caps and connect the wires. One box rested at the entrance to the small tunnel. As she set the caps she could feel the red mist flowing out of the hole. It burned her skin as it crept out. Images of her professor's fiery face returned to her mind, and it became difficult to stay in that mist. But she knew it had to be done, so she gritted her teeth and tried to ignore the burning. By the time the caps were placed and the wires secured her hands were throbbing with pain from the mist, and she noticed that blood was seeping from between her fingers and at her knuckles. It was almost as if she had lowered her hands into a vat of acid.

She set the second box near the entrance to the cave, at the side which Cal determined to be the least stable. When everything was in place she brought the roll of wire out to Cal who smiled at her.

"I couldn't have done this by myself," he said,

"I don't think I'd be alive right now if I'd left you," she replied. "Thanks."

Helene smiled and held out the roll of wire. "Let's do this."

The sun had set, but the ground reflected the soft eerie glow which was gathering in the sky above. The mist was coming together and growing thicker. Now it appeared like a thick, red, glowing fog and it hovered about a thousand feet above the ground. It seemed to cover the sky in all directions, though it actually did have a border of some kind to the east and west which it did not cross.

Cal told Helene to keep the roll of wire and get in the truck. Then he had her hold it out the window as he backed slowly away from the cave. His arm hurt as he used it, but there was no choice. He would ask Helene to drive later, after the explosion. He backed away until they were over a small rise in the land, within sight of the property line and the road. They could no longer see the cave, but they could see the glowing red mist now which seemed to be hanging together longer before dissipating and regrouping in the heavens.

Cal handed Helene the detonating device and told her which wires to fasten to which posts. Then he looked in the direction of the cave and told her to turn the handle clockwise.

6

The explosion was more than Cal had counted on. Pieces of rock were thrown hundreds of yards as the cave collapsed on itself. Debris rained on the truck for almost ten seconds as the ground shook for the second time that evening.

The two of them looked toward the cave and waited.

The mist was no longer coming from the cave.

Then there was another rumbling of the earth, and the skies grew suddenly thicker. Deep red clouds were quickly forming and churning. It was as if a violent storm had come out of nowhere.

Then Helene saw it in the distance. There was a red column, something like a tornado. It stretched from the ground to the clouds and seemed to be injecting them with the terrible mist.

When she pointed it out to Cal he knew what had happened.

He traded places with Helene and told her to drive for the highway.

7

Buzz was climbing up out of the pit to haul out another load of rocks when the explosion hit. First dirt and dust flew up out of the hole. Then the ground began to shake. The rock he had been stepping onto shook from its place and rolled down the hill. Buzz quickly looked for another, but they were all moving, and he went to his knees. He held firmly to the rope, but rocks began pelting his head and his shoulders.

Then he heard the scream.

He didn't want to look. Somewhere inside he knew what he would see. The spell that had driven him for the past week was beginning to weaken, and he knew that suddenly he was no longer needed.

Then he looked.

A red mist was seeping from the hole at the bottom of the pit. It wound its way through the rubble and toward the surface. It oozed past his legs, and he felt its grip as it pulled him downward.

The rope burned in his hands. The rocks were striking his neck and the back of his head.

Then a large rock near the top of the pit came loose and rolled straight for him. If he had turned to see it he might have been able to avoid it. But he did not turn, and the stone struck him firmly on the top of his head .

He saw blackness and stars, and he felt the earth rolling around him as he tumbled toward the bottom of the pit and the waiting hole. He felt the stones as they poked and prodded him on his descent. His arm burned, his face felt hot, the blackness of unconsciousness came and went.

When the world finally stopped moving he found himself in a broken heap at the bottom of the pit. The hole was beside him, and the air which seeped from it was very hot. The rocks had stopped falling, and the skies above him lit up the inside of the pit with an eerie red glow.

He tried to move, but one of his arms was broken, and his knees and hips hurt. He felt his face and was shocked at how small and angular it had become, and at the wet redness which was covering it.

Then he felt the rumbling deep within the earth. The rock beneath him felt as if it were shifting and sinking. He tried to roll away from the hole, but it was moving toward him. Rocks fell into the hole, then more rocks fell to replace them. The earth around him was disappearing into the hole, faster by the second. He turned and tried to crawl up to the rope, but he felt his wounded legs as they turned beneath and led him slowly downward. He screamed out as the coldness wrapped around his ankles, then his legs. He tried to pull at the earth with his hands, but the earth around him was also heading downward.

Then everything gave way. The walls of the pit separated from the surrounding stone, and a one-hundred-foot cross section of the earth collapsed into the cavern. For a moment Buzz felt free and light as he floated through the air, down into the depths of the earth. For a moment he saw the men again, the dancing naked men.

Then tons of earth and stone crushed and buried his body in the ancient cavern.

The column of redness rose like a tornado from the ancient cavern, feeding the thickening skies.

Eleven

1

Before the thick clouds had come, Michael had looked for Helene at her motel. There had been no one in the front office, and she hadn't answered her door. Michael kicked the door in and found a few of her things, but no sign of Helene or where she might be.

Now he stood at the abandoned gas station with a dead phone in his hand. The second loud explosion that day rumbled from the north, and then the clouds began to grow thick and churn. The air quit moving and became too hot to bear. The pavement was becoming hot under his shoes, even though the sun had already set.

He was nearly hysterical. Helene was here somewhere, but he had no idea where to go now. He had stopped for only a moment at the police station but had caught on to the sheriff's insanity before it became too dangerous. The station had smelled badly, like death getting old. The sheriff had sported a stupid grin and vacant eyes and said he had never heard of Helene and that she was a stupid broad for being out in this weather anyway. Then Michael had decided to make some phone calls, but not from there.

The receiver grew hot in his hands, and he dropped the useless piece of plastic to his side. What was happening? When would it stop? Where was Helene?

Then he noticed that smoke was coming from the rubber hoses on the gasoline pumps and decided to get away from there.

As he ran down the opposite side of the road, pump number three blew, then the gasoline fumes ignited and the underground tanks exploded, one after the other. The impact of the explosions threw him to the pavement and burned the hair on the back of his head. The flames leapt across the street and consumed the five and dime, along with two old women who had just come out, puzzled at why the store was open but no one was there.

Still there was no movement in the air. But the flames moved as if whipped up by the Santa Anas. Michael got to his feet and looked back only for a second. His hands were red, burned by the heat of the pavement. He ran ahead of the fire, limping slightly on his wounded leg, leaving the flames to consume the small downtown area. Ahead of him he could see more smoke from fires which had started in other places. If Helene was here he couldn't help her now. But what was he to do?

He looked around for a car, but the town had shut down and there was no one around. Then he decided to head back to the roadblock on foot. There the walls of the canyon would protect him from the flames, and he would be safe, as long as the man with the rifle wasn't there waiting for him.

2

Sheriff Rodriguez looked out his window and into the streets of town. To his right the flames from the fire station spread out to cover the small shops where the inhabitants of Comstock had made their meager livings for over a hundred years. He had seen fires before, but none like this one.

It was over. There was nothing more for him to do.

He walked back to the jail cells and regarded about a dozen of the luckier people from the small town. They had died quick deaths, most of them anyway. Now death of a different kind had come, one he was not prepared to face himself. He had helped it come, and though he did not know exactly why, there was an old albino woman near the center of town who did. He noticed that his deputy was still alive at the back of the cell, handcuffed to the bed just like he had left him there. The deputy was watching him with calm, intent eyes. Always looking for a way out. Never one to panic. That's what he'd always heard about Sam

Barnes, and that's how he'd always been on the job. The sheriff grinned at the man, then threw him his keys before returning to his desk.

The deputy heard the gunshot just before he got the cell door opened. On his way out he looked just for a moment at the man he had once admired. He had been a good man, and something had turned him sour. Now he smelled like piss, and blood covered the side of his head where his brains had come out. Sam reached forward and closed the sheriff's pained eyes. Then he headed to the side of the station where the cars were parked.

3

John Justin could see that the town was burning from a mile away. The town was glowing with the yellow glow of fire, and the skies were glowing red. The clouds churned and bubbled, and he decided that he'd seen enough.

He gathered his dog and his gun and headed for his truck. He could see that the red clouds ended both to the east and the west, and he was going to leave until they had passed. He had never seen anything like this, and he didn't think it was safe. It looked to him like a nuclear explosion had hit somewhere downtown, only he knew it would have been louder than the explosions he had heard. But still those clouds were ominous, and they gave him a bad feeling.

His nearest neighbors, Ken and Jenny Lusky, were half a mile away. They, too, saw the fire and the skies. They, too, decided that it would be best to leave until it passed.

But Frank Harper had been bitten by the madness and he only stared out his window and giggled while the town burned. A funny thought came into his mind, so he ran to the closet and grabbed his fiddle so he could play it while Comstock burned down. It wasn't quite right, though, so he lit his own curtains for a better effect. He bounced madly about his living room, dancing and laughing while his wife sat stiff with dead eyes smelling badly on the living room couch.

4

By the time Helene got to the main road, traffic was already backed up past the intersection. Horns blared and some larger vehicles simply drove on the shoulders and along the fence rows as they crowded toward the western exit. But the traffic was only building up. It didn't seem to be going anywhere.

Then she saw Michael.

He was limping through the traffic, heading westward with the vehicles. In moments he would be straight across from her. One car lurched forward and knocked him over, but then he was back on his feet, running as if he had never gone down.

There was a rumble, and the clouds began to turn a bloodier shade of red.

Helene rolled down her window and shouted to Michael as he approached. But he did not hear her. The traffic was too loud, and his mind was set on one thing, and he ignored his surroundings as he headed for that goal. So she jumped out of the truck and waved her arms as he passed on the other side of the road. At first she thought he didn't see her. Then he glanced her way for a moment but continued to run.

Then he stopped.

He looked back at her with confusion on his face. He looked back toward town, then up to the churning skies. Then he ran across the road to her and grabbed her into his arms.

"What's happening?" he asked her.

"I don't know, but we need to get out of here."

Michael looked back down the road. "These cars aren't going any-where. I came in that way. The road's been blocked by some wrecked vehicles, and there's a man with a gun trying to keep it that way."

Helene remembered the man shooting at them when she and Cal were at the cave and hoped that this was the same man. "I think he tried to shoot us earlier, but Cal got him with his own gun."

Michael looked confused again for a moment, then he noticed that a man was inside the truck, leaning toward them.

There was another explosion which came from town. Some of the cars on the road were burning now, and tires were beginning to melt.

Michael decided that the questions could wait. "Come on!" he shouted. "We can only get out of here on foot."

Helene leaned into the truck and explained to Cal what had happened. Cal got out of the truck and followed as Michael led them through the maze of cars.

Others began to follow. Ahead some others had already gotten out and were heading west on foot as well. The skies had begun to move. They were coming down now. The wave of terror swept through the people as they hurried toward the border of the blood red skies, hoping to get there before the clouds consumed them.

And as they ran Helene knew that's just what the clouds meant to do. Cal knew it too. He had seen it in Buzz's eyes, and he knew that whatever had been in the red mist which had escaped from the ancient cavern had waited a very long time for this day. It would not stop until it had done all it had come to do; all they had come to do.

Together the three of them ran toward the edge of town, slipping through and around and over the parked cars. Some people were moving quickly, some were moving very slowly. Cal spotted a young mother carrying her child. He knew she would not make it. He ran then, ran to the mother he had known for years. He took her little girl from her and threw her on his back. He signaled for Michael and Helene to go on ahead as the mother cried out for him to go, run with her little girl. The woman's leg was burned badly, and she could not run very quickly. She would not make it out like this, but all three of them would die if he helped her too. So he ran, he ran like the wind with the little girl on his back and the red clouds continued to descend and the world around him became like a fiery furnace.

5

Helene and Michael climbed down the side of the rig which lay across the highway, and they continued westward. There were about six people in front of them, Lord knew how many were behind them. They were all faring better than those who had decided to exit by the east end of town. The rocks there were piled high, and only a few younger men had been able to scale the mass. But even they would not make the border of the clouds before the red death descended.

But Helene and Michael could see the border. It was an indistinct line where the clouds stopped. The clouds were now only ten feet above their heads, and the heat was tremendous. Behind them the cars were beginning to explode, and in moments the gas tanks on the big truck would go.

But as the clouds crept downward they ran past the border.

The heat was gone. Suddenly the coolness of the night air hit their blistered faces and arms. It was soothing.

There were cars here. Cars which had come from Del Rio, and which had stopped at the roadblock, then backed away as the red clouds had descended. One man was in a truck, and he had already started a message back to Del Rio for some help. In less than an hour the ambulances would come. Before then there would be other cars and trucks to take the most seriously injured back toward Del Rio.

Helene stopped and turned around. The clouds were very low now. She didn't think she would have been able to stand under them, if she had wanted to. But she certainly didn't want to.

And where was Cal?

She watched and waited as two more people came running from the red mass as it lowered itself slowly to the ground. The man was screaming and patting his head. The woman was barefoot, and you could smell the burnt flesh on the bottom of her feet.

But no Cal.

Helene watched and waited.

And she said a short prayer.

6

Cal leapt across the hood of the last car between him and the big truck. The people behind him were beginning to scream, and he could feel the heat on his back. The little girl was crying, but she did not scream. The clouds were low, and he had to crouch down to keep her head out of them. He knew what waited there, and he knew that it would not spare even this little girl.

But the truck was too tall. The clouds had already settled on its top side, and the tires had caught fire. The hot metal of the tank was popping as it changed shape in the furnace which was descending.

Cal took the girl off his shoulders and carried her under his arm. He ran to the front of the truck and crawled between the tank and the truck. The space was tight, but it was enough. The metal seared his back as he squeezed through, and the little girl screamed out as her arm brushed against the hot tank.

He could see the border. There were no more cars in the way. He tucked his head and ran as the fire burnt his head and his shoulders. He felt real flames break out on his shirt, and his head hurt.

The clouds descended. Behind him the screams of burning people were cut short by the explosion of the big rig's gas tanks.

The explosion threw Cal forward to the hot pavement. He dropped the girl and her head hit the pavement firmly. The clouds were upon them.

Cal crawled to the girl and grabbed her in his arm. Then he rolled out of the inferno, away from the clouds and the death they brought. The air felt suddenly cool, and there was no more fire above him.

He heard the pavement sizzle as the clouds came in contact with it. He lay still, the unconscious girl beside him, less than three feet from the red clouds which now rested on the ground. But they did not move toward him. The clouds remained within their border as they burned and destroyed and consumed the people and the places of Comstock.

The air felt cool.

But his whole body burned.

And he closed his eyes.

Epilogue

Epilogue

1

Cal looked out the window of the small hospital. He would be leaving in a few hours. The burns had been treated and he had spent only one night in this bed. But that night had been filled with dreams of the fire that fell from the sky.

The little girl was okay. She had sustained a slight concussion and some burns from the fall, and one of her arms had broken, but she would live. Her dad had been out of town on business and had come by to thank Cal in person. Her mom had died in the fire.

Her mom had been taken in the fire. Cal knew that was a better word for it. She had been taken, along with all of the other people who didn't make it out. And only about a dozen had.

And he had heard the stories. In a little while he would go see for himself. But already he knew that they were true. He had known before anyone had said anything to him. He had known as he lay on the pavement looking into the redness as it swallowed the town.

2

Helene and Michael drove into Austin late that afternoon. They had answered all of the questions from the police and the reporters. They had seen the pictures on the news. They had not gone back, however. Helene had insisted that they leave as soon as possible, and Michael had not argued.

It had been a nightmare. But it was over now. In a few days she would put the horror behind her and get on with her life.

But it would never really be completely gone. Even now she caught herself looking up into the skies again, almost expecting them to be coming down upon her.

She didn't understand what had happened. Nobody really did. What had become of Comstock was a puzzle, one which she might return to someday. There were still caves in the hills, and she had a feeling that some of the answers lay in the paintings which were probably still in those caves, still intact after the disaster. Those paintings were not a part of what had been destroyed .

And what had been destroyed? She knew that it was more than cars and buildings, it was something on a different level. The town would not return. And they were still trying to find out exactly what had replaced it.

Helene looked to her boyfriend, and he squeezed his hand. They would work through this together. It was good he had come. Now she had someone to talk to who would understand. She would keep in touch with Cal too. She knew that of all of the people who had survived, Cal perhaps understood it all the best.

She looked out the windshield and felt the comfort of familiar surroundings. It was good to be back.

3

The sun was setting as Cal drove westward on Highway 90, toward Comstock, or what had been Comstock. The drive seemed too long, and wild thoughts ran through his mind. As he got closer to that place something inside of him awakened and urged him on, pushing him to go there, to see, to become a part of it.

The voice would never leave him, and someday he would learn to live with it.

He turned the last corner and slowed down. A mile ahead he could see what everyone had been talking about. The television crews had come and gone. The scientists would be here next week. But no one was here now.

He slowed his car and approached the construction blockades which sealed the end of the road.

Beyond this there was no pavement.

But there was something.

Instead of gutted cars and melted asphalt there were trees and under-brush. They stretched for as far as he could see. He got out of his car and walked to the edge of the road. He disregarded the warning signs and walked past the blockades, entering the forest.

The air turned sweet and fresh. And it was full of bird song. The ground beneath his feet was cool and soft, things were growing out of it as if they had been doing so forever.

As he walked he began to understand. He was the white hawk. They all were. *They* had been the terror, not the clouds of fire. He didn't understand what this meant, but he knew that it was true.

He followed his own path which led him toward where the town used to be. There was no sign that modern man had ever set foot here. There was no rubble. There was no debris.

But then the setting sun glimmered off something shiny which lay near his feet.

He bent down to pick up the object.

It was an arrowhead. It looked new.

In the distance he heard the rumble of a thousand buffalo hooves.

www.ingramcontent.com/pod-product-compliance
Lightning Source LLC
Chambersburg PA
CBHW050331160726
48002CB00001B/264